"Resorting to threats now, my lord?"

"Whatever is necessary." Langston leaned forward so that his face was close to hers, his masculine scent teasing her nostrils. "I won't let Deverell ruin his life by marrying you."

She blanched at his cruelty. She should have expected this. As an actress, she was considered a fallen woman, the type no decent man would take to wife.

"And if I told you I have no intention of marrying your brother?"

He moved away and arrogantly looked her up and down. "Hoping for richer prey? No one else would be foolish enough to offer marriage, and I think you are clever enough to realize that. No, I think you have every intention of accepting Deverell's offer."

"Not everyone is avaricious. But perhaps, my lord, you do not know that," she said with false sweetness.

"You are an actress, and we both know that is just a front for a more…lucrative profession."

Sam clenched her hands to keep from slapping the man. "Then my more lucrative profession will make it all the worse for Lord Deverell to be in my clutches, won't it?"

His mouth thinned. "Ho

"You don't have enough.

"We shall see," he said.

ABOUT THE AUTHOR

Georgina Devon began writing fiction in 1985 and has never looked back. Apart from her prolific writing career, she has led an interesting life. Her father was in the United States Air Force, and after Georgina received her B.A. in social sciences from California State College, San Bernardino, she followed in her father's footsteps and joined the USAF. She met her husband, Martin, an A10 fighter pilot, while she was serving as an aircraft maintenance officer.

Georgina, her husband and their young daughter now live in Tucson, Arizona.

Books previously published by Harlequin

Untamed Heart

Scandals

Georgina Devon

Harlequin Books

TORONTO • NEW YORK • LONDON
AMSTERDAM • PARIS • SYDNEY • HAMBURG
STOCKHOLM • ATHENS • TOKYO • MILAN
MADRID • WARSAW • BUDAPEST • AUCKLAND

ISBN 0-373-83322-9

SCANDALS

Copyright © 1996 by Alison J. Hentges.

PROLOGUE

Langston Castle,
Kent, England, 1805

"AHH...!" The scream of agony penetrated the heavy oak door.

Standing in the dark hallway the Marquis of Langston, Jonathan Gervase Maurice St. Simon, ran his long fingers through his already disheveled hair. It was all he could do to keep himself from bursting into the room where his wife lay giving birth to their child. If only it were over, he thought. If only Annabelle did not have to suffer so.

Fast on the heels of that came the even worse realization that she might die. He froze, appalled at the possibility.

"My lord." The hushed voice of the doctor intruded on Langston's dark introspection.

"Is she all right? The babe?" Langston felt as though he'd been riding his stallion, bent on reaching hell, for the past twenty-four hours.

"You've a fine son, my lord," the doctor said. "But my lady has lost a good deal of blood. She is asking for you."

Langston's chest tightened painfully. Annabelle, his beautiful, vivacious wife of one year. He loved her with an intensity he had never thought to experience. He took a deep breath to steady himself before entering the room. He did not want her to see his fear.

As he stepped inside, a blast of heat assaulted him. The fireplace was an inferno, and the draperies were pulled against the weak winter sun. In the large four-poster bed, Annabelle lay like a rag doll, a small white bundle at her side.

"Annabelle," Langston murmured, striding to her side.

"My love." Her voice was weak and he knew the effort it cost her to speak.

Always a pale-complected woman, she was now whiter than the linen sheet covering her. Her glorious black hair spread over the pillow, free as he had never seen it before. Her blue eyes were deep, dark pools of pain.

His chest tightened even more. She was the light of his life, had been since the first time he'd seen her at Almack's. It seemed an eternity ago.

"Love," she whispered, her eyes unfocused.

He took her hand, so frail and thin that the blue veins showed through the skin. If only he could give her his strength.

"Where are you, my love?" Her voice was a rasping plea.

He could barely hear her. Lifting her fingers to his lips, he was shocked by how cold her flesh was. An heir was not worth losing his wife...his love.

"I am here," he whispered, trying to comfort her. "All is well. You just need to rest."

Her mouth, once blood red, now dry and pale, twisted. "I am dying," she said with a soft sigh. "I am dying without knowing what it is like to live."

He choked back a denial, knowing it would do her no good to hear it. Knowing she spoke the truth.

"The babe..." She paused to regain her breath, her chest rising and falling alarmingly. Her ravaged face held him prisoner. Her voice lowered. "You must not tell Langston. Promise me you will not."

The marquis stared at her. What was she talking about?

"I am here, Annabelle. With you."

She reached for his arm, and the grip of her slender fingers was powerful in its tenacity. "Shh. The servants must not know, either. They will tell him."

Perplexed, Langston laid his fingers over her cold ones. She must be suffering delirium.

"Annabelle, calm yourself. Everything will be all right." His voice caught on the last words. He was lying, and he knew it. There was nothing he could do for the woman he loved except to stay with her and comfort her.

"Do not tell...him...about the...babe," the thin thread of her voice continued. "He will disown him, and I could not bear that. The child...the child is innocent."

Langston stared down at his dying wife. Her words were beginning to make a dreadful kind of sense.

"Why would he not want the child?" he asked, afraid of her answer, yet knowing he had to ask.

Her head twisted from side to side, sweat glistening on her brow. She bit her lower lip before speaking, as though a fresh pain held her in its coils. "He is arrogant...proud." The breath soughed between her parched lips. "He could not bear the knowledge that his heir is another man's get."

Unable to look at her, Langston closed his eyes. He wished he could close his ears to the soft words she spoke. When at length he opened his eyes, it was to see her lying exhausted, the babe at her side starting to squirm in discomfort.

"Ah...love," she said faintly. "Hold me. One last time, hold me."

Langston stared down at her, seeing the fine bones beneath her translucent skin. How he had loved her, loved her even now as her betrayal sank into his soul. She thought he was another man.

Holding the agony at bay, Langston carefully picked up the child and set him in the crib positioned nearby. Then he lay down beside Annabelle and took her into his arms.

"You are...warm," she said against his chest, her teeth chattering. "I am so...cold."

He held her tighter, telling himself not to ask her anything else. But he could not resist. "Why did you marry Langston?"

Her eyelids lifted, showing pupils so large he saw his face, ravaged by pain, reflected in their depths. He knew her answer before she said it.

"He...will be a...duke someday." Thin and reedy, the words spilled from her. "But I wanted...to marry you. I wanted to be...Mrs. Huntly." A soft smile curved her bloodless lips.

Huntly! His hands curled into fists, and his nails bit into the palms. "Your parents made you accept Langston." His tone was flat.

She nodded, her fine black hair catching on the collar of his shirt. "Our babe..."

Hers and Huntly's. The ultimate betrayal. Langston swallowed the words of denial. Annabelle, the woman he loved, had never loved him. And she had lain with another man.

Taking a firm grip on his emotions, he said, "You are delirious, my love. Wait until you feel better. Things will be better soon."

Even as he spoke, her eyes drifted shut, and her head lolled to the side. The child began to cry.

Instinctively Langston released her and rose, going to the babe. He must be hungry. The wet-nurse would have to be called.

Lifting the corner of the blanket from the baby's face, Langston gazed into the unfocused blue eyes of his heir; fruit of his wife's womb—another man's son.

CHAPTER ONE

London, 1815

THE MARQUIS OF LANGSTON, heir to the Duke of Rundell, watched the Drury Lane actress perform. His mother, Alicia, Duchess of Rundell, said the woman was a hussy bent on leading Deverell, her youngest son, into ruination. Deverell said she was exquisite. The *ton* said she was the next Sarah Siddons. Langston agreed with them all.

Chestnut hair shot with bronze cascaded down her back, making him itch to run his fingers through it. Langston had not felt such an urge in years. The actress's face was delicately molded, with high cheekbones, a wide brow and a teasing cleft in the chin. Her mouth was full and a trifle wide for the current taste, but he found it intriguing. It was a mouth made to be kissed.

From this distance, and in the stage lighting, he could not tell the color of her eyes, but Deverell had told him often enough. Dev called them "honeygreen," which meant they were green with streaks of golden brown. Langston smiled to himself. Dev was nothing if not poetic when his affections were engaged, which was often.

Her figure was faultless, as well, he admitted to himself as his gaze roved over her supple limbs. Tall and willowy, she was being toasted by the bucks of the *ton* as the Divine Davidson. The ladies were more reserved in their praise.

Langston understood why. No woman in her right mind wanted to compete with Samantha Davidson for a man's attentions.

"I say, Jon," Dev said in his pleasant tenor, "she is magnificent, isn't she?"

Deverell had sandy hair, hazel eyes and an engaging grin. A major in the hussars, he held himself with a military bearing that still managed to be graceful. But he was too volatile by half and always had been. He was also quick to forgive, unable to hold a grudge longer than a fortnight.

Langston gave his brother an indulgent look and nodded. "She is rather extraordinary. Thinking of making her your next mistress?"

It was a loaded question and Langston knew it. Dev had a weakness for beautiful and talented women. This woman was both in spades. However, she was *not* marriage material.

Dev's hazel eyes glinted recklessly. "I'm thinking of making her more than that."

Langston sucked in his breath. So his mother was right. He'd accompanied Dev tonight at his mother's urging. The duchess was in a dither about her youngest son's intentions toward the actress. Sons of dukes did not marry women who trod the boards.

He kept his voice neutral as he asked, "Just what sort of arrangement are you contemplating?"

Dev flushed with irritation. "Mother's been talking to you. Don't deny it."

"Mother talks to me constantly, Dev," Langston replied in a tone laced with mild humor. "To which particular conversation are you referring?"

Dev's flush deepened, and his mouth thinned. "Don't play the innocent with me. I have watched you in the Commons too much to underestimate you. You know perfectly well that she does not want me offering marriage to Sam."

"Sam?" Langston quirked one dark brow at the masculine nickname Dev was giving a very feminine woman. When Dev frowned fiercely, he added, "So 'tis true. You intend to ask that actress to marry you." Langston shook his head in exasperation. "I told Mother she was mistaking your intentions, that you would never be so gauche as to line a fortune-hunter's pocket."

"Sam's no fortune-hunter," Dev retorted, his voice rising so that several women in the box beside them glanced their way.

Seeing their interest and knowing no good would come of any gossip, Langston smiled at them. It was a dazzling display of perfect teeth that managed to be at once beguiling and dangerous. It was a smile to which many a woman had fallen victim.

"I trust you are enjoying the play, ladies?" he asked them, his gaze lingering briefly on each woman's face.

All three fluttered their fans and simpered. They turned back toward the stage, although it was obvious from their covert glances that their attention was really on the two eligible sons of the Duke of Rundell.

Langston looked at Dev and said in a low, firm voice, "Don't make a cake of yourself. Lower your voice, or your intentions will be all over Town by tomorrow."

Reckless by nature, Dev fisted his hands on his black pantaloons. "I have nothing to be ashamed of. If those old biddies choose to spread tales, there is nothing I can do to stop them." His chin rose. "And I have no cause to wish to."

"You're a fool, Dev," Langston said. "Take the woman for your mistress—everyone else does it—but don't ruin yourself by marrying her."

Sitting straighter in his chair, Dev said, "I would never insult Sam by offering her *carte blanche*. She is a lady and deserves my respect and love in a union before God."

Langston's mouth thinned in disgust. "Righteous indignation doesn't suit you, Dev. You have had more mistresses than most men have had horses, and the current object of your affections is undoubtedly making a comfortable living by supplying rich men with the very commodity you are determined to sample only by marriage."

A burst of applause drew Langston's attention back to the stage. Samantha Davidson was performing the part of Lady MacBeth so superbly that she rivaled the renowned Edmund Kean, who shared the stage with her. Langston wondered what it was about the actress that incited Dev, a normally light-hearted young man bent on purely carnal pleasures, to offer her respectability.

She was undoubtedly a stunning woman. There was a litheness about her limbs and movements that drew all eyes to her. Or perhaps it was her manner of speech, that low, whiskey voice, that induced mystery and created in one a curiosity to delve deeper into her personality.

Langston grimaced. He was being as stupid about the woman as Dev, and *he* was not besotted with her. For he had no doubt that the Divine Davidson's favors went to the highest bidder; every woman's did. And Dev's offer of marriage made him the highest bidder. It was a situation he, as older, wiser brother, would have to change.

In the most reasonable tones he could summon, Langston said, "She is striking, Dev, but enjoy her bed without utterly losing your head. Don't let her press you into marriage."

Dev jumped to his feet, flipping his chair backward. "You are cynical and narrow-minded. Just because Annabelle cuckolded you, you think every woman is deceit personified." He drew himself up to his full six feet. "Well, you are wrong. Sam is different."

Langston felt his shoulders stiffen with anger. It was a reaction beyond his control. However, he managed to keep his voice cool. "If you will think beyond your nether parts, Deverell, you will realize that all women are out for the best opportunity. They marry the wealthiest, highest-ranking man available. If they are not marriage material, then they seek to be *kept* by the wealthiest, highest-ranking man. Your actress is no different from Annabelle."

"I pity you," Dev said, the anger of seconds before replaced by sadness. "Because of that one betrayal, you will deny yourself the happiness of finding someone you can care for, someone with whom you can spend the rest of your life.''

Langston kept his voice level in spite of the mounting bitterness that threatened to choke him. ''My past has nothing to do with this, Deverell. This actress is only after your position and money. She cares nothing for you, and marriage to her will ruin your life.''

''I don't care,'' Deverell said, the sadness superseded by defiant determination. ''Sam is worth it.'' With an abrupt twist of his body, he left the box.

Langston consciously relaxed his shoulders as he watched Deverell. But Dev's words had brought back the memories.

A sharp twinge in the back of his neck told him to let the memory and the anger go. His marriage had been a painful lesson in the machinations of the female mind, but he had learned. He would never again make the mistake of trusting a woman.

Now Dev was about to make the same mistake. He was playing into the actress's greedy hands. And the scandal would devastate their mother, not to mention what it would do to Dev's standing among the *ton*. Even his fellow officers would laugh at him after their initial envy abated.

The son of the most powerful duke in Britain did not marry an actress. Lesser members of the aristocracy might do so, but a Rundell . . . never. And when the woman realized that marrying a duke's son did not gain her wealth and cachet, the love she professed for Dev would be supplanted by derision. No, it was a misalliance that would only cause Dev pain.

When his mother had first told him about Deverell's intention to marry the Davidson woman, Langston had laughed and told her not to worry. Dev was too busy sowing his wild oats to settle on one woman. That had been two weeks ago. In that time, Dev had attended Drury Lane every night, coming home after the sun was up. Langston assumed he spent the time with Samantha Davidson.

Watching her with narrowed eyes as she moved gracefully about the stage, her voice a low purr that sent shivers down his spine, he understood Dev's reasoning perfectly. She was a woman any man would long to possess.

Perhaps there was a way to persuade her to let Dev go.

"Langston," said the deep voice of Andrew, Lord Ravensford, as the man came into the box, "mind if I join you?"

"Be my guest," Langston said as his friend righted the chair Deverell had sent tumbling.

Ravensford was a tall, powerfully built man who dressed impeccably and could charm the chemise off a doxy without a farthing changing hands. Red hair and piercing green eyes lent him a distinction few others possessed. He was an old friend of Langston's and of the same political persuasion, sitting in the House of Lords while Langston was the member of Parliament for Northumberland.

Langston would not be legally considered a peer until he assumed his father's title. Therefore, Marquis of Langston was a courtesy title only, taken from one of his father's lesser dignities. Which meant that he could run for and hold office in the House of Commons until he became the Duke of Rundell. Meanwhile, he and Ravensford were touted as the Whig coalition to replace the late Charles James Fox and Lord North in Parliament.

Ravensford sat down and said, "Have you heard that Huntly plans to run for MP from your district?"

"Bloody hell," Langston breathed. "The man is a cockroach." *The man is the father of my dead wife's son.* He pushed the painful thought aside.

"And sure to spend the blunt buying votes," Ravensford added in disgusted tones. "He nearly beat you last time. This time he won't be as circumspect. The man is dangerous."

Langston groaned, the problem with Dev temporarily put on hold by this news. "Huntly is a Tory, in favor of the King retaining power over Parliament. That is something I cannot countenance. George III is insane and the Prince of Wales is irresponsible.''

''True,'' Ravensford agreed. ''Not to mention the Poor Laws you are trying to get through the Commons. Huntly will drop them if he is elected to your seat.''

''Bleak indeed,'' Langston muttered. ''Well, I shall have to campaign for the votes as never before.''

Ravensford, in an attempt at levity, added, ''Too bad the Duchess of Devonshire is gone. Otherwise you could ask her to give away kisses for you as she did for Fox.''

Langston chuckled. ''By now the bloom would be off her beauty. I shall have to find another diamond of the first water to garner votes for me.''

''And I know just whom you should choose,'' Ravensford said, his voice husky.

Langston glanced sharply at his friend. When he saw the direction of his friend's gaze, his stomach knotted. If even a man of Ravensford's experience could be caught by Samantha Davidson's beauty, what hope was there for Dev—or himself?

Much as he preferred to deny it, he had to admit that the constriction in his chest was caused by jealousy. Ravensford could have his pick of the demireps, and Mrs. Davidson certainly fell into that category.

"She is very likely as expensive as Harriette Wilson," Langston said sardonically and instantly regretted his words. No woman would come between him and a friend.

Detecting the strain in his companion's voice, Ravensford dragged his gaze from the stage. "You could afford her, Langston, but with Cynthia as good as betrothed to you, I know you would never take a mistress."

"Honor's damned inconvenient at times," Langston said wryly, trying to ease the tension that had formed between them.

"And speaking of honor," Ravensford said, rising, "I see my sister waving at me." He grimaced. "Got her usual flock of beaux and wants me to ride roughshod over the lot." He sighed dramatically, his grin a slash of white in his swarthy complexion.

Langston watched his friend leave before reluctantly turning his attention back to the stage. His shoulders tensed once more as he watched the Divine Davidson sink into a graceful curtsy. The worst part of this entire situation was the attraction he felt for the woman, an attraction he would deny to the bitter end.

SAMANTHA DROPPED into a final curtsy as the curtain fell. The excitement she always felt after a successful performance was quickly gone, and exhaustion rode her like a fury. All she wanted to do was go home and be with Amalie. Her child made everything worthwhile.

"You are a hit—as usual," Timothy Jones, who played Banquo's ghost, said, *sotto voce*.

"We are all a success," Sam said, intentionally ignoring the envy Timothy had long since stopped attempting to hide. "The whole company deserves praise."

But Sam knew that the audience had come to see Edmund Kean and herself. London was touting her as the successor to the great dramatic actress Sarah Siddons, who had retired in 1812. The comparison pleased Sam, but more important, her success gave her security—for the moment.

Popularity was fleeting on the London stage. Today she was everyone's darling. Tomorrow she would be nothing.

A large part of her success was due to the men of the *ton,* an indisputable aspect of her life that she did not like but grudgingly accepted. Those men would be waiting for the cast members in a back room of the theatre.

She made her way there, feeling clammy and dirty in the pale high-waisted dress she'd donned for the last act. She wanted to be anywhere but here.

The young and not-so-young bucks crowding the room were not seeking her company because of her acting ability. Her gift was of no moment to them, and she knew it.

But her gift mattered to her. She was good at what she did, and proud of her skill. But she was pragmatic enough to realize she could not get by without socializing with and humoring the male members of her audience. It was a small price to pay for the ability to support herself and her small daughter.

Immediately upon her entrance she stopped by a vase of red damask roses. She plucked one and secured it in the ribbon holding her hair in place. To the London audience it was an affectation they associated with her. To Sam it was a little piece of calm and beauty in a world that was too often harsh and deadly. The rich fragrance was a tonic to her tired mind.

She needed the calming influence when an aging roué accosted her with his terrible jokes. After the first two, she murmured, "Excuse me," and tried to slip away. Before she got very far, another man detained her.

"I say, Mrs. Davidson." The man put a hand on her arm, forcing her to stop. "Join me for supper?"

Sam stared pointedly at his fingers until he released her. Knowing she had to make amends for the silent order to be unhanded, she smiled at him.

"Thank you, Lord Drake, but I am afraid I am already engaged."

His mouth turned down. "Perhaps another time?"

She widened her smile. "Perhaps."

Turning away, she was confronted by two more men, one of them the Honorable David Huntly. He was a tall, slender man, impeccably dressed, with brown hair cut in the fashionable Brutus style. His thin lips smiled while his blue eyes devoured her.

"Mrs. Davidson," Huntly murmured.

Sam took an unconscious step back. The movement did not prevent Huntly from taking her unoffered hand and raising it to his lips. Chills chased up her arm and made the hair on her nape rise.

"I hope you have reconsidered your answer?" he asked softly, the heat in his voice at odds with the cold glitter in his eyes as they roved possessively over her person.

Sam's chill intensified. Huntly had been importuning her to become his mistress for weeks. It took a great effort of will to meet his gaze squarely. "My answer is unchanged and will remain so."

His smile hardened, and for an instant Sam thought he might strike her. Then the expression was gone and he was his usual urbane self. Still, he and his companion blocked her way, so she was forced to remain. She knew by the smirk on his face that Huntly understood exactly the position she was in.

Smiling coolly, Sam decided that the rest of the night would only cause the headache growing in her temples to become worse. But she would not let Huntly cow her.

Huntly took a champagne flute from a passing servant and held it out to her. She took it because there was no way to decline graciously, but she merely touched the rim to her lips while Huntly's companion tried to entertain her with amusing anecdotes.

Meanwhile, Huntly's perusal of her person continued, growing more thorough and insulting by the second. It was too much, and the increasing pain in her temples made it easy for her to eye him coldly.

If only men would see her as a person and not an object to be purchased by the highest bidder! And Huntly was the worst of the lot. All he wanted was to share her bed. No loving relationship, no lifelong commitment.

She wanted nothing to do with such a man. And while she needed a father for Amalie and a husband for herself, even that was not enough. She also wanted a man she truly loved, and who loved her equally in return.

A soft sigh escaped her. Dreaming was lovely, as long as she realized she was doing just that. No man would offer her marriage—at least no man she could care for as she should.

Her mouth quirked up at one corner. Deverell St. Simon had offered her marriage, and she was a fool not to accept him. He was sweet, and she liked him. But she could never shackle him to a socially unacceptable marriage where only one of them loved.

"I believe Mrs. Davidson finds us boring," Huntly murmured, his insinuating tone penetrating Sam's musings.

This was an untenable position, she decided. It was past time to make her excuses and leave the party.

Just then, she sensed a change in the men's posture. Her curiosity piqued, Sam casually turned to look behind her. The movement became an awkward twist.

For not more than three feet away, and looking directly at her, was the most arresting man she had ever beheld. He was formidably handsome, with broad shoulders and lean hips. Her throat closed, and she had to remind herself to breathe.

Blond hair, burnished by the candlelight, swept back from his high forehead. His nose was classically strong. His deep-set eyes were dark, the hard, glinting brown of a bird of prey as it focuses on its victim.

Sam swallowed, her gaze dropping to his mouth. His lips were full, firm and well shaped, putting the lie to the coldness in his eyes. Unaccountably they made Sam wonder how they would feel on her skin.

Chiding herself for such susceptibility, a susceptibility she had never suffered before, she straightened her shoulders and looked up at him. An imposing man, he stood easily a foot taller than she, and she was not a short woman. He also towered over most of the men present.

He moved with controlled power, and she had no doubt he would make a dangerous enemy—or an exciting lover. Color infused her cheeks at the reckless thought.

He was close enough for her to see the fine fan of thick brown lashes, which were an interesting contrast to his fair hair. His eyes held hers captive.

He bowed curtly, and his mouth curled up at one corner. "Mrs. Davidson," he said, his voice deep and mesmerizing. "I am delighted to meet you at last. I feel I already know you."

Sam's chest tightened in a strange premonition. The gleam in his eyes was both mocking and derisive. But why? She had never seen him before this moment. Such undisguised dislike made her hackles rise.

Her voice cool, just short of rude, she said, "Then you have the advantage, sir."

His mouth twisted higher, giving a sardonic cast to his features. "Allow me to introduce myself. I am Langston. Deverell's older brother."

Understanding dawned like a newly lit candle in a dark room. He was here to warn her not to accept Lord Deverell's offer of marriage. Doubtless he thought her a fortune hunter. She pushed the disillusionment away; she should be used to men thinking the worst of her.

"How delightful," she murmured, turning away from the confrontation she knew he wanted.

To turn her back was the cut direct, but she did not care. Exhaustion weighted her shoulders, and all she wanted was to go home.

Huntly snickered and murmured provocatively, "Met your match at last, Langston?"

The marquis, for Sam knew his title from her conversations with Lord Deverell, smiled disdainfully at him. "I see you have not changed since Eton, Huntly."

The other man turned brick red. "Nor have you, Langston. But contrary to past experience, your position and wealth will do you no good with this lady. Prinny himself has already tried and been refused."

The marquis quirked a brow. "I am not the Prince of Wales."

Sam lowered her lashes to hide her growing exasperation. The three men were behaving like little boys arguing over a toy. She used their absorption in one another to slip away. The last thing she wanted was to be a party to a disagreement or, more correctly, to be subjected to the confrontation she knew the Marquis of Langston intended.

The door was a mere step away when a large hand settled on her arm. Tingles spread down her spine. Langston.

She felt an odd urge to move toward his strength. She shook her head slightly to banish the foolish idea, dislodging the rose from her hair ribbon.

He caught it before she could. Raising it to his face, he breathed deeply of its heady scent.

"A beguiling affectation, Mrs. Davidson," he murmured, replacing it without asking her permission.

He was unbearably close. Sam felt suffocated, her pulse beating too quickly. She retreated from him until her back was pressed against the door.

As haughtily as she could manage with the blood pounding through her veins, she said, "You must have something you think very important to say to me, but—" she forced a brittle smile to her lips "—I do not wish to hear it."

His eyes narrowed. "At this point, Mrs. Davidson, it does not matter what you wish. I intend to speak to you and you *will* hear me out."

Sam saw the implacable line of his jaw and the tension in his features. This man was used to being obeyed. But she refused to be browbeaten—particularly by a man she was so disturbingly responsive to.

With a shrug, she stepped to the side. "There is nothing to discuss."

His fingers moved to her shoulder. "I do not take kindly to opposition," he murmured.

Sam stiffened with outrage. "I do not take kindly to being detained. Unhand me, sir, or I shall scream."

"Do so," he said, his voice low and carrying no inflection, making his words that much more potent.

Nonplussed, Sam was momentarily at a loss. He must have sensed her confusion, because he took the opportunity to maneuver her out the door.

The darkened hallway was deserted, and Sam felt her pulse quicken until she thought she might faint. She was not afraid he would harm her, but there was something about his lean, muscled form towering over her that was both exciting and terrifying.

Lifting her chin so that the cleft became more visible, she said, "Do you find brute force an effective means of getting your own way?"

A gleam entered his eyes. "I use whatever means are at hand."

Sam silently acknowledged his determination as he angled her farther down the shadowed hall. Instead of trying to evade him, she would meet him head on. After all, this confrontation was not totally unexpected. In a family like the Rundells, someone was guaranteed to take exception to a younger son's marriage to an actress. Sam just wished the person taking exception was not Langston. The man's potent masculinity was far too disturbing.

They stopped where a lone candle flickered. Sam felt angry, yet invigorated. She had not felt this way in the presence of a man since she was sixteen. No, in truth she had never felt this heady blend of excitement and keen awareness of another person. It was almost frightening, and most surely a mistake.

Langston released her and stepped back. "Mrs. Davidson, I am sure you know why I am here tonight. I have no intention of letting you trick Deverell into marrying you."

Sam froze. It was exactly what she had expected, but it did not ease the anger and, yes, the pain of being thought a conniving female.

Her voice sharp, she said, "Are you your brother's keeper? I would not have thought you the biblical sort."

These were not the words she had intended to say, but something about Langston raised her ire. She would not permit him to dictate to her. Nor would she grovel before him and waste time and energy trying to convince him that he had wrongful notions about her. It was obvious he had made up his mind, and nothing she said or did would change it.

Fury emanated from him. She saw it in the tense line of his broad shoulders under the perfectly fitted black coat. It gave her a modicum of satisfaction.

Very quietly he said, "I do not believe you understand just what you are undertaking. I have vast resources at my disposal. You have nothing."

Raising one brow, she murmured, "Resorting to threats now, my lord?"

"Whatever is necessary." He leaned forward so that his face was close to hers, his masculine scent teasing her nostrils. "I won't let Deverell ruin his life by marrying you."

She blanched at his cruelty, but she should have expected this. As an actress, she was considered a fallen woman, the type no decent man would take to wife.

"And if I told you I have no intention of marrying your brother?"

He moved away and arrogantly looked her up and down, his gaze lingering for one heart-stopping instant on the fragrant rose nestled in her curls. "Hoping for richer prey? No one else would be foolish enough to offer marriage, and I think you are clever enough to realize that. No, I think you have every intention of accepting Deverell's offer."

Sam swallowed her ire, knowing it was futile to berate Langston further. "Not everyone is avaricious. But perhaps, my lord, you do not know that," she said with false sweetness.

"You are an actress, and we both know that is just a front for a more... lucrative profession."

Sam clenched her hands to keep from slapping the man. Sarcasm dripping from every word, she said, "Then my more lucrative profession will make it all the worse for Lord Deverell to be in my clutches, won't it?"

His mouth thinned. "How much do you want?"

Sam had thought he could not make her angrier, but she had been wrong. Blood pounded in her ears. "You don't have enough."

"We shall see," he said.

Sam recognized a threat when she heard it, and she had no intention of remaining for more of the same. Before he could speak again, she spun around, eluding his grasp, and sped down the hallway.

She would not allow the arrogant Marquis of Langston to rule her life.

CHAPTER TWO

LANGSTON WATCHED the woman rush away from him. There was a sway to her hips and an elegance to her slender back and long neck that drew him in spite of himself. She was like the rose in her hair— lush and beautiful. It was just as well she was not right for Deverell. To covet his brother's wife would be to live in hell.

He sauntered to the backstage room they had recently left and collected his beaver hat and gold-tipped walking cane. Shrugging on his many-caped greatcoat to ward off the winter chill, he left.

Outside, the frosty air made the half moon appear rimmed in silver. The scent of soot hung heavily in the air.

"Jon." Deverell's voice caught Langston's attention.

Langston slowed enough for Deverell to reach him. "Been lurking in the shadows waiting for your lady love to leave?"

Dev flushed. "Perhaps." Then his hazel eyes narrowed in suspicion. "I never expected to see you coming from that room. Thinking of taking a mistress before you tie the knot with Cynthia?''

A small spurt of guilt over his reaction to Samantha Davidson tugged at Langston before he told himself not to be ridiculous. He was not betrothed to Cynthia, and he was not attracted to the Davidson woman.

"I am not in the market for female entertainment, Dev. I leave that foolishness up to you.''

Dev laughed, but it was strained. "You know me too well.''

"I thought I did,'' Langston said, resuming his brisk pace.

"What were you doing in the back room, anyway?'' Deverell asked suspiciously. "It ain't your style to chase lightskirts.''

Langston gave Deverell a disgusted look. "True. But sometimes family obligations come before taste.''

Deverell skidded to a halt on the slippery walk. "I ought to have known. You were talking to Sam! I never should have left in the first place.''

Ignoring the accusation in his brother's tone, Langston continued on his way. Again he heard Deverell rushing to catch up. It did not surprise him to feel Dev's hand seize his coat and pull him to a stop, but his renowned patience was wearing thin.

"'Tis damnably cold out here, Dev. Leave it until we get home."

"I bloody well won't!"

Langston removed Deverell's hand from his coat. "Then you will rant and rave to yourself, because I am not standing out in the weather for anyone."

A fine sleet was coming down, melting as it hit the ground. It glistened on the rim of Langston's beaver hat and sparkled on Deverell's shoulders before sinking into the woolen cloth of his coat.

Deverell dropped his arm. "Have it your way."

Langston ignored Deverell's sullenness and left him to follow or not as he chose. It was not long before Dev caught up again.

"What did you say to Sam?" Deverell asked, his voice heavy with suppressed anger.

Langston did not bother looking at Dev. He knew what he would see. Ever since they were boys, Deverell had chafed at the restrictions placed on him. As a young man he was close to becoming a rakehell. It worried everyone except their father, who said Deverell would settle down in time.

"I told the woman you were not available for marriage."

"You had no right!"

Deverell's words rang out in the quiet street. Langston kept moving, determined to reach home before it began snowing in earnest. "Damn," he muttered. "Wish I'd had the carriage brought round."

"Are you listening to me?" Deverell demanded.

"The whole world is listening to you," Langston said wearily. He was tired of battling, first the Divine Davidson over Dev, and now Dev over the Divine Davidson. He was beginning to detest the chit.

Deverell paused in midstride. "I am going to marry Sam, no matter what you say."

Langston sighed in exasperation as he turned to face Deverell. "She is an actress, Dev. Or have you taken complete leave of your senses? No doubt she has had more men than you have had women, and that is no small accomplishment."

"Bloody hell!" Deverell exclaimed, slipping on the wet cobbles. "You are a righteous bastard."

Langston knew there was nothing to be gained by taking his frustrations with the woman out on Dev. Dev was going to be difficult enough to handle as it was.

"Do your name and family mean so little to you that you would drag them through a sordid marriage to such a woman? A marriage that can only end in failure."

"Sam is as honorable as any *ton* miss. The only difference is that Sam earns her living. And she is a sight more honorable than Annabelle was."

"That was a low blow, Dev," Langston murmured, forcing himself to let go of the old, destructive anger. Annabelle's betrayal was in the past, but it had taught him a lesson he intended never to forget.

"I fight to win," Deverell said softly. "The army teaches a fellow that. And I intend to win Sam."

Langston suppressed a groan. "So you admire the actress because she supports herself. Think. Marriage to you will be a windfall to a woman like that. She will snap you up like a fox after a chicken."

He shook his head and walked more quickly. They were almost at Grosvenor Square, where the Duke of Rundell's impressive Town house was situated.

"I admire Sam because she is her own person, Jon. She has made a success of her life despite her situation." Dev's voice softened. "And she is kind. You would not expect it in a woman in her profession, but she is genuinely kind. I saw her give a beggar her last shilling. Show me one toast of the *ton* who would do the same, and I will show you a monkey in Prinny's livery."

Langston chuckled at Dev's comparison. The Prince of Wales was a law unto himself. But he sobered quickly. "Did you offer Mrs. Davidson money to tide her over?"

"Of course I did," Dev said immediately before seeing the sardonic twist on his brother's mouth. "Ah. You tricked me into that, didn't you?"

"You tricked yourself," Langston said, his voice laced with sarcasm. "She expected you to give her money, and you very likely gave her much more than she gave the beggar."

"I tried. She refused my offer," Dev said triumphantly. "Sam is not mercenary."

"Enough," Langston said, mounting the steps to the double doors of their father's residence. "Right now, I am cold and tired, and I am fed up with arguing. 'Tis obvious the woman has you wrapped in tick and tucked away for a cold winter's night."

Pushing open the doors before the butler could reach them, Langston strode ahead of Dev. Disgust was something he seldom felt for his scapegrace brother, but he felt it now.

He had not gotten ten feet into the foyer when his mother's personal maid accosted him. With a curtsy, she said, "If it please your lordship, Her Grace wishes to speak with you."

"Tell her I will be there shortly," Langston said.

He was not surprised by his mother's summons. It was one of the reasons he had come here, instead of returning to his Town house, the other being that his residence was still under renovation and there was no decent bed to be had.

When he entered his mother's boudoir minutes later, she was reclining on a silver-brocade settee. Even after having three sons, the eldest of whom, Langston, was thirty-two, Alicia, Duchess of Rundell, was still a beautiful woman. Her black hair, as yet untouched by gray, was cropped fashionably short in the front and piled high on her head in the back. Her eyes were large and gray, ringed in black lashes, and her dressing gown of royal blue, embroidered with silver thread, enhanced them.

"What did she say?" the duchess asked.

Langston smiled. Dev got his impulsiveness from their mother. "Aren't you going to offer tea and biscuits or something equally fortifying before you start putting me through the Inquisition?"

"Do not be provoking, Jon," she said. "'Tis past midnight."

Without notice the door on the west wall opened. It connected the duchess's suite with her husband's. The duke sauntered into the room, his gaze going from his wife to his son and back again. He was a tall, slim, elegant man, very like his eldest son. Only where Langston's hair was burnished gold, the duke's was paler, owing to gray at the temples. Their eyes were identical—deep brown and piercing.

Gervase St. Simon, Duke of Rundell, gazed at his wife and then his son, a smile tugging at the corners of his mouth. "A powwow, as the American aborigines would say?"

Alicia rose from her seat and went to her husband, hands outstretched. "Dearest, I did not know you were back from Brooks's."

"That is obvious, my love." His smile turned wicked. "Otherwise you would not be entertaining another man in your boudoir."

Langston rose, feeling uncomfortable by the desire his parents made no effort to hide. There had been a time, not so long ago, when they barely spoke. Then his mother had run away with her lover. The duke had realized he loved his wife and did not want to lose her. He had brought her home, declared his feelings, and things had changed.

However, for the first twenty-seven years, his parents' marriage of convenience had been a disaster. Langston's own marriage had been a debacle. He did not need a crystal ball to see that Dev's planned marriage to an avaricious actress would be doomed, as well.

"Excuse me," Langston said quietly, wanting to leave the room. "I will be on my way, Mother. We can talk in the morning."

The duchess whirled around, her brows drawn into a frown that did nothing to mar her beauty. "Don't be silly, Jon. Your father can discuss this problem with us." She tugged the duke to the settee where they sat close enough for his arm to circle her shoulders. "You must know, Rundell, that I am worried about Deverell. He is chasing a Drury Lane actress—offering marriage!" she finished in appalled tones.

The duke's amused eyes met his son's while his hand tightened on his wife's shoulder. "Deverell is much too conscious of his name and position to be serious, my dear. You have nothing to fret about."

Alicia's mouth thinned and her gaze hardened. "'Tis what I expected you to say. Honestly, Rundell, just because you were aware of your duty at an early age does not mean your sons are."

The duke's face sobered. "Alaistair seems to have done very well for himself, even if he did initially marry Liza because of her brother's suicide. And Jon here has already wed once and has an heir. But a second son would be nice, so he is on the brink of betrothal to the eldest daughter of the Earl of Sandring." He grinned wickedly. "Dev is not even twenty-six. He, too, will eventually settle down with the right woman. No doubt the actress is being recalcitrant with her favors, and Dev hopes to soften her by offering more than monetary gain. He wouldn't be the first young buck to do so."

It was on the tip of Langston's tongue to ask his father if the duke had done such a thing in his youth, but there were his mother's feelings to consider. At the moment, the duchess looked scandalized.

Instead, Langston said, "I think Dev might be more serious than you credit him, sir." It was as close as he could come to contradicting his father. While they got along well enough, the duke had raised him to understand that a son did not argue with his father.

"Well," Rundell said, standing, "I leave it to you to save him from himself." Bending down to kiss his wife, he murmured, "As for you, I will be waiting, my love."

The duchess blushed prettily, but her eyes boldly met her husband's. "I shan't be long." As soon as the duke was gone, she sighed. "Now, Jon," she said in her mellow alto, which was, Langston noted, disturbingly similar to Samantha Davidson's, "you still have not told me about *that woman.*"

Langston knew he could not tell her everything about the actress. To hear that Samantha Davidson was the most attractive woman he had ever seen would only make the duchess worry more. And if she knew he wanted the woman for himself—and to his disgust, he did—his mother would suffer a case of the vapors the likes of which he never hoped to witness.

He compromised. "She is a remarkably handsome woman with a genuine talent. 'Tis obvious why she is being touted as the next Sarah Siddons.''

The duchess jumped up and began to pace the room, her silver-embroidered robe swirling about her legs like liquid metal. "Stop skirting the issue, Jon. This is not the House of Commons. I am your mother and we are discusing your youngest brother's ruination." She stopped and stared him down. "Is she going to release Dev?"

Never one to allow an opponent the advantage, even when the opponent was his mother, Langston rose and strode to the hearth, where he propped one elegantly shod foot on the grate. The fire was comfortably warm after the chill of outside, and he was suddenly tired.

When he spoke, his voice was calm and level, much as it was when he carried a motion in the Commons. "She will eventually release Dev. 'Tis merely a matter of making it worth her while."

"So true," the duchess said, resuming her seat. "Women such as she understand only one thing: blunt. And the more of it, the better their comprehension." Her gaze shifted to Jon. "See that she is convinced."

"I intend to do so, ma'am," he replied, taking this as dismissal.

She rose and came to him, kissing him on the cheek. "You were always my dependable one, my sensible one who knew what to do and when to let something languish. That is why you do so well in the Commons.''

She moved to her dresser and picked up one of several jars. A delicate shudder ran through her slight frame as she gazed morosely at her reflection in the bevelled glass.

"Do whatever it requires, Jon. We cannot have a St. Simon marrying an actress. There has been quite enough scandal in this family.''

Her attempt to run off with a man who was not his father had ended in the biggest scandal of the past ten years. He knew it continued to trouble her, even as it continued to perplex him.

Langston left the room determined to prevent Dev from making an alliance that could only end in disillusionment and pain.

THAT SAME EVENING, Samantha opened the front door of her small home in Covent Garden. She had bought the house after her first season as a leading lady at Drury Lane. It was modest, and it needed repair. The furnishings were cast-offs and the rugs threadbare, but it was hers and it was a respectable place to raise her nine-year-old daughter.

With a sigh of relief, Sam took off her cape and laid it across the chair situated in the foyer for that purpose. She tucked a wayward lock of chestnut hair behind her ear and considered making herself a strong cup of tea to help her think. For think she must.

It was obvious that the Marquis of Langston intended to hound her. She was no green girl, unaware of the power and influence such a man wielded, and he would bring it all to bear against her.

But even this knowledge, serious as it was, could not dim the remembrance of his proximity and her reaction to his touch.

She stiffened her spine. He was not importuning her for her favors, far from it. If only he were interested in her for something different. If only he did not think of her as an ambitious tart out to bilk his younger brother. She sighed again. And if only gold could be made from dross.

Picking up the candle Lottie had left burning, Sam mounted the narrow flight of stairs to the first floor and the bedrooms, the notion of hot tea forgotten. She eased open one of the doors and slipped inside. It was a small room, with a highboy against one wall and a bed against the opposite one. The bright yellow gingham curtains were closed to the moonlight, but the candle she carried allowed her to see Amalie.

She crossed to the bed and gazed down at her child. Setting the candle on the nearby table, she gave in to the urge to smooth her daughter's hair back from her forehead. Suddenly overwhelmed by love, Sam sat on the bed and gathered Amalie into her arms.

"Mama?" Amalie sleepy voice asked.

"Yes, sweetheart," Sam murmured, relishing the feel of her child's slight body against her heart. " 'Tis only me."

Amalie snuggled closer and Sam rocked her, crooning a lullaby. She knew Amalie had fallen back to sleep, but she hoped that her nearness now would help to make up for the time she had to spend away.

She loved her daughter so much it hurt.

Amalie's wealth of golden hair and large blue eyes were a strong reminder of the girl's father. Charles Davidson had been an actor, and he had left her when Amalie was six months old. Sometime later Sam heard he had drowned when the ship he was taking to America sank. His memory had long ceased to be painful.

Settling Amalie into the nest of comforters and bedclothes, Sam dropped one last kiss on the girl's cheek. It was time she herself went to bed, or tomorrow would be torture.

AND IT WAS, Sam decided some hours later as she levered herself onto her elbows and peered into the dim light of the room. A remnant of last night's headache still plagued her, no doubt made worse by the knowledge that Langston intended to make her life miserable. She flopped back onto the pillows and flung an arm over her eyes.

It would be so easy to give in to Langston's demands, particularly since she had no intentions of marrying Lord Deverell in the first place. But she knew she would fight the marquis. If she did not, she was afraid she would succumb to the attraction he held for her.

A whirling dervish chose that instant to fling open the chamber door and launch itself at her bed. Sam caught Amalie just as the girl hit the spring-green bedcover.

"Amalie," Sam said, laughing, "you certainly know how to roust me from bed."

Amalie giggled and wrapped her arms around her mother's neck and squeezed. "I thought you would never get up today. Lottie said to leave you be until you did."

"That was very nice of Lottie."

Sam set Amalie on the bed and rose to don a frayed emerald-green wool robe and slippers. The sooner she got up, the sooner the lingering headache would dissipate. Hugging herself against the chill, she crossed to the coals laid in the fireplace and lit them, then lowered herself into the chair in front of the hearth.

"Mama," Amalie said from her perch on the bed, "Lottie's bringing your chocolate, and then will you please take me to see the wild animals in the Tower?"

Sam suppressed a sigh. She had to attend an early rehearsal and there were things to do about the house. It would be nice to have some time just for herself, but her daughter needed her more. There was nothing she would not do to ensure Amalie's happiness and security.

"Of course, Amalie," she said. "But we shall have to hurry, and we shan't be able to stay long."

"Oh, thank you!" Amalie said, climbing off the bed and jumping up and down in her exuberance. "I shall get my pattens and we can be off."

Sam chuckled. "I have to dress, and I would like my breakfast."

"Now, missie," Lottie said from the doorway, where she stood holding a tray loaded with a steaming pot of chocolate and a plate of scones, "I told you not to bother your mama about that today."

Nearing fifty, Lottie was tall with a robust figure and thick gray hair worn in a severe bun. Never a pretty woman, she had aged into distinction. Rectangular spectacles perched on a nose that was too small for her round face. Her bright blue eyes missed nothing, and Sam loved her dearly.

Sam took the tray from the older woman. "Thank you, Lottie, but how many times must I tell you I can fix my own breakfast?"

"Tsk," Lottie said with an affronted air. "I'm the servant, Miss Sam, not you."

Shaking her head at her old nurse's stubbornness, Sam resumed her seat with the tray on her lap. "And I am the one who won't hire a cook and scullery maid to help out."

"'Course not," Lottie said matter-of-factly. "You're saving money to support us in our dotage, far-off though that may be."

A smile tugged at one corner of Sam's mouth. Lottie's refusal to admit she was getting older was a constant source of banter between them.

"And I hope to save much more," Sam said, "but I do not expect you to shoulder all the burdens in this house."

Hands on her ample hips, Lottie stated, "You work most of the night and part of the day as it is. 'Tis only right that I do what needs to be done here."

It was an old argument, and one that Sam never won. She took a sip of the hot chocolate and let its rich warmth slide soothingly down her throat.

"Thank goodness you make the chocolate. I have not the patience to do it."

Moving to make up the bed, Lottie sniffed. "You've patience enough when 'tis something you want to do. Did you not spend months convincing the leader of the acting troupe to make you part of it, after your good-for-nothing—" She stopped, her gaze darting to Amalie.

But Sam knew what was unsaid. After her husband, an actor, had deserted her and Amalie, she had returned home, begging for shelter. Her stepfather had refused, turning her away to fend for herself and her child. She would never forgive him, but his cruelty had hardened her resolve to succeed.

And she had.

Putting the unpleasant memory from her mind, she spread jam on one of the warm scones and handed it to Amalie, who was now sitting on the floor beside her.

"Mmm," Amalie said. "May I have another?"

Sam smiled indulgently. "Of course, but chew with your mouth closed."

The smacking stopped immediately.

Having been raised in genteel poverty—her mother was the youngest child of a minor baron—Sam insisted on good manners.

"Don't be wiping those sticky fingers on your dress," Lottie said sternly from the side of the bed she was tucking in. "I just washed and starched that pinafore yesterday, and I don't do laundry again for a week."

"Yes, ma'am," Amalie murmured, taking another scone.

While Amalie ate, Sam began to dress. "I was going to do the upstairs floors today, Lottie, but Amalie and I are going to the Tower. I will do them tomorrow." She stared at the nurse. "Do not clean them while we are gone."

Lottie looked away.

"I know what that means," Sam said. "Do *not* do them."

"There's a note for you, Miss Samantha. 'Tis down by the front door. I forgot about it."

Sam knew this was Lottie's way of avoiding the issue, but she did not press her further. "Who is it from?"

"Don't know. A footman in blue-and-gold livery brought it round. Didn't recognize the colors as belonging to any of your admirers."

A sense of foreboding raised the tiny hairs on the back of Sam's neck. She quickly dressed in a serviceable Pomona-green walking dress and sturdy half boots, then left the room.

The note, written on heavy vellum, lay on a tray on the small table in the front hallway. As she picked it up, Sam noticed that her fingers were shaking.

She grimaced. It was not as though she even recognized the paper or the coat of arms embossed on it, so why did she feel so faint-hearted?

Inserting a nail under the sealing wax, she opened the single sheet. The sender had written in bold, black script: "I shall call on you at three of the clock today. Langston."

The breath she had not realized she was holding escaped from her parted lips. He wanted to berate her again about Lord Deverell's proposal of marriage. The arrogant man had enough nerve for a dozen dukes' heirs.

Glancing at the watch pinned to her bodice, she saw that it was one o'clock. Normally she brought Amalie home before going to the theatre for rehearsal, but that might place her here when Langston called. And she had no intention of receiving him.

Let him suffer a little longer, thinking she intended to marry Lord Deverell. It was small recompense for the way he had treated her. Jaw clenched and chin elevated, she strode back up the stairs.

"Lottie, I want you and Amalie to meet me at the theatre at three o'clock. Amalie may watch for a while and then you can bring her home."

Lottie glanced up from the clothes she was folding. "Something in the note?"

"Nothing I cannot resolve," Sam said, pacing to the fire and back. "And the sooner he realizes that, the better."

Amalie, oblivious to the undercurrents of her mother's mood, jumped up and squealed. "May I really come and watch you, Mama? How grand!" She caught Sam's hand and squeezed. "Someday I am going to be a great actress just like you."

Sam's chest tightened as she looked at her child. How do you tell your daughter you want better for her when you know it is not possible? Her gaze slid to Lottie's worried face. The older woman knew how she felt.

Smiling, Sam gathered Amalie to her breast. "Well, today, will you settle for just being my audience?"

CHAPTER THREE

SAM'S SATISFACTION at having avoided Langston was short-lived. He had not come to the theatre after her, but his brother had and had followed her to the post-performance party.

"Please, Sam, say you will marry me," Lord Deverell St. Simon pleaded.

Sam gave him a bittersweet smile and allowed him to retain one hand in both of his, even though she knew they were being carefully observed by the jaded rakes populating this Drury Lane Theatre room. Deverell had confronted her here when she refused to meet him privately. She sensed a desperation in him that made her long to comfort him as a mother would a child, but that, she knew, would only make the situation worse.

"Thank you very much for the great compliment, my lord, but you know I cannot accept." She spoke coolly in spite of her sympathy for him.

"Sam, don't say no," Deverell said, his voice breaking. "Don't refuse yet. Think about it."

Regret overwhelmed her. If only she could accept him. He would provide security for her. More important, he would provide it for Amalie. He could give Amalie the life Sam knew she never could.

Still, he was too nice and too decent for her to accept him. Although his reputation was that of a rakehell, she sensed an innate goodness in him. One day he would make some woman a fine husband.

But not her. She knew the world of the *haut monde* well enough to realize that as a younger son Deverell would benefit most from marrying an heiress, preferably one from a titled family. Barring that, he could marry a tradesman's daughter if her dowry were large enough. But he would be a fool to marry her. Doing so would bring him nothing but ridicule.

Besides, she did not love him.

Unbidden, a picture formed in her mind: a strong face with a broad forehead and hawklike deep brown eyes. Langston. She sighed. He cared nothing for her.

"I say, Mrs. Davidson," came a languid drawl from behind her, "mind if I procure you another glass of wine?"

Glad for a respite from Deverell's persistence, Sam turned to the Earl of Ravensford. He was a devastatingly handsome man with a wicked, lopsided grin. Gossip said he was a crony of Langston's. Her initial feeling of relief evaporated.

Nevertheless, she managed a smile.

"Thank you, my lord. I should very much like that."

"Sam..." Deverell pleaded.

In a deceptively mild voice, the earl said for Deverell's ear alone, "Don't make a cake of yourself, Dev. She is not interested."

Deverell frowned, his hazel eyes darkening. But he said nothing further, only watched the couple disappear into the crowd.

"Thank you, Lord Ravensford," Sam said softly. She did not elaborate, having no desire to belittle Deverell.

Ravensford grinned down at her. "Dev's a firebrand. Always has been and always will be. The army is a good place for him."

The smile she gave him this time was genuine. Despite his being a friend of Langston's, she found that she liked this tall, swarthy man, whom many said was one of the most powerful up-and-coming politicians in the country.

However, when Ravensford deposited her in an out-of-the-way corner as she requested while he fetched her a glass of wine, she took the opportunity to slip from the room. 'Twas past time for her to be home. She was tired and she was melancholy.

Entering her small dressing room, she took hold of her thick woolen cape and swung it around her shoulders. In so doing, she knocked over a crystal paperweight, one of the few gifts her husband had given her. It was in the whimsical shape of a unicorn. Charles had said it was to protect her maidenhood from his advances. A shiver chased down her spine at the memory. She had been young and naive.

As she righted the paperweight, she noticed the thick sheet of paper it had covered. It was the Marquis of Langston's note, which she had placed there earlier. She frowned in irritation. He could send her enough notes to paper Drury Lane and she would still ignore him.

Langston was dangerous. Instinctively she knew he could hurt her—in any way he chose.

But enough of such thoughts. It was time to be off.

With one hand she drew the hood up over her head, while with the other, she picked up her reticule. It felt comfortably heavy. Inside was a small, single-barrel pistol.

To save a few shillings, she always walked home from the theatre. It was several blocks, usually not more than twenty minutes of brisk walking, but the Covent Garden area could be dangerous after dark.

However, it was a risk Sam was willing to take in order to better provide for Amalie. A penny saved was a penny earned.

She left the theatre through one of the side entrances. The cold air formed halos around the gas street lamps and frost nipped her nose. She clutched her cape closer and set off.

She did not get very far before the sound of carriage wheels on cobbles made her breath catch. Ordinarily, the noise would mean nothing—this was, after all, a well-traveled area—but she found herself inordinately nervous, a state she blamed on Langston.

Sam walked faster.

A black carriage pulled up beside her. The door opened, revealing the figure of a man. A very big man.

Sam took a deep breath and told herself it was mere coincidence that the coach had stopped beside her. Still, she had learned to be cautious.

She continued walking. The bump of the reticule against her thigh was reassuring.

When the vehicle rolled forward just enough to keep pace with her, perspiration broke out on her forehead, despite the cold air. It was becoming obvious there was nothing chance about this encounter.

She fumbled with the strings of her reticule. Before she could open it and get her fingers on the pistol, the forbidding figure leapt from the open door of the vehicle and landed nimbly in front of her. Sam jerked to a halt and spun around, intending to make a dash for the theatre.

His hand shot out and circled her waist. She twisted like an animal in a trap, and just as helplessly. Then he lifted her off her feet and tossed her into the carriage, where she landed awkwardly on the floor.

She screamed, but it was no use. In seconds, the man was beside her, the door was closed, and the carriage was in motion.

Sobs of frustration and fear escaped her. She bit her bottom lip to stifle them and struggled with her reticule.

"You have powerful lungs, Mrs. Davidson," said a deep, familiar voice.

Sam froze in the act of ripping apart her reticule. "Langston!"

"Who else?" he drawled.

"A cad and a bully," she spat, her fear now replaced with fury.

Her anger, in fact, was so intense that when her fingers finally closed over the butt of the pistol, she was fully prepared to pull the trigger. It was too small to seriously hurt the fiend, but might deter him.

Before she could get the pistol completely out, Langston's fingers closed firmly on her wrist. "I think not," he said softly.

"Let me go," she said with as much calm authority as she could muster when her entire body felt as though lightning were arcing through it.

He released her, his lips parted in a grin that had nothing to do with amusement. "You are a spitfire, Mrs. Davidson. Very like Deverell in that respect."

Sam's fury eased to a simmer that was no less strong, simply less volatile. "Only when provoked. You have no right to abduct me like this."

"You left me no other alternative." His voice deepened, the baritone Sam found so disturbingly seductive taking on a marked grittiness. "You failed to meet with me."

"So you resort to brute force," Sam said, taking a seat on the plush cushions opposite him and smoothing her skirts.

His smile widened, showing straight white teeth in the light from the carriage lanterns. He looked decidedly dangerous.

"I used the means available." His eyes narrowed to slits and the smile left his face. "You will find that I get what I want."

Sam's pulse quickened and she felt oddly elated. It was the speed of the vehicle, she told herself.

"You will find yourself disappointed, then," she said, her voice not as strong as she would have wished. "I take orders from no one."

He shifted so that the broad outline of his shoulders faced her squarely and his knees pressed against hers. Sam felt distinctly nervous.

"You will take mine."

Sam tossed her head defiantly. "I do not believe so, my lord."

"Oh, yes, you shall." His voice hardened. "Or you will rue the day you did not."

Sam took a deep breath and clenched her shaking fingers under the cover of her cape. "More threats?"

"If that is what it takes to make you release Dev from your scheming wiles, yes."

When she did not reply, Langston leaned forward until his warm breath fanned her cheek. Sam felt a tremor shudder through her, and she had to lower her lashes to hide the enormity of her reaction from his cynical stare.

"Let Dev go without further trouble, and I will give you a thousand pounds," he said softly.

Sam bit her lip to stop the scathing reply she longed to fling in his arrogant face. Pulling as far away from him as the confines of the vehicle allowed, she blinked back the moisture forming in her eyes. She would not let his derision hurt. She would not! Instead, she would fight back with the only means available to her. She would not let him belittle her without making him suffer in the process. No matter that she had no intention of carrying through with what she was about to demand.

"You hold your brother's future lightly," she said, disgusted at the wobbly quality in her voice. Straightening her spine, she turned to face him fully. "I should think that Lord Deverell's rescue from a fate worse than death would be worth at least ten thousand."

The hands resting on his thighs fisted. "You hold yourself in high esteem."

"Someone must," Sam retorted. "For 'tis obvious that you do not."

"Five."

Sam forced a smile to her stiff lips. "Ten, and not a tuppence less."

"Damn you!"

She heard acquiescence and fury beyond measure in the two words of capitulation. Tomorrow she would laugh in his face as she refused his money and told him not to judge others by himself. *She* did not share his greed.

It was a brilliant plan. The small pain of disillusionment she felt at his belief in her culpability was nothing. Nothing at all.

Turning away once more and gazing out the window, she saw the familiar buildings of Covent Garden. She realized with a start that he was taking her home. There was something forbidding and exciting about Langston taking her to her door. Something intimate.

"Stop the carriage and I shall walk the remaining distance." She jumped to her feet, only to be bounced back down when the wheels hit a rut.

His countenance was enigmatic. "The streets are too dangerous."

A nervous laugh escaped her parted lips. "I walk these streets all the time. I can take care of myself. That is why I carry a pistol."

One dark brow rose. "You can?" he murmured, taking the reticule from her suddenly trembling fingers. With sure movements, he pulled out the pistol and examined it. "One shot and you are through. Not much protection."

"Enough," she muttered, extremely uncomfortable under his gaze.

His perusal moved over her face, lingering at her full lips. "Not enough," he said in a tone that implied she was a fool. He returned the small weapon to her reticule.

She lifted her chin angrily. "Not all of us are fortunate enough to be rich as Croesus and able to afford our own carriage."

"True," he drawled, handing the reticule back to her. "Some of you are women who tread the boards waiting for some unsuspecting dupe to come along to marry you. Unfortunately for you, you picked the wrong man this time."

Sam bristled. "I picked ten thousand pounds' worth of the wrong man," she said haughtily. "Fortunately for you, I do not love Lord Deverell. For if I did, I would not give him up for any amount of money."

Langston scowled, the yellow flames from the lantern glinting in his eyes. "And you consider yourself honorable because you will take money to keep from ruining a young man's life?"

His scorn was like a sharp blade drawing blood.

"I have as much honor as a man who uses his superior strength and position to intimidate a woman."

Langston narrowed his eyes as he surveyed the defiant tilt of her face. Admiration for her spirit was a hard pill to swallow, as was his body's response to her. No matter what he told himself about her morals, he wanted her. It was unsettling. He had not reacted like this to a woman since Annabelle. Perhaps not even her.

He was saved having to respond to her when the coach drew to a stop. Not waiting for the footman, he opened the door and jumped down. The area was not lit, but the outside lanterns of his carriage provided a hazy illumination, and there was a soft golden glow in the front window of her house. Someone must be waiting up for her.

He turned to offer his hand, but she ignored it and jumped to the ground as he had. In his examination of the area he had forgotten to lower the steps for her, something his footman normally would have done.

"Damnation! Is that you, Jon?"

Langston swung around. Deverell was bearing down on them, a hackney coach already disappearing into the night.

"What the deuce? Deverell, this is none of your concern."

"Lord Deverell," Sam said in a small, surprised voice.

Langston glared at her only to wish he had not. Her widened eyes and softened mouth were altogether too inviting for comfort.

"So," Dev said, planting himself in front of his brother. "You are the one who kidnapped her. I would not have believed it if I had not seen it. When I followed Sam from the theatre and heard her scream just as a man tossed her into a carriage, I thought she had been abducted by a villain.''

"Don't be melodramatic," Langston said, his patience at an end. "I needed to speak with her, and it was the only way I could get her to listen."

"Bloody outrageous," Deverell said, his fists on his hips. "I ought to call you out for this."

Irritation replaced exasperation as Langston stared at his brother. "That you would even consider such a thing is beyond belief. The woman is an *actress,* Deverell, and I have done nothing to her."

"The devil you haven't," Deverell said, his voice rising nearly to a shout. "You kidnapped her and, if I don't miss my guess, threatened her."

"Please," Sam said, stepping between the brothers. "Please, this is all so unnecessary."

Deverell put his hands on her shoulders and pinned her with his gaze. "Are you saying he did not abduct you? That he did not threaten you?"

Caught in the intensity of his interrogation and unable to deny what his brother had indeed done, Sam looked away. "He did not harm me."

Langston saw Dev's hands on the woman and the look of possessiveness in his eyes. It was too much for his self-control. Reaching out, he grabbed her arm and yanked her from his brother's hold.

"Enough, Deverell. Go home now, before there are repercussions that cannot be mended."

"Repercussions be damned! This is *my* business, not yours. Sam is the woman I intend to marry, and Napoleon will rule Europe before I leave her to your mercy... *brother*."

The hair rose on Langston's nape. Things were moving too quickly, too furiously. He had to conquer the unreasonable emotions that had him in their grip. Deverell must not marry this woman, and that was all that mattered.

Taking a deep breath, he said quietly, "All I am trying to do is convince Mrs. Davidson that she would be better off accepting my offer of money than marrying you."

Dev took a step closer, his eyes blazing. "You have gone too far, damn you."

"Dev—"

Deverell swung his fist with all his might. Langston saw it coming in time to jerk his head to the side. Dev's fist connected with nothing.

"Gentleman Jackson has stood you in good stead," Dev said heavily, swinging again.

With lightning-fast reflexes, Langston reached out and grabbed his brother's wrist. "Stop it, Dev. She is not worth this."

Deverell stilled. "She is to me. I am going to marry her no matter what you do." His entire body tensed. "And if I find you importuning her again, I swear that I will call you out—brother or not."

Langston let go of Deverell's wrist and cast a venomous glance at Samantha. She stood not five feet from them, a look of horror on her face.

"No wonder everyone lauds your thespian skills, madam," Langston said bitterly. "I would almost think you were appalled by the sight of brother against brother, and all of it your doing. Should he challenge me and one of us be killed, it will be on your head."

CHAPTER FOUR

Two DAYS LATER, Jonathan St. Simon, Marquis of Langston, rapped smartly on the weatherbeaten mahogany door of Samantha Davidson's house. It was a row house typical to Covent Garden, worn and badly in need of repair. He wondered who'd been such a skinflint as to put her up in a house like this. Most of the men he knew considered it a matter of pride to provide extravagantly for their mistress.

The culprit was probably Huntly, he decided, frowning fiercely. He had not thought her the type to fall for the man's slick good looks and polished tongue, but then, she would not be the first to do so. And he had seen Huntly pursuing her in Drury Lane.

His stomach churned at the picture of her in Huntly's arms. He pushed it from his thoughts.

His concern was Deverell, and he would soon put an end to it. A draft for ten thousand pounds sat in his pocket.

He knocked again and felt the aged planks tremble under his force. The anger he had carefully
banked after the confrontation with her and then
Deverell two nights before flared anew when she did
not answer. He had sent around another note today, sure that she would meet with him this time.

When no one answered his third knock, his
shoulders tensed. He had learned a modicum of
patience in the House of Commons, but it was fast
deserting him.

What game was this lightskirt playing? Did her
absence signify that she had changed her mind?
That ten thousand pounds was not enough? He
should have known better than to send her the note
telling her his intended time of arrival. He should
have just shown up on her doorstep at dawn.

Regaining the iron control that was the envy of
his enemies in the Commons and the delight of his
friends, he pushed the tip of his beaver hat back
with the end of his walking stick. Brows knitted together, he stared into the gathering dusk.

Where could she be at this time of day? With her
lover? With Huntly? Or worse, with Dev?

Langston's mind filled with dark thoughts, the
sort best left to the deepest recesses of the night.
With a determined effort, he took a deep, calming
breath, a technique he had learned his first year in
the Commons.

Drury Lane was the only place he could think that she might be where he could follow. He signaled his coachman and gave directions.

The ride took a matter of minutes. Inside, the theatre was dark except for the stage, where Samantha Davidson and the rest of the troupe were rehearsing.

As he walked toward them, he studied the woman Deverell thought himself in love with. He noticed again her elegant grace. Was it part of her stage persona or was it natural? Scowling at his curiosity, he reminded himself he was not here to learn about her.

Yet she held his interest. He remembered seeing Sarah Siddons perform. Samantha Davidson was better. He could not decide what the subtle difference was. She had the same rich voice, the same ability to wilt or glow depending on the part. But there was more, a determination . . . a desire.

A part of him found that desire intriguing. Did she bring it to her private life? To a lover?

"Bravo! Bravo!" a light, childish voice shouted as the actress sank into a graceful curtsy and the scene ended.

The shout tore Langston's thoughts from places they should never visit. Glancing in the direction of it, he saw a young girl sitting in the front row of seats beside a heavyset older woman. The girl had a long, blond braid and a pale, heart-shaped face, dominated by large eyes. There was a certain grace and elegance in the way she held her shoulders and head that reminded him of the actress.

Suspicion narrowed his eyes. He looked to the stage where Samantha Davidson was moving with her fellow performers into position for the next scene.

"Excuse me," the girl's voice called to him. Frowning, he looked back at her. "Oh, pardon me," she said, drawing back into the safety of the older woman's shadow. "I thought you might be a friend of Mama's."

Langston's mouth curled. *A friend of mama's.* Definitely the actress's daughter.

A sigh of exasperation came from the woman sitting beside her, who Langston realized must be her nurse, followed by a stern reprimand. "Amalie, how many times must I tell you not to speak to strangers! Now hush, or we'll go home right this instant."

The girl fell silent, but as he took a seat, Langston noticed her stealing bold peeks at him. Clearly she had not been cowed by her nurse's reprimand. In spite of knowing whose child she was, he admired her determination.

But who was the girl's father? Had Samantha Davidson been married, or was the child illegitimate? It was hardly unheard-of for such women to have children by men who were not their husbands.

His fingers flexed as he sat on one of the benches and tried to ignore the girl's interest in him. It was not easy. She squirmed in her seat and constantly whispered to her nurse. A fleeting picture of his son, Stephen, about the same age as this girl, flashed through his mind.

Stephen, with the black hair and blue eyes of his dead mother. The boy was at Langston Castle in Kent with a tutor. He was due to visit his son there again. He found himself missing the child, despite the fact that the little boy was a constant reminder of his wife's betrayal.

A spate of girlish applause pulled Langston from his ruminations. The rehearsal, it seemed, was over. He rose and vaulted onto the wooden platform, determined to end this farce Samantha Davidson had prolonged.

"Mrs. Davidson," he murmured, "a word in private, if you will."

Sam had known he was here before he spoke. She had seen the late arrival in the dimness of the theatre, and chills had chased down her spine. His voice was merely confirmation of what her body had already sensed. She swallowed hard to banish the disconcerting realization that she was so attuned to him that she could intuit his presence.

She sensed the other members of the troupe watching them avidly. They wanted a show. She did not.

Determined to put the best possible face on the confrontation she knew was coming, she turned and studied Langston. "Persistent, aren't you, my lord?"

He sketched a mocking brow. "Scheming, aren't you, madam?"

Her indignation rose. "Acting, sir, is my livelihood. You should have consulted with me on a convenient time, instead of sending your commands around without a by-your-leave."

Gathering her skirts, she made to sweep past him. His hand shot out like a whip and wrapped around her wrist. She stopped in her tracks. It was that or have her arm wrenched out of its socket.

Briefly, Sam considered making a scene and causing her fellow performers to come to her rescue. The brittle hardness in the marquis's brown eyes decided her against it. He was not going to back down, no matter what she did.

"If you will release me, I will give you the satisfaction of a discussion." Her gaze shifted to the hand gripping her wrist before returning to his countenance. "Or are you determined to make me pay for not being at your beck and call by bruising me?''

The flush that rose into his cheeks gave her some small satisfaction. But his eyes didn't flinch and his hold didn't ease.

A thump followed by the scramble of feet warned Sam seconds before Amalie's small body careened into Langston. He stumbled backward, releasing Sam as he clutched Amalie to him to keep from knocking her down as he flung out one arm for balance.

Wrapped in his embrace, Amalie pummeled him with her fists. ''How dare you! How dare you hurt my mother!''

The few remaining cast members chuckled, but Sam feared her daughter would be hurt. She yanked Amalie out of Langston's arms and pushed the child behind her.

''Don't touch her, or you will regret it,'' she said, agitation making her chest rise and fall rapidly. ''She was only trying to protect me.''

Langston's brows rose. ''You think I am cad enough to harm a child?''

Sam forced her breathing back to normal, keeping a secure grip on Amalie, who was wriggling in an attempt to escape her mother's grasp. Eyes wary, Sam said, ''I think you are a man who is not accustomed to being crossed. I have learned through experience that such men are not to be trusted.''

He stepped back and made a show of calmly brushing dust from the sleeve of his immaculate black coat. But Sam saw the strain in his face and realized he was giving himself time to control his fury at her accusation.

When he looked back at her, his eyes were hard. ''I am a man of honor. I would no more hurt a child than I would cheat at cards.''

Sam knew how the aristocracy prided themselves on not cheating at cards. It was a matter of honor to them, as important as their name and lineage. Her lips twisted. ''Very noble of you, I am sure.''

His mouth tightened into a thin line. ''Quite.''

''Miss Sam,'' Lottie said, puffing from the exertion of hurrying up the steps on the side of the stage. ''Miss Sam, he was watching you the whole time. Don't trust him.''

Langston clenched his hands into fists before consciously relaxing them. Turning to Lottie, he said in his most level voice, ''My good woman, many men watch your mistress. Most of them with less honorable intentions than I.''

Lottie sniffed, her spectacles catching the light. ''Honorable is as honorable does.''

Deeming it time to intervene before her faithful servant succeeded in angering the marquis to the point where he could not refrain from action, Sam said, "'Tis all right, Lottie. His lordship merely wants to talk with me."

Lottie sniffed even louder and gave Langston a warning look, but then she pulled Amalie to her side and began to lead her away. From the safety of Lottie's skirts, Amalie stuck her tongue out at Langston. He couldn't suppress an appreciative smile. It was so typically childish, and exactly what he would have done at her age. Exactly what Stephen would do.

His response infuriated Amalie, who planted her feet firmly, resisting Lottie's efforts to keep her moving. "Don't try grabbing my mother again," she said. "I . . . I shall scratch your eyes out if you do."

Langston made her a bow free of mockery. "Very noble of you." When at last the child was out of sight, he extended his arm to Sam as though she were a lady he wished to escort. Her daughter's spunk had taken the edge off his anger. "If you will come with me, I will take you home in my carriage. 'Tis dusk and, as I told you before, the streets of Covent Garden are dangerous."

Sam stepped away, keeping her arms at her sides. "Then I am sure you will excuse me if I decline. I must take my child home."

She saw him swallow beneath the pristine whiteness of his cravat.

"Your daughter and servant are included in my invitation. When we reach your house, you may invite me in and then we will conclude our business in private."

Sam considered refusing him, but knew it would only postpone the inevitable. It would, of course, be no small pleasure to watch his face when she refused the ten thousand pounds. The question was whether she would let him continue to think she intended to snare Lord Deverell or whether she would tell him the truth.

"As you wish," she said, sweeping around him and going to fetch Amalie.

Langston watched her stride away. It was too bad that Deverell had seen her first and now must be disentangled. He would not be averse to becoming her protector if the circumstances were different, if she were different ... if he were.

He grimaced at his weakness. He was ten times a fool to allow himself such thoughts. There were Deverell and Cynthia to consider. Not to mention that Mrs. Davidson was the type of woman he deplored: grasping and untrustworthy.

Minutes later, Sam entered Langston's coach with as much bravado as she could muster. It was the same vehicle he had used to abduct her two nights previously, and it brought back a rush of emotion reminiscent of the fright she had felt. Instinctively her right hand went to the reticule where her pistol resided before she forced herself to be calm and think of the present.

She hoped to sit beside Lottie and Amalie, but one glance in the sleek vehicle told her there was not enough room. Someone would have to sit beside Langston. Amalie would not, nor could she expect the heir to the Duke of Rundell to take his seat beside a servant. With a sigh of resignation, she motioned Amalie and Lottie to the maroon velvet cushions across from her.

Langston eyed the seating arrangements sardonically. Sam lifted her chin and met his gaze.

"Very considerate of you," he murmured, sitting beside her so that his thigh touched hers.

Shock held Sam motionless. Her heart sped up and her mouth went dry. Never had a man's closeness affected her so. She was appalled that he made her tingle from the bottom of her stomach to the tip of her toes by doing nothing more than brushing his leg against hers.

Taking a deep breath to calm herself, Sam tried to inch away from him. It was to no avail. Even as she moved away, he seemed to shift closer. An impossible situation!

"Mama," Amalie said, breaking into Sam's agonized thoughts, "why are you allowing this strange man to take us home? You have never done anything like this before."

Langston cocked one brow and murmured under his breath, "I find that hard to believe."

But Amalie heard him. "I am no liar!"

"I beg your pardon, miss," Langston said. "But perhaps you are not aware of everything your mother does."

Sam wanted to throttle the man. "Amalie is only nine years old, my lord. She has certain expectations of life and the people around her. Your condescending remarks are not part of them."

"Perhaps," he murmured, letting the matter drop. He had no argument with the child and found he admired her spirit.

They reached her house not more than ten minutes later. Sam was thankful the trip was short. There was no telling what Amalie would have said next or what Langston would have replied.

"Lottie, take Amalie to the kitchen and give her supper," Sam said when Langston opened the vehicle's door.

The marquis hopped down before the outrider could reach the door, and extended his hand to help first Amalie, then Lottie. Part of him viewed his behavior as inappropriate—he had servants to do this—but another part of him needed the activity.

The child scowled at him, and it took all his willpower not to grin at her, something he knew would be taken as a great insult. The nurse bobbed a brief curtsy, but vouchsafed no smile. When they were safely on the ground and started toward the door, he turned to assist Sam.

Staring down into his strong-boned face, Sam found herself licking dry lips. His brown eyes were opaque, any emotion he felt carefully hidden. But his mouth, with its well-defined lips that hinted of sensuality, was mocking.

He held his hand out for her. The last thing she wanted to do was touch him, but to ignore his gesture would be to admit his power over her.

Girding herself for the shock of feeling his heat, she gingerly put her hand in his. Suddenly her legs refused to support her weight. It was a reaction she had never before experienced and one that was alarming in its intensity.

Sam lurched forward and would have fallen had Langston not caught her. Embarrassment at her unwelcome susceptibility stained her cheeks as she pushed against his chest to be free.

"I can walk on my own," she muttered, trying desperately to avoid such proximity, to get away from the electricity of his very masculine body.

"It did not appear that way a moment ago," he said softly. His eyes had a wicked gleam that hinted at a smoldering awareness of her as a woman.

Sam's stomach did somersaults. Confusion made her bite her lip. He was here to pay her off, not to seduce her.

Straightening her spine, she skirted around his disturbing presence and bade him to follow her into the house. As she entered with her head held high, his presence behind her was so unsettling she did not need to hear him close the door behind to know he was there.

She strode into the parlor, which at this time of year was not much warmer than the out of doors. Too bad Langston's being here precluded her lighting the meager pile of coal in the fireplace. But she did not want to take the time to fiddle with it because she wanted him gone as quickly as possible.

Resolutely she turned to face him. She had learned long ago that timidity did nothing but put her in a weak position, a place she had learned to avoid the hard way. Her stepfather and husband had been excellent tutors.

Calmly she said, "Now, my lord, I presume you have in your possession a ten-thousand-pound bank draft?'

His eyes narrowed, but he said nothing. One elegant, long-fingered hand reached into his coat pocket and withdrew a sheet of paper, which he held out to her.

It was the draft, the ultimate insult. Sam felt her chest tighten painfully. If only things could have been different. If only Charles hadn't deserted her. She'd still be married, Amalie would have a father and security, and this man wouldn't be standing before her now, paying her to stay away from his brother.

"I see you have stood by our agreement," she murmured in a voice made husky by the effort not to cry.

He stepped back, his hands dropping to his sides. "I would not do otherwise."

Sam's melancholy was suddenly replaced by intense anger. She ripped the paper in two, then did likewise with the halves, again and again, until nothing but confetti remained, floating to the threadbare carpet beneath her feet.

"This," she said in a voice that caught in fury, "is what I think of your money!"

Before she knew what he was about, Langston's fingers gripped her upper arms and his face was inches from hers. His warm breath fanned her flushed skin. Tremors skated down her spine.

"You would press a saint to violence," he said, his voice deep and rough, "and I am no saint. So be careful how you bait me."

She knew his words were no idle threat. But the woman in her sensed more than anger in the grip of his fingers, the hooded glitter of his brown eyes. She saw desire.

She took a deep breath, tortured by the urge to follow the dark path of passion he offered, passion without love or respect. She needed to run.

His eyes darkened and his face lowered. He was going to kiss her. He was going to pull her down into the maelstrom of emotions reflected in his eyes, and she knew with a sigh of surrender that she would not fight him.

He crushed her to his chest, and his mouth covered hers. His kiss devoured her. Sensations she had never experienced before engulfed her. Her head spun and she fell into him, drowning in the passion.

Without warning, he pushed her away, his lips tearing from hers and leaving her feeling bereft. She stared at him, not fully comprehending. His face was set in harsh lines, his mouth a thin slash.

"See the power you wield?" he asked, his voice low. "Deverell has not a chance against you." He clenched his hands in denial. "Even I am unable to resist you, and I know you for what you are."

She slapped him then, a violent crack of sound.

Horror at her action held Sam motionless as she watched the red marks of her fingers on his cheek. She bit her lower lip to keep it from trembling. "I...I have never hit another person, but I am not the type of woman you think. Your condemnation of me is unpardonable."

Fury emanated in waves from his stiffly held body, but his voice was steady and dangerously calm. "Then why did you destroy the draft on my bank? I think 'tis because you never intended to accept it. I think you plan to trap Deverell into marriage no matter what you say." His mouth twisted. "I would probably do the same, were I in your position."

Sam swayed, the cruelty of his words compounded by the emotions he had so recently evoked in her. She put a hand on the back of a chair, seeking comfort in the familiar feel of frayed cloth.

"You judge me by your own standards, Lord Langston. You have said as much. But your standards are not mine. I never intended to take the money from you because I never intended to wed your brother. Lord Deverell is an amiable and affectionate young man—but I do not love him. I will not marry a man I don't love."

Even as she tried to explain her feelings, Sam berated herself for trying. It should not matter what he thought of her. It should not matter if he believed her. But it did. She could not deny that it did. That realization was enough to make her crumble inside.

"Fine words," Langston said, stepping to the door, "but I am sure you won't be surprised to learn that I do not believe them." He paused on the threshold. "You have not heard the last of me. I shall ensure that Deverell will never marry you."

Just as Langston stepped into the small, dimly lit foyer, there came a loud banging on the front door.

"Let me in," Deverell's voice demanded. "I know you are in there, Jon—your carriage is right out front. I won't have you threatening Sam again."

Langston turned on Sam and snarled, "You knew he was coming here. You planned this."

Frantic, furious and determined to avert the catastrophe she saw looming, Sam whispered fiercely, "Don't be an ass. I knew nothing of the sort. You are the one who came for me in Drury Lane."

His dark brows raised in mocking doubt, he turned to the door and whipped it open. The anger twisting Lord Deverell's handsome features made Sam gasp. Never, not in her worst nightmare, had she thought it would come to this, not even after the brothers' earlier confrontation.

Deverell barged into the foyer and slapped his gloves across Langston's face. "I challenge you, brother."

Sam gasped. "Oh, no," she pleaded, rushing between the two men and confronting Deverell. "This is ridiculous. Langston was only trying to do what he thought best for you. Don't do this terrible thing."

Langston's fury only increased when Sam stepped between him and Deverell. Damn her! He wanted to throttle her even as he wanted to do other things that would merit Dev's challenge. Instead, he forced himself to stay motionless. No good would come of further enraging Dev.

Over her head, he held Deverell's gaze with his. "Do not let her make us enemies . . . brother."

"She does not need to do so," Deverell stated. "You have done that by your actions. I told you to leave her alone."

Desperately Sam turned to Langston. "Stop him. You are the elder—you must do something!"

His gaze flicked over her, rage tightening the skin around his mouth. "This is no concern of yours."

"What's going on here, Miss Sam?" Lottie stepped into the foyer. "I heard voices when I was in the kitchen, and that's something, seeing as 'tis so far." Her shrewd eyes shifted between the two men. "They fighting over you?"

The urge to fly into Lottie's arms and be wrapped in her voluminous hug was intense. Instead, Sam pulled herself together and stepped away from the two men. She could not stop them, and she did not want their quarrel to bring Amalie. Her daughter was too young to be subjected to such unpleasantness.

"As you say, Lord Langston," she addressed him formally, "'tis none of my affair. Therefore, I must ask you to conduct your quarrel in a place other than my home."

Lord Deverell flushed and made Sam an elegant bow. "I am sorry, Sam. You are right. This is not for a lady's ears." Without further word, he turned and stalked from the house.

Langston began to follow, then spun round and pinned her with a frigid gaze. "Brother against brother—an ugly situation." He took a step toward her, then paused, his countenance fierce. "I trust you are satisfied. 'Tis a certainty that unless I kill or maim my brother in this idiotic duel, he will marry you regardless of what it does to his life or to his family."

Sam watched him leave, her face devoid of color.

CHAPTER FIVE

SAM PULLED the hood of her grey kerseymere cape closer about her face and wondered for the umpteenth time what she was doing here. She had no interest in politics and had never before set foot in the House of Commons. As it was, she was conspicuous as the only woman present.

It was foolhardy even to be here, especially after last night. But she had had to come. All night she had tossed and turned, plagued by nightmares. Langston was here. She had to speak with him. Perhaps between them, they could find a way to stop the duel.

In an effort to avoid attracting undue attention, she moved to a far corner where the light of the numerous candles from the magnificent branch of luster did not penetrate. From here she could not see the floor, but she could hear the speakers.

Pinpricks of anticipation chased down her arms when she heard the speaker recognize Jonathan St. Simon, member of Parliament for Northumberland. The urge to move forward in order to see him was great, but Sam knew she must resist it. She did not yet wish to reveal her presence.

When he spoke, his voice was rich and evocative, its powerful tones holding one's attention and commanding respect. Sam shivered at the emotions he called forth in her.

"Respected members," he began, "as you all know, the last few years have seen a number of changes in our country. We have enclosed lands that were once public domain, we have enacted Corn Laws to protect the prices of our grains, and we have developed industry that provides many jobs and wealth to our nation."

His voice lowered, becoming even more forceful, if that were possible. "These changes have also brought greater poverty. Our Poor Laws were originally developed during Elizabeth's time, and I move today that they are no longer adequate to meet the needs of our people."

A low rumble of noise began, rising in volume until the Speaker of the House had to rap for silence.

Sam held her breath in anticipation of what would happen next. She knew, even with her limited experience, that what Langston proposed was revolutionary. Whatever else, she thought, he was a strong man who had the courage to stand up to his peers for a cause he believed in. She could not but admire him.

"Fellow members," Langston began again, his voice as commanding as ever, "before you speak against me, think of your own constituents. How many go hungry in winter? How many throw themselves on the mercy of the parish only to find the parish has neither the money nor the will to provide for them?" He paused, allowing his words to penetrate. "How many of you have seen small children starving in the streets, begging for a mere crust of bread?"

Sam blinked to clear the moisture from her eyes. This was not the arrogant man who threatened her with vengeance. This was a man filled with compassion for those less fortunate. He was showing himself to be true, honorable and noble, and she found herself wanting to cheer for him. The wall she had built around her heart to protect her from the frightening attraction she felt was crumbling.

The realization was a shock. She barely knew Langston. Yet the man speaking below her, the man fighting for others, the man who abhorred her, was a man she could respect.

Langston ended with, "We must enact new Poor Laws."

The room burst into a cacophony of men talking and shouting, fists pounding on wood. Sam could tell from the reactions that Langston would have difficulty in getting his changes, but she believed he would fight to the death for them.

Her mind reeling from the discovery of this facet of his personality, she left, her intention of speaking with him forgotten. She needed time to consider the man she had just heard, the man to whom she was dangerously drawn against her better judgment.

Holding her cape tightly about her body, she skirted the small groups of men in the gallery and made for the exit. Outside, the sky was overcast, but the watery winter sun struggled to break through, just as Langston had struggled to break through the wall of indifference the comfortably situated had erected between themselves and those who were not.

She walked briskly down the street, her mind a jumble of conflicting thoughts and emotions. She longed for him to win his battle, for she believed in what he fought for. She had once been a recipient of parish charity, and it had been a bitter, miserable pill to swallow, with no genuine kindness or compassion to sweeten it. And it had never been enough to feed Amalie, let alone herself. Those had been long, cold despondent days.

Sam stopped and took a deep breath of the soot-tinged air. Her lungs expanded slowly and she exhaled softly, glad of what she now had in life. She had fought for everything, just as Langston was now fighting for others. What would happen to his crusade if he dueled with Lord Deverell? She had no doubt that word of the meeting would spread. The scandal sheets would pounce on it, and while she knew Langston would shoot into the air if he chose pistols or fail to draw blood if he chose swords, she was not so sure about Deverell. And there was no doubt that the resultant scandal of a duel with his own brother would not help his cause.

Perhaps it would ruin him in the House of Commons. And even if his motion passed the Lower House, what would happen to it in the House of Lords? Would the members of the peerage reject a motion brought forward by a man tainted by such action? She did not know.

But she did know she was the cause of the rift between the brothers. It was her responsibility to try to close it; for the sake of all the people Langston was trying to help, if for nothing else. It was the right thing to do.

She felt lighter of heart and there was a spring in her step that had been missing for some time. Lifting her chin and squaring her shoulders, she decided she would call upon Lord Deverell the next day. He was the one who had issued the challenge, and she knew enough about such things to realize that he was the one who must withdraw it.

SAMANTHA FACED DOWN Lord Deverell's land-lady. "I am here to see his lordship. Please tell me which set of rooms he occupies."

Iron-grey hair pulled back into a severe bun accentuated the doughy contours of the landlady's face. She drew herself up in an attempt to look down her nose at Sam, whom she clearly considered a bolder-than-brass bit of muslin. The effect was mitigated by the woman's short stature and rotund stomach.

"I won't be lettin' the likes of you into my place."

Sam stiffened at the woman's insulting words. It was the same disdain Langston exuded. Part of her wanted to turn around and walk away, but she had spent too much time learning Lord Deverell's whereabouts and crossing palms in the process. It seemed that Deverell had left his parents' Town mansion the same day he had challenged Langston.

Taking control of the situation, Sam strode past the older woman and into the hallway, stating plainly and unequivocally, "If you do not show me Lord Deverell's rooms, you will force me to knock on every door here." She paused to let the implication sink in. "I do not think you want that."

"Harrumph!" The woman turned crimson and her deep-set eyes sparked. "I keep a respectable 'ouse, I do."

Sam knew she had won this round when the landlady edged past her, careful not to touch any portion of Sam's person. Sam followed her down the hall.

Pausing at a door, the woman muttered, "Dunno as 'e's in." She eyed Sam with loathing. "See that you doan go wanderin' around 'ere. If I sees you do, I'll call the Watch on you."

Sam lifted her chin. "'Tis a pity your mind is so small that you think badly of people whom you do not even know."

Angling around the woman, Sam rapped smartly on the door. She sensed the landlady's wrath, but ignored it.

Deverell's man answered the knock, his eyes as large as sovereigns. "Mrs. Davidson! Ah, his lordship..."

Seeing the man's distress, Sam said gently, "Please tell your master that I am here on a matter of concern to both of us."

Rather than wait for the servant to gather his wits and usher her in, Sam stepped forward and closed the door behind her—in the landlady's disapproving but curious face. She kept her countenance cool and slightly aloof while the manservant gaped at her.

"Please be seated, Mrs. Davidson," he finally said in a voice that spoke volumes. Nevertheless, he did not attempt to evict her.

Sam sat in the chair he indicated. It was beside a small drum table in front of the fireplace. Looking round, she was amused by the homely clutter of the room. Two stuffed chairs sat by one wall, a gaming-table between them with a deck of cards strewn across its surface. Several books lay on other tables. There was a decanter and two glasses on a sideboard. The furniture was obviously rented with the room, but the disarray came from its current occupant.

The door that Sam knew led to sleeping quarters opened with a bang. Deverell stood framed in it, his face a mask of shock and concern.

"Sam, whatever is the matter that you would call on me in my rooms? If anyone has seen you, your reputation will be in shreds." As he spoke, he strode toward her.

Sam smiled. He was like a little boy in his undisguised concern and disorderly appearance. One thick lock of brown hair fell into his hazel eyes. His white shirt was open at the throat and looked as though he'd slept in it. His Hessians were unpolished.

"Deverell," she said calmly, hoping to allay some of his dismay, "'tis perfectly all right. No one saw me, and—" she shrugged "—my reputation is already assured by my profession. Nothing else I do will make a difference."

"*I* will," he stated firmly, towering above her, his brows drawn fiercely together. "When I have put a stop to Langston's threats to you, I will marry you. No one will dare to malign you after that."

He was so like his older brother in his capacity to feel emotions strongly, yet so different in whom he felt them for. Deverell judged people by who they were. Langston judged people by what he thought them to be.

Sam rose gracefully, deciding to take the conversation in hand before her swain got beyond reason. "Lord Deverell, I appreciate your concern on my behalf, but there is nothing for you to defend. Your brother has done me no harm. However, I believe your challenge to Langston can do great harm."

"That's rot!" Deverell stepped away from her and went to pour himself a glass of port. "Would you care for some?" he asked belatedly. "Don't have sherry."

"No, thank you."

He downed the ruby liquor in one gulp. "Langston is beyond anyone's reach. He will inherit the premier dukedom in England and all the solidity and respectability that confers." He laughed harshly. "No, my little confrontation with him will do no harm. But it will avenge your honor."

Sam sighed in exasperation. The young man was as pigheaded as his older sibling. It must run in the St. Simon family.

"Lord Deverell," she said, keeping her frustration out of her voice, "Langston is trying to get some new Poor Laws through the House of Commons. They are changes that will benefit people who cannot help themselves, and I believe they are very important. I am afraid that dueling with his own brother will adversely affect his efforts."

She paused to see if she had captured his attention. Indeed, his expression *was* a bit sheepish. She began to hope her mission would succeed. "I fear that the scandal sheets will pick up this story, and the people who would otherwise support his Poor Laws will not then do so because of this rash act. It would be a great loss if what he is trying to do for others is ruined by a challenge that has no cause."

Instantly Lord Deverell's mouth thinned, and Sam knew she had erred in her choice of phrase. She took a step toward him, but was stopped by his fury.

"No cause? Do you know that he has convinced my mother not to give me the parure of emeralds she holds for my future bride? I wished to give you the ring as a sign of my devotion."

Sam found her exasperation exceeding her fondness for this young man. "Lord Deverell, we have discussed this matter before. While I am conscious of the honor you do me, I do not love you, and I will not marry where I do not love. That is why this should not be a matter of hard feelings between you and your brother."

"Well, it is." He fell to his knees. "I want to marry you, Sam. There is so much I can do for you... do for your daughter. And I will, I promise. Only say you will marry me!"

Sam closed her eyes briefly. What a temptation! To never again have to worry about Amalie's future would be bliss. But not this way.

Taking a deep breath, she said, "You know the answer, Lord Deverell. It has not changed and it *will* not. If you still feel you must meet Langston, then I am truly sorry." She moved to the door.

"Sam," he pleaded, jumping to his feet and following her. "Please."

Gently she said, "'Tis better this way, Lord Deverell. We are not meant for each other."

Before he could voice the denial she saw in his eyes, Sam opened the door and slipped out, closing it behind her with a finality that could not be mistaken. Minutes later, she stood outside the building and gazed about her. The street was filled with people. On the corner a young girl called, "Chestnuts. Piping 'ot chestnuts."

The smell was wonderful in the cold air, tempting Sam to the extravagance. Rationalizing that this was a once-a-year treat, she bought a twist. The child's pinched face and grateful smile prompted her to pay twice the asking price. The look of surprised gratitude was well worth it.

Chewing slowly to prolong the pleasure, Sam looked at the small watch pinned to her spencer. The gold timepiece was simply designed, with no filigree or precious stones, but it held strong memories for her. It had been a gift from her mother, one of the few remaining reminders of her childhood.

It was early afternoon, and she had several hours before the rehearsal. She had time to walk to Grosvenor Square, where she knew Langston's house was located. She did not relish another confrontation with him, but it was necessary. It appeared she had not gotten through to Deverell, and talking to Langston was the only way left to try to avert the duel.

Now if only her heart would slow to its normal rate.

"DAMNATION," Langston muttered as the sound of voices penetrated his library door, interrupting his concentration.

He lifted his head and realized that his neck muscles were tight and sore. The mantel clock struck four. He had been working on the changes to his bill for the past three hours. He tidied the papers and set them neatly on one corner of his mahogany desk.

He leaned back in the maroon leather wing-chair and rubbed his neck. His gaze went, as always, to a large portrait hung over the mantel. Sir Thomas Lawrence was the artist; Langston's dead wife was the subject. Annabelle had been three months pregnant and not yet showing when the painting was done. The artist had captured her translucent beauty and flawless complexion to perfection, and her eyes seemed to sparkle like brilliant sapphires. At the time the portrait was done, Langston had thought they reflected inner joy. Later he'd realized it had been hectic excitement, brought on by the illicit affair that had brought the child she carried into existence.

He kept the painting prominently displayed so that he would never forget her duplicity, would always be reminded that women were not to be trusted.

The voices outside rose in volume, piquing his curiosity and drawing his attention from his dead wife's glowing face.

Suddenly he identified one of the voices. "I *will* see Langston," Samantha Davidson stated forcefully and unequivocally in her husky whiskey voice.

Tension pooled in Langston's gut. What was she doing calling on him? No woman called on a bachelor, not even his mistress.

Standing, he told himself to make her wait. Let her deal with the footman, who appeared to be as adamant that she would not see him as she was that she would. Langston rolled his shoulders and stretched his spine. A modicum of calm settled over him.

His mouth curled sardonically as he reached the only conclusion possible as to the reason for her call. Apparently she had not accepted Deverell's generous offer of marriage yet. She was here to coerce him into offering more than the ten thousand. That would explain why she'd so cavalierly torn up his original bank draft.

He smiled. He had some very unpleasant news for her.

Making a split-second decision, he strode to the library door. "Peter," he said to the footman, "direct Mrs. Davidson in here."

The young man could not hide his relief, and he hastened to do his master's bidding.

Langston did not wait for her to enter. Instead, he moved to the fireplace and set about stoking the fire. The room was growing chill. He didn't examine his motive for deciding to alleviate that chill at this particular moment.

"Mrs. Davidson, milord," Peter announced formally.

"Thank you," Sam murmured, giving Peter the sort of smile no man could resist.

Langston watched her charm his servant. Against his will, he felt his own blood heat. His lips thinned as he fought his attraction.

"You may go now, Peter," he said more harshly than he had intended. When the door was closed, he added, "I see you never fail to entice, Mrs. Davidson."

She eyed him with dislike, her fine brows raised in disdain. "I see that you are your normal congenial self as well . . . milord." The last word came out soft and taunting.

Langston refused to give her the satisfaction of responding, for he was in no mood to accommodate her. Ignoring the way his senses clamored with awareness of her, he studied her dispassionately.

She was clothed plainly in a grey wool cloak, the hood fallen to her shoulders. The light from the chandelier glinted on the rich tones of her chestnut hair. Red, gold, russet and bronze mingled to create a color as striking as that of any precious metal. An insidious desire to release the thick twist of hair and bury his fingers in its depths besieged him.

He reminded himself harshly that she was his adversary. She was the reason his brother had called him out.

"What brings you here, Mrs. Davidson?" he asked coldly. "Have you come to accept my offer, after all?"

Her chin rose. "I have not."

"Ah. Another matter, then." He moved to a table and poured himself a glass of golden liquid. "Would you care for some? 'Tis Scotch whiskey. A liquor my brother Alaistair introduced me to several years ago."

"No, thank you," she said.

The words were level and her voice calm, but Langston saw the look in her eyes as she watched him swallow. "You don't approve?"

"'Tis not my place to approve or disapprove. And 'tis certainly not the reason for my visit."

Plainly spoken. Against his will, he felt a stirring of respect for her.

"Then why are you here?" He set his glass down and moved to the fireplace, where he propped one Hessian-clad foot on the grate.

Sam never shifted her gaze from him as he moved about the richly appointed room with an ease born of familiarity. In his perfectly tailored brown coat, immaculate cravat and buff breeches, he was everything an aristocrat should be. But there was more to him than his position and power. He cared about others.

Which did not mean she had to like him.

Still, she respected what he was trying to accomplish. That fact kept her from stalking out of the room as his insolent gaze roamed over her.

"I have come to ask you to reconsider your duel with Lord Deverell. I..." She found it difficult to continue when contempt twisted his mouth. "I think it would be detrimental to the bill you are trying to get through the House of Commons."

There. It was out, and damn his eyes for looking at her as though she were dirt. She drew herself up proudly. Being here was the right thing, no matter what he thought of her.

"Mrs. Davidson," he drawled in his deep voice that never failed to send shivers of pleasure down her spine. "I never intended to meet Deverell. And if you are so concerned about my work in the Commons, then 'tis more than I would have thought of you. More likely, you are using this as another ploy to raise my offer above the ten thousand pounds we agreed upon."

Heat stole up her cheeks, and she berated herself for allowing it. She should be inured to his scorn by now. It took her several moments to clear the obstruction in her throat.

"You are a beast, but I do believe there is some compassion in you for others. I heard your speech in the Commons yesterday and found myself moved by your eloquence. I even found myself wanting you to succeed."

For an instant an emotion other than mockery flickered in his eyes, but it was gone so quickly that Sam decided she'd been mistaken. Her wish for him to see beyond his superficial impression of her was deluding her into seeing things in his face that were not there.

"Very noble of you," he murmured, cementing her decision that he had not changed his opinion of her. "But I assure you there will be no duel with my brother, since I have no intention of meeting Deverell and have taken measures to ensure that the duel does not take place."

"You have taken measures?" Sam echoed.

"Yes. I have friends who are as concerned about the passage of this bill as I am. They are equally concerned about Deverell's well-being. Therefore, he is being sent to Wellington in Brussels as a courier. His departure is imminent, leaving no time for a duel. And Brussels is crowded with members of the *ton* and alive with the resultant parties. Dev will enjoy his visit and very likely forget all about you."

He pushed away from the grate and moved to stand closer to her. She could smell his citrus-and-musk scent, and it did strange things to her equilibrium.

"Very clever," she murmured. "And very convenient for you. You are a man who takes advantage of his opportunities."

"I am a man who protects his own," he said softly, iron underlying each word.

"I never doubted it for a second," Sam said, goaded by his unspoken warning and determined not to be intimidated. Stepping back to put more distance between them, she said, "It seems that you have everything well in hand and that I have wasted my time and risked my reputation for nothing. Good day."

Without waiting for him to grasp the initiative once more, Sam spun round and strode from the room, through the polished marble foyer and out into the evening dusk. She badly needed the release of a brisk walk. Her nerves were raw from the encounter with Langston, and her mind was a welter of desire and denial.

Thank God she would not have any further dealings with him.

CHAPTER SIX

"MAMA," Amalie's high, sweet voice called from the back door. "Mama, do come! There's a package for you!"

Sam smiled at her child's exuberance. Her daughter had a sunny disposition that found pleasure in all of life's experiences. The arrival of another present was not unexpected. Many men sent Sam gifts, some large and expensive, necessitating their return; others were small and delightful, and these she usually gave to Amalie. Roses were a particular delight because everyone in the household could enjoy them.

Getting up and wiping the worst of the dirt from the apron covering her plain wool gown and spencer, Sam removed her work gloves and glanced about her tiny garden. This was where she found peace. Rosebushes surrounded her, their winter-dormant stalks rising bravely from the frost-nipped ground. Right now, she had to keep them mulched for protection. Her work would be rewarded in the summer when they would burst forth in all their glory, and the thick, heavy scent of the damask roses and the lighter scent of the small climbers would welcome her.

She smoothed her apron again and moved toward Amalie, who was impatiently hopping from foot to foot.

"Do hurry, Mama. Two men brought this package, and just look at the rose attached to it. It smells heavenly and, oh, this must be important!"

"Slow down," Sam said gently.

She picked up the gift. The child was right. The heavy scent of damask ascended from the red bud residing in splendor against the gold foil wrap. The rose was from a hothouse. Clearly someone had put great care and expense into this gift.

Setting the box back down, Sam disconnected the flower and carefully anchored it in Amalie's golden braid, where it looked even lovelier than it had on the gift. "There, now *you* are the special package," she said, kissing her daughter's pink cheek.

"Oh, Mama," Amalie said, "do be serious. I am dying to see what's inside the box." She shook the package so that it rattled, which made her blue eyes sparkle even more.

Beginning to feel decidedly curious herself, Sam deftly undid the outside paper to reveal a square container. Inside reposed a blue velvet jeweler's box. Her pleasure evaporated.

Another importunate gift meant for a man's mistress. She did not want Amalie to see the expensive piece of jewelry she knew the box held.

"Amalie," she said calmly, closing the outside lid to block the view, "please go in and tell Lottie to serve us tea in the parlor. 'Tis nippy out here, and a bit of hot tea and buttered bread would be lovely." When Sam saw Amalie's chin set in stubborn protest, she added, "We can pretend we are grand ladies."

This was a charade Amalie never tired of. Sam did not know why it appealed so, and she didn't allow the charade very often, since there was unlikely to be any such future in store for her daughter. But right now it was more important to protect Amalie from the cruel reality the contents of this beguiling box represented.

"Oh, very well," Amalie said grudgingly, her gaze on the gift. "But I still want to know what you got."

Sam smiled gently. "We shall see, love. Now run along and do as I asked."

When Amalie's small figure was gone, Sam pulled out the jeweler's box and flicked it open. Inside would be a note telling her who sent it. There always was.

But she was momentarily diverted by the gift itself. It was a particularly exquisite gold ring set with two diamonds, the brilliance of which testified to their value and perfection. It was a ring any woman would long to wear. It was a bribe no man would expect to have refused.

Sam's mouth thinned as she opened the accompanying note and read Lord Deverell's black scrawl:

Dearest Sam,

Please forgive my cowardice in sending this as I have. You will receive this pledge of my devotion as I am crossing the Channel. I did it this way knowing you would not be able to return it to me post haste and hoping it will encourage you to think long and objectively about my suit. Please wait for my return before making your decision. I am, as always, your devoted servant.

Anger flared in Sam, quickly followed by pity for the young man. He was a child of his privileged world, accustomed to getting what he coveted. Of course she would return the gift.

But to whom? Since Lord Deverell was out of the country, the only people left were his parents or his brother. The thought of meeting any of them face-to-face was more than she cared to consider.

She could hire a boy to take it to one of them, but the ring was very valuable and she did not want to be responsible for its possible loss. Nor would she put such a task on Lottie. She herself must return it. And better the devil she knew than the one she did not...which meant Langston. Besides, she would not ask to see him, merely leave the gift with his servant.

That decision made, Sam closed the jeweler's box and dropped it into her apron pocket. First, she had to entertain Amalie at tea.

LANGSTON SCOWLED at the twin diamonds winking at him in the light. The doxy had nerve, bringing him the ring. Why return what was obviously a very expensive gift? If she did not want to commit herself to Dev, why not pawn the ring?

A knock on the library door interrupted his musings. It was Peter, who announced that Winkly, the Bow Street Runner Langston had summoned, was here. His brother Alaistair had used the man very successfully in dealing with the deceased Earl of Bent's attempt to kidnap Alaistair's wife. Winkly had been in the Peninsula with Alaistair, and the two were as close as an aristocrat and former guttersnipe could be.

"Send him in," Langston said to his manservant.

Moments later a thin, weasel-faced man ambled into the room. "Evenin' guv'nor...er, pardon me, yer lordship," he said, doffing his wool cap. "I understand as 'ow you wanted me services."

"I certainly do, Winkly." Langston stood and walked around to the front of his desk. "There is an actress I want you to investigate. Find out her past and where her husband is, or if she was even married to the man who fathered her daughter."

"Righto, guv—" He grimaced at his overfamiliarity with the heir to the powerful Duke of Rundell. "Pardon me, milord. Ain't used to mindin' me *p*s and *q*s."

"That's quite all right," Langston said, smiling.

Winkly grinned. His missing front tooth gave him the look of an urchin. But that was a misleading impression. Winkly was one of the best Runners in the business.

"How soon will yer be needin' the information?" he asked, his face sobering.

Langston frowned. "It cannot be soon enough."

Winkly's brow rose, but he made no comment. He knew that no matter how courteously the Quality behaved, when one of them was angry, it was best to stay clear. "Quick as I can, guv. 'Oo's the lady?"

"She is no lady," Langston stated with flat coldness that went beyond fury. "She is an actress and no better than Harriette Wilson."

A low whistle escaped Winkly's thin mouth. Lord Alaistair's brother was dangerously angry.

"Her name is Samantha Davidson."

Winkly would have given another whistle, but fortunately caught himself in time. The Divine Davidson was the talk in all the pubs, not to mention all the gentry's drawing-rooms. This was a rum case if he'd ever seen one. Still . . .

"Righto, milord. I'll be gettin' right on it."

"Thank you," Langston said.

Recognizing dismissal in his tone, Winkly took himself off. Too bad about this, he thought. He hadn't ever heard ill of the actress. Too bad by half.

After Winkly left, Langston sat back down at his desk. Ravensford would be here shortly to discuss the revised version of the Poor Laws bill before taking it to the House of Lords. Much as Langston disliked it, he'd had to make certain changes to his bill, but he was savvy enough to realize that compromise was critical in politics. It was better to take small steps at first, because over time they added up to a giant stride forward. It was a principle he tried to remember in his private life, as well.

But who was he fooling? He slammed down the sheaf of papers. He could think of nothing but Samantha Davidson. The quill he had been using to make changes to his bill snapped. He dropped it to the desk, noting the spatter of ink over the papers, but for once not caring.

He was obsessed with the woman.

"I told Peter not to bother announcing me," came a deep rumble from the doorway.

Startled by the sound of the Earl of Ravensford's voice, Langston inadvertently knocked over the ink well. "Bloody..." He stood before the black ink flowed from the desk top onto his breeches. Taking out a pristine handkerchief, he quickly mopped up the worst.

As Langston sighed and dropped the ruined square of linen into a wooden wastebasket, Ravensford took the opportunity to study him. "Deep in contemplation when I arrived?"

"Yes, but not the kind you imagine."

The earl grinned roguishly. "It would not concern a certain delectable actress who is the talk of the Town, would it?"

Langston scowled, but not for long. The rakish twinkle in his friend's eyes was too hard to resist. He smiled. "Yes, you scoundrel. How did you know?"

Now it was Ravensford's turn to scowl. "When a woman visits a bachelor's house, 'tis soon the on-dit of the ton. Very likely the scandal sheets will pick it up next." He paused. "Cynthia won't be pleased."

"I never thought she would be, but this is family business, and Cynthia is not yet part of the family." It was a coldhearted statement and he knew it, but he refused to allow any woman to control his life. Not after Annabelle.

Grimacing, Langston went to the side table and unstoppered a decanter. "Whiskey or port?"

"Whiskey," Ravensford answered. "'Tis a damned barbaric drink, but it suits my mood."

Langston nodded agreement and splashed the amber liquid into two tumblers. He handed one to his friend and motioned toward a pair of large leather chairs pulled up before the fire. He paused at his desk to pick up the jeweler's box, then took a seat and propped his booted feet on a leather stool. Ravensford did likewise.

Raising his drink, Langston said, "Here's to the passage of our Poor Laws and the downfall of all scheming females."

They both drained their glasses.

In a quiet voice, Ravensford said, "I did not think you intended to take Mrs. Davidson as your mistress. You know Deverell is besotted with her, and Cynthia is in daily expectation of your proposal."

"Her damned visit was to try to get me to avoid meeting Dev in a duel." He banged his empty glass down on the table between them. "The woman is not and never will be my mistress. What sort of man would seduce the woman his brother wanted? Even if Deverell is wrong to desire her and I am determined to keep him from her, I would be no brother if I took her for myself."

Ravensford gave his friend an almost pitying look, but held his tongue. He knew better than to contradict Langston when he was in one of his moods.

"As for Cynthia's feelings, I am sorry for the situation, but Mrs. Davidson is outside my sphere of influence."

"Ah," Ravensford murmured, watching the flames leap in the grate. "She is a woman with a mind of her own."

"So it appears," Langston said, rising. "Care for another?"

"Whiskey grows on a chap," Ravensford said.

"Alaistair says so." Langston poured two more glasses. Sitting, he added, "But Mrs. Davidson's visit was not my first reason for asking you to come." He smiled wryly. "I had intended to give you my revision of the Poor Laws bill. But—" he waved a hand in the general direction of his desk "—as you can see, 'tis no longer possible today. Therefore, let's go to the second reason."

"By all means," Ravensford said.

"Mrs. Davidson." Langston's voice deepened and his fingers tightened around his glass. "Something has to be done about the woman. Deverell is obsessed with her."

"Deverell?" Ravensford's quiet word seemed to echo in the room.

"Deverell." Langston picked up the jeweler's box and tossed it to his friend, who caught it with a deft flick of his wrist. "Open it and see if you don't agree."

Ravensford gave a soft whistle. "Impressive."

"Quite. And inappropriate unless the woman is his *chère amie,* which I know she is not." He paused to sip his whiskey, savoring the fiery sensation in his throat as he swallowed. "He had that delivered to her after he left the country."

"And she returned it? Could she be after *you?*" Ravensford countered with a knowing gleam in his eye.

"I don't offer marriage, Dev does." Langston bit the words off. "And we all know what happens when a woman marries a man for his position alone."

Ravensford shook his head. "You will have to let go of your anger someday, my friend. Annabelle did nothing that is so unusual, after all. Many people have affairs, as well as quite successful marriages."

"But Annabelle bore me an heir not of my body." Bitterness permeated every word. "Most women in a marriage of convenience manage to give their husband an heir of his body before they take a cicisbeo."

"Yes, that was badly done, but Stephen is a delightful boy and a credit to you." His voice lowered, but was nonetheless firm. "He will make a good Duke of Rundell when the time comes."

Langston's mouth twisted. "A Duke of Rundell with not a drop of Rundell blood in his veins." Not even Ravensford knew who Stephen's sire was. It was the one secret Langston kept from everyone. He could only hope Huntly continued to do likewise.

"Rare, but not the first time something like this has happened. Let it go, Langston, so you can live and enjoy the rest of your life."

Langston glanced at his friend and saw the worry and concern Ravensford made no effort to hide. "Thank you."

"Now," Ravensford said, "what do you intend to do about Mrs. Davidson?"

"I have a plan that should put paid to her chances with Deverell once and for all, but I shall need your help."

"If I can morally give it, 'tis yours."

Langston smiled. "I am planning a house party at Langston Castle. Mrs. Davidson will be invited to perform in the small theatre there, an offer I trust her to accept for the monetary remuneration. Your job is to seduce her."

"A very pleasant task, but why?"

"Deverell won't want her if he knows she has been your mistress."

"And you?"

The taunting inquiry in his friend's question brought a flush to Langston's countenance. "I shall shortly be engaged to Cynthia. And if that is not enough for you, I have no wish to make Deverell hate me more than he already does because of that woman."

Ravensford nodded. "It does indeed appear that I am the only man for the job." Rising, he drained his glass and set it down. "Well, I won't have it said that I ever shirked my duty to my country or my friends."

Langston gave a hearty laugh, and felt an enormous release of tension. He rose and clapped his friend on the shoulder. "I knew you would come through. I will have a fresh copy of the bill sent round tomorrow. I think you will agree with the compromises I have made and see that they are small in comparison with the good brought about by getting this through the Lords."

"I am sure I shall," Ravensford said, "but in the meantime, how about a game of whist at Brooks's? Your brother Alaistair and Tristan Montford have asked us to meet them."

"Glad to," Langston said, thankful for occupation that would keep him from thinking about the actress for at least a little while. "After that, let's drop in on Drury Lane. There is no time like the present to start our campaign."

CHAPTER SEVEN

SAM SENSED HIM in the audience. There was an electricity in the air that made the hair at her nape rise and her skin tingle.

But why was he here? She had thought that by returning the ring she had severed all connection between them. Surely he was not here because he still thought she intended to wed his brother!

She missed a line and immediately chided herself. He did not have to be here because of her; he could be here for any number of other reasons. He could even be here to enjoy the play, which was receiving excellent reviews.

Yet when she entered her dressing-room hours later, she still worried about the reason for Langston's presence. It took the scent of roses to penetrate her concern.

A large bouquet of hothouse-grown damask rosebuds cascaded over the single wooden chair in the room. A gasp of surprised pleasure escaped her as she hurried to them and picked one up to smell. Delightful.

She searched for a card, but did not find one. A secret admirer? A frown marred her delight. Subterfuge was the last thing she needed now, and it left her two choices: throw the flowers out or enjoy them in spite of the manner in which they were delivered.

She took another sniff of one exquisite bloom and caressed its satiny petals with a finger. She *would* enjoy them, and the devil take the consequences.

As she was fastening one perfect bloom in her hair, a knock sounded on her dressing-room door. She drew her green wool wrapper closer about her suddenly trembling body and called huskily, "Who is it?"

"Langston."

She was not surprised. From the moment she had realized he was in the theatre, she had known this would happen. Everything she told herself to the contrary was only wishful thinking.

There was no bolt on the door because she had never before felt the need for one. She kept no valuables here, and the other cast members respected her privacy. Now she wished there were *two* bolts on the door.

"I do not wish to speak with you," she said, pleased she'd kept the tremor from her voice.

"But *I* wish to speak with *you*," he countered in the lazy drawl that made her head spin.

She knew that if she defied him, he would open the door without her permission. Once that happened, she would be at his mercy—unless she decided to scream for help, something she would never do.

On silent, slipper-covered feet, she crossed to the door and opened it a crack to peer out at him. He was magnificent in his evening dress. The black jacket and black pantaloons hugged the musculature of his shoulders, hips and legs. In the light from the wall sconces, his hair was like burnished gold. And when his gaze traveled the length of her person, revealed in the small opening and a wicked gleam entered his hooded brown eyes, Sam knew she was lost.

"Go away," she said breathlessly. "I am not dressed."

"I don't mind if you aren't," he murmured.

Blood pounded in her ears. She licked suddenly dry lips. More than anything she wanted to let him in, wanted to feel his lips on hers and discover if her memory of them was as pleasurable as the reality. Somehow she managed to deny the urge. "I have nothing to say to you now that Lord Deverell is out of the country and your duel with him cannot take place."—

"But I have a proposition to put to you." He lingered suggestively on the word that could mean a multitude of things. "It will be worth your while."

No matter what happened between them, it always came back to his belief that she was a money-hungry tart. "Nothing concerning you is worth my while," she said tightly, trying to push the door closed.

It was an impossible task because his foot was wedged in the opening.

What did he want of her? Sam wondered in dismay. "Please," she cried, "leave me alone."

His smile did not reach his eyes. "I believe we are going to talk, after all, Mrs. Davidson."

Slowly, inexorably, he pushed the door open until he was in the tiny room with her, his presence overwhelming her senses. He closed the door softly and advanced on her. Sam backed up until her thighs pressed against the small dressing-table.

The smell of greasepaint and damask rose mingled with his musk and spice to make her feel dizzy. Her fingers gripped the edge of the table, and her chest rose and fell rapidly with her labored breathing as she tried to control her unruly susceptibility to his nearness.

He towered over her, his eyes missing nothing as he looked around the cluttered room, lingering for a moment on the roses. "Have you ever heard that cleanliness is next to godliness, Mrs. Davidson?" he asked, his attention back on her.

"Too many times to remember, my lord," she said, feeling pinned in place by the intensity of his gaze. "However, I am sure the desire to deliver that little homily was not the reason you forced yourself on me."

His expression gave away nothing of his emotions. "I have not forced myself on you, and you were the one to seek me out last."

Sam's fingers tightened their grip on the wood. "I had an excellent reason."

"The debate is whether or not your reason was valid. Particularly to call on a man to whom you have no relation . . . not even as a lover."

The rebellious thought that he would make a wonderful lover made her flush. The memory of his lips pressed hungrily to hers, his tongue demanding her surrender, heated her blood and made it impossible for her to stare him down. She looked away, fully aware that she was getting the worst of this encounter.

Pulling herself up straight, she let go of her death grip of the table. "There is nothing to debate, my lord. I did what I had to, and I would do it again."

He took a step toward her. "There won't be a second time."

The small room was normally cold, but Sam felt as though she were standing next to a roaring fire. His proximity was most unnerving, and it made her rash. "You are right. There won't. 'Tis obvious that you consider yourself above average mortals. Nothing can hurt you or your Poor Laws. For the sake of the people you are trying to help, I hope you are right about your invincibility."

An unsettling observation, he thought, but not unsettling enough to make him forget his purpose for being here. "I am here to offer you employment when the theatre season is over."

She arched one perfectly formed brow in mock query. Her hair tumbled about her shoulders in disarray, and her wrapper revealed the deep valley between her breasts. Her face was rosy, as though she had just made love. The spurt of irritation he felt was quickly followed by a flash of desire so intense it took his breath away. A heavy tightness settled in his loins.

"I believe I have already turned down one offer more advantageous than any you are likely to make."

Her voice was husky and her eyes smoldered. He wondered if she realized how seductive she was. Probably not, or she would be pulling out her little pistol in an effort to keep him away. But he was not here for that, either, and he would never make such a proposition to her. Never.

"I am here to ask you to perform for my guests during a house party I am planning. It will be at Langston Castle for two weeks' duration, and the remuneration will be more than you earn in a season here."

Her eyes widened briefly. He saw her bite her lower lip and wished she would not. It was all he could do to stick to his resolution.

When she tried to skirt around him, he moved so there would be no contact between them. The last thing he wanted was to touch her; his control was precariously fragile.

One of her slender white hands clasped her wrapper tightly around her throat; the other moved to caress a crystal unicorn sitting on her dressing-table. He thought it a whimsical object for so practical a woman.

"Very generous," she murmured, her husky voice causing unsettling sensations that he was unable to suppress. "I am sure you will understand and be unsurprised when I refuse your offer." Her gaze rose to meet his, challenging him to argue with her.

"I suggest, Mrs. Davidson, that you give yourself a couple of days to consider. Remember you are a mother, with all the responsibilities that entails.

Not to mention the fact that my brother's offer no longer stands. Deverell will not return from the Continent for some time."

"Gracious of you, my lord, to give me a second chance at your magnanimous offer," she murmured provocatively.

He made her a curt bow of acknowledgment, when what he really wanted to do was take her in his arms and kiss her until both of them forgot what lay between them. "Then you will take my advice?"

She whirled away from him, her dressing-gown flowing behind her, the scent of damask rose following in her wake. With her back to the door she said, "I won't accept your generous offer. Money is not everything in life."

He gave her a penetrating look. "For most people, it is. I cannot believe you are different."

Sam hardened her voice. "Hell will freeze over before I accept anything from you."

Sparks shot from her eyes, and her porcelain complexion became suffused with a becoming color. Langston's desire for her grew, despite his knowing that to succumb to it was to court disaster.

"Damn you and damn me," he muttered, swiftly closing the distance between them. "We are nothing to each other, and my brother desires you, yet..."

His hands settled on her shoulders in a grip that was at once firm and tender. Passion vibrated through his body like the strings of a harp stroked by commanding fingers.

She stared up at him, her pupils dilated, her lips parted. She was a woman caught in a man's ardor and unable to deny her own response.

"Damn you," he muttered again. "This is a mistake." His head lowered and his mouth sought hers.

Sam melted against him, even as her mind screamed for her to push him away. He was right; this was a mistake. A mistake neither of them wanted, yet both seemed unable to resist. As he deepened the kiss, his hands skimmed over her shoulders, moving with a restlessness that spoke of desire beyond control.

When he could stand it no longer, Langston twined his fingers in her thick, luxuriant hair, pulling out the pins. A groan escaped him as the silken strands spilled into his hands. "You don't know how I have longed to do this," he murmured against her lips.

He lifted his head and stared down at her. She looked wanton with her hair streaming down her back and her face blurred with passion. The dressing-gown she wore gaped at the neck, revealing the top curves of her breasts. The sight was more than he could endure. One hand left the satin welcome of her hair to skim down her arm, taking the robe's sleeve with it. He wanted more.

"You are a witch," he murmured, taking her lips again.

When at last he tore his mouth from hers, she stared at him with glazed eyes, seeing the dark passion he made no effort to hide. It was a fleeting instant, and then his lips were at her throat and one hand was at the small of her back, fitting her to his arousal while the other hand tangled deeper into her hair.

A whimper of desire and denial escaped her lips as her head lolled back against the door. His mouth moved lower, skimming the rising mound of her aching breast. She went taut in response.

"Samantha," came a man's voice from the other side of the door.

Sam stiffened in shock. Timothy Jones had come to escort her to the post-performance gathering.

Langston froze, his mouth pressed to the swell of her breast, his loins fused to hers. It was all he could do not to utter the groan rising in his throat. He lifted his head and gazed down at her dazed features, and only then did he fully comprehend where he and this woman had been headed. If the man on the other side of the door had not interrupted them, he would have taken her here on the floor! He would have driven the final wedge between himself and the younger brother he loved. And he would have done it because of this woman.

"Sam!" The voice behind the door had taken on an edge of worry. "We are waiting for you to appear in the back room. The men are beginning to grumble."

Sam gulped hard, then brought her hands up to Langston's chest and pushed. Nothing happened. If anything, he held her closer, making it impossible for her to take a deep breath. The expression on his face was enough to make her wish Timothy Jones to the devil, even though she knew his intervention had been timely. She was no fool. The light in Langston's eyes was desire, bold and untrammeled.

The hunger in his face was matched by that in her soul. She squeezed her eyes shut against the sight of him, against the reflection of her desire in his dilated pupils.

"Sam?" Timothy rapped hard on the door.

Somehow she found her voice, although it was so husky it was almost unintelligible. "I . . . I'm fine. I shall be there shortly."

"Are you sure you are all right?" he asked again, tentatively jiggling the doorknob.

Langston pressed her into the door, preventing the man outside from easily opening it. She suppressed a gasp as the cloth of his shirt and embroidered vest rubbed against her breasts. When she reassured Timothy, her voice was barely audible.

"If you insist," Timothy muttered, sounding unconvinced.

It seemed an eternity before they heard his footsteps retreat down the hall. Only then did Langston release her. Sam sagged against the door, thankful for its support. The last thing she needed was to dissolve into a puddle of desire at the man's feet.

"Will you go now?" she asked, appalled at the weakness of her voice.

He stepped back, his hooded gaze traveling up and down her body, the passion of seconds before no longer evident. "For now," he said, and once again his deep baritone sent a shiver of pleasure through her.

She lifted her chin and said in a stronger voice, "I see that you are yourself to the bitter end."

A smile of appreciation curved his lips. "I am a man, Mrs. Davidson, just as you are a woman. Unfortunately for both of us, we desire each other." His voice roughened, sounding like the muffled roar of the ocean crashing to shore. "But I will never make love to you. You are not the woman for me, just as you are not the wife for Deverell.''

Sam grasped her robe in one hand while the other clutched at her throat, which was closing in pain. Dignity was all she had left; he had already seen her passion and was throwing it back at her. She drew herself up and, with squared shoulders and innate grace, moved away from the door.

''Get out, Langston.''

For a moment he paused, and she thought he meant to say something to her. Then he opened the door and left.

As soon as the door closed behind him, Sam seized the chair and dragged it across the room, sending the roses spilling to the floor and spreading their heady scent through the tiny room like opium smoke. Only when the chair back was wedged under the doorknob did she take a deep breath, trying to stop the shivers that racked her like an ague.

Every time he came into her life, he created havoc. And now this. What was happening between them? She did not try to fool herself that this was love; they did not even like each other. And what about his offer?

Sam picked up the roses from the floor to give herself time to think. Certainly the money would be welcome. She did not absolutely need it, but raising a child involved so many unforeseen expenses.

And then there was the attraction between her and Langston. It was growing out of control. She should never have allowed him to kiss her. He should have never wanted to kiss her. Yet it had happened.

Another rap on the door interrupted her. "Sam," Timothy said again, "I thought you were coming immediately. Several of your more eager swains are threatening to fetch you themselves."

Sam's hands clenched. That was so typical of the aristocracy. They thought their wealth and lineage entitled them to anything they desired. Langston was no different from his kind.

"I shall be there shortly," she said as she slipped out of her robe and into a simple empire-waisted gown of fine muslin.

She heard his footsteps recede as she secured one of the roses in her hair. Her audience awaited her, and they would expect the rose. Besides, she needed the soothing scent of the familiar flower. She draped an Indian shawl over her shoulders and left.

Sam paused at the back room's entrance to gather her wits. Male members of the *ton* crowded the area as usual, and the cast members fawned upon them as usual. She felt a headache beginning in her temples. 'Twas always the same.

"Mrs. Davidson." Huntly's suave tenor added to her discomfort, causing a sharp stab of pain that made her wince.

Sam steeled herself and turned to him with an inquiring look. "Mr. Huntly?"

His brown hair was perfectly styled and his cravat was tied with precision, if not flair. His evening dress, in the black that was *de rigueur*, was immaculate, if uninspired. She did not like the man. He had a veneer that was too smooth, too perfect, making her want to scratch the surface and see what slithered out. She shuddered and clutched her shawl more tightly around her.

"Would you care for a glass of champagne?" he asked, handing her one before she could reply.

"Thank you," she murmured, wondering why he persisted in seeking her out. Just last week she had refused his offer of protection, the word he had used to phrase his proposition.

"Would it be possible to go to your dressing-room?" His eyes glittered as his mouth smiled, showing straight white teeth. He was a predator, no matter how urbane his style. Sam's skin crawled. He was not forcing himself on her, as some did, and yet . . .

"I believe anything you wish to say to me can be said here, Mr. Huntly." She kept her voice low and her tone reasonable in spite of knowing what was coming next.

His mouth tightened, the smile slipping. "I am sure you know exactly what I wish to discuss. I am asking you again to come to my country estate when Drury Lane closes for the season. I will make it worth your while and don't even mind if you bring the child and the old woman."

"You do not?" she asked, her voice deceptively mild. "That is very generous of you. Not many men would allow their mistress's child to accompany them to the love-nest."

His smile reasserted itself. "I pride myself on not being like most men."

"I understand perfectly," Sam murmured, angling away from him. She racked her brain for some phrase, some witticism, that would allow her to escape without making an enemy of him. Enemies were a luxury she could ill afford in her position, and a man like Huntly did not take kindly to being refused.

The Marquis of Langston chose that moment to approach. "Mrs. Davidson," he said, his eyes smoldering. "How fetching the rose in your hair is. A beguiling effect that I am sure your other admirers appreciate as much as I do."

"Langston," Huntly cut in, his tone just short of challenging. "I should have known you would be pursuing the Divine Davidson. You and I seem to have many tastes in common."

There were no outward signs, but Sam sensed Langston tensing. He had an alertness about him that told her better than words that these two men had a past. Something had happened between them, and now they hated each other.

As though to put the lie to Sam's perception, Langston drawled, "You think so, Huntly? It just goes to show how one can be mistaken. Mrs. Davidson and I are in the process of resolving a business arrangement. Were you doing the same? Somehow I did not think so."

Huntly's mouth thinned and some of his smoothness deserted him, making his voice hard. "Mrs. Davidson and I were coming to a mutual agreement, the nature of which is none of your concern."

"I am sure it is not," Langston said, his gaze contemptuous. He turned to Sam. "I trust you will give my offer due consideration." Without another word, he sauntered off.

Sam went crimson to the roots of her hair. How dare the man do this to her! His words made her look like a demirep caught between two lucrative offers.

"As I was saying Mrs. Davidson . . . Samantha," Huntly said, his voice once more smooth, "I think we would do well together, and I would make the remuneration worthy of your position. You would no longer have to act on the stage."

His smile, so cultured on the surface, did nothing to hide the feral gleam in his eyes.

"I am extremely appreciative of your offer," Sam said, hoping she would not choke on the lie. Huntly could damage her if he set about it. He was possibly influential enough to make the Drury Lane management think twice about renewing her contract.

The idea stiffened her spine. She was through being manipulated by others. She did not have to accept his offer, just as she did not have to continue appeasing him. She would survive, whatever he did. It could be no worse than being seventeen and having a baby to care for with no husband or parents to support her.

No, Huntly might try to ruin her career, perhaps even succeed, but she and her child would survive. There was, after all, Langston's offer if need be.

"Then you accept," Huntly stated, reaching for her hand.

Quickly Sam reached for the champagne glass, preventing him from touching her. She did not

think her acting skills were great enough to cover
her aversion to him.

"At this time, Mr. Huntly, I fear I cannot accept." She saw the first glitter of anger in his eyes
and knew she was doomed to fail in placating him.
"I am a mother, and my child's upbringing is the
most important thing in my life. I do not want
Amalie to see me living with a man to whom I am
not married."

"Perhaps you will reconsider. I shall be staying
in town after Parliament adjourns. Send word to
me when you change your mind."

Sam forced herself to smile. She had made a
dangerous enemy, and had no one to protect her
from his retribution.

Except—should she choose to accept his offer—
the Marquis of Langston. It was a frightening realization.

CHAPTER EIGHT

SIX DAYS LATER Sam fought back tears as she watched Amalie moan and thrash in the throes of a fever that would not abate. If only the doctor would arrive!

Worry and exhaustion weighted Sam's arms as she dipped the rag in the cool water and sponged Amalie's heated face again. It seemed she had been doing this forever, but Amalie's condition remained unchanged.

Dear Lord, she prayed silently, *do not take her from me, I beg of you. She is my life.*

"Miss Sam, the doctor's here," Lottie said from the doorway. She stepped aside to allow him to enter.

"Thank God," Sam breathed, dropping the rag and rising. "Sir Reginald, thank you. I..." She glanced at her daughter's pale face and wasted body and then looked back at the physician. "I cannot seem to help her." Her voice caught on a sob.

Sir Reginald, with his capable hands, strong-boned face and piercing blue eyes, was the best in

London. Without waiting for permission, he edged Sam away and sat in the chair by the bed. As Sam watched, he examined Amalie from head to foot, making no comment in the process.

When he was finished, he pulled the coverlet back over the child and turned to Sam with a worried frown. "She has an inflammation of the lungs. We must keep her warm and apply a poultice to her chest, which must be kept on at all times. I will prepare the ingredients for a tisane that she must take three times a day."

Sam nodded, determined to pull her daughter through this. She had to.

THREE DAYS LATER, Sir Reginald pronounced Amalie out of immediate danger. "However, that does not mean I advocate your staying in London. The air is bad for her, and she will recover much more slowly here. If possible, you should take her to the country."

Sam gulped and nodded. "Of course. If that will restore her health. Anything."

Then Sir Reginald named a fee for his services that made her gasp. Fortunately she had the money in a savings account, but there would be precious little left. Still, the doctor's service was worth every guinea.

Only after he departed did Sam allow herself to collapse on one of the overstuffed, threadbare chairs in her parlor. She buried her face in her hands. All the tears she had been holding back ran between her fingers and fell on the skirts of her wool gown, only now she cried from relief.

In the aftermath of released tension, she dozed off. When she awoke, the room was dark. The draperies on the windows were open, and Sam got up and looked out into the cold winter night, considering her options.

She had only one. If Amalie was to recover completely, she had to be in the country, and Langston's offer could make that possible. Sam decided to call on him tomorrow. She would accept his invitation to perform at his house party with the proviso that Amalie be allowed to accompany her.

She shivered slightly in the chill room. She decided to look in on Amalie.

Just as she put her foot on the first stair, there was a knock on the door. Who could be calling at this hour? When she did not immediately answer, there was a louder knock.

Going back into the parlor, she looked out the front window to see at the curb a carriage with a familiar crest. Langston.

He rapped a third time before she reached the door. Slightly breathless, she pulled it open and blurted out, "What are you doing here?"

His heavy-lidded eyes traveled over her as he stepped into the house without asking. "You look dreadful, so it must be true."

Bewildered by his words and arrival, yet finding a sense of warmth and security stealing over her at his presence, Sam automatically shut the door. No matter how he reviled her, she always felt a peculiar sense of safety with him.

"You have not answered my question," she stated baldly.

He scowled. Moonlight filtered through the fanlight above the door, the cold glow making his features harsh and haunting. Sam caught her breath in awe. It was an unwelcome emotion.

"I went to Drury Lane to repeat my offer of last week. They said you had not been in for nine days because your daughter is gravely ill."

He said the words evenly, but she detected his concern. He was genuinely worried about Amalie. She should have expected this of a man who had created a bill like his Poor Laws. He had compassion for others—as long as they were not his enemies.

Sam raked her loose hair back from her face and prepared herself to ask him if his offer still stood.

"Yes, the doctor was here earlier. She is on the mend, thank God, but she is far from totally recovered. Sir Reginald..." She paused to study Langston, to see if there was any softening in his features that would make it easier for her. There was nothing, but she went ahead regardless. "Sir Reginald says she must go to the country. If your offer is still open, I accept it, provided my daughter may accompany me."

There, she had all but pleaded. Sam released the breath she had unconsciously held and waited for his response.

"Fine. The two of you will leave the day after tomorrow for Langston Castle. I will send a coach."

He spoke tersely, matter-of-factly, but Sam did not miss the scrutiny he subjected her to, as though he expected her to collapse at any moment. She must truly look awful.

"Thank you, Langston," she said, her voice hoarse with unspoken emotion. "I had hoped your offer still stood."

"I do not make offers I do not intend to honor."

No, she thought, looking at the stern lines of his face, he would not. He was a proud man, arrogant, but he stood by his word, and somehow she knew he stood by people he cared for or felt responsible for. Was she one of those? When had that happened?

And what of the passion that flared between them? Sam knew that going to Langston's home would only make it harder to resist.

SAM PEERED OUT the window of Langston's well-appointed coach. Frost sparkled on the glass, making the bare tree limbs and the dead winter grass appear crystallized. It was a stark, yet beautiful scene.

A grey rabbit gazed inquisitively at the passing carriage from the cover of a holly bush. It was such a bucolic sight that Sam instantly found herself feeling as though she were leaving the cares of the world behind.

"Mama." Amalie's voice made Sam smile. "Are we almost there? Is Lord Langston going to be nice to you?"

Sam looked at her daughter, in surprise. Why would she think Langston might *not* be nice? Only one thing came to mind. Amalie must have overheard the shouting between the brothers going on in her parlor that evening when Langston had driven them home from her rehearsal. It must have frightened Amalie; hence her current apprehension.

Despite that, Sam was relieved to see that the three long days of traveling had not done Amalie any harm. Her color was still good. She had, in fact, improved daily, and pray God, would continue to.

"Sweetheart, Lord Langston is my employer and will treat me with respect." Or so she would insist. She owed him a great deal, but that did not mean she had to allow him to treat her with anything but courtesy. "And we are on his drive right now."

Amalie's eyes became as round as two blue moons. "We are? But I see lots of trees and no house."

"Now, missy," Lottie said, pushing her spectacles back up her nose, "this is a rich man's home. 'Tis not for the likes of Lord Langston to have his house visible from the road. We will go some distance before seeing it, and all will be his lordship's land. After all, he is an influential man."

Amalie cocked her head in puzzlement. "What does 'influential' mean?"

Sam turned aside and brought her grey-gloved hand up to cover her mouth. With luck, Lottie would think she was hiding a yawn and never know she was silently laughing at the situation Lottie had gotten herself into. Now the nanny would have to explain the word, and then the next, and the one after that. Illness had not blunted Amalie's inquisitiveness.

"Well...influential means powerful," Lottie said, her brows drawn together in concentration.

"What is powerful?" Amalie asked, determined to get to the real meaning of what Lottie had said about the man.

"You know," Lottie said, exasperation beginning to creep into her tone. At Amalie's innocent head shake of denial, Lottie said, "Someone who has control of everything."

Sam's grin widened. The interrogation was bound to last all the way to the marquis's door.

The pair were still at it when Sam's gasp of admiration interrupted them. Ahead, surrounded by extensive lawns now brown from winter's cold, was a sprawling Elizabethan mansion, its many-paned windows sparkling in the winter sunlight. It was large enough to house the entire village in which Sam had grown up. For the first time since meeting Langston, the true magnitude of his wealth and power were brought home to her.

She felt like a gnat that has just met up with a rolled newspaper. And to think she had stood up to him, still intended to do so. She thought of all the comfort and security she had turned down when she refused Lord Deverell. Still, she was not sorry about that.

As the coach pulled to a stop and a footman dressed in blue-and-gold livery rushed down the front steps to open the door for them, Amalie said in awed tones, "Mama, isn't this grand? Just the most grand?"

Sam shook her head in amusement as her impulsive daughter fairly leapt into the footman's extended arms. She knew she should subdue Amalie's high spirits, but she hadn't the heart. After such a close brush with death, the child deserved all the enjoyment she could get.

Sam stepped down without assistance, feeling the frost crunch under her boots. "Mrs. Davidson." Langston's deep voice resonated through her body as he approached. "And Amalie and Mistress Lottie. Welcome to Langston Castle. I shall do everything possible to see that you are entertained."

"And that I entertain," Sam muttered under her breath.

She had not seen him come from the house and only realized as he drew nearer that he must have come from the stable. He was dressed in riding clothes. Buff leather breeches scandalously clung to every muscle in his thighs, while the neck of his white lawn shirt opened at the collar to reveal golden curls. The sight was nearly her undoing.

"Yes," he murmured wickedly, "and that you entertain. After all, Mrs. Davidson, I did not invite the premier actress of London here merely to look beautiful.''

His flattery was so out of character that Sam gave him a sharp look. There was a gleam in his eyes that sent a shaft of pleasure shooting down her spine. If she had not known better, she would have thought he was flirting with her.

Amalie, however, was completely taken in. "My lord, now that we are here, I know you will be nice to my mama, won't you?" she said with such innocence it would have taken the devil incarnate not to agree.

Langston found himself smiling at the child even as he recognized she had positioned him so that he had to agree with her. Yet, seeing the clearness in her blue eyes, he realized she was not trying to trick him; she was simply asking for his affirmation that he would treat her mother well.

"It seems you are much recovered from your illness, Amalie, for 'tis obvious you have not lost any of your brashness." He continued smiling as he spoke, because he found himself genuinely fond of the little girl. "I promise to do my best not to be unkind to your mother," he added when the girl's chin took on a stubborn tilt.

Amalie beamed. He looked from child to mother. Mrs. Davidson was smiling at her daughter with such softness and love in her eyes that

Langston found himself envying the girl. It was a sensation he pushed away to concentrate on the qualities he did *not* admire in Mrs. Davidson—such as her use of Deverell.

He turned abruptly to the footman. "Michael, take Miss Amalie and Mistress Lottie to their rooms, then arrange for them to have something hot to drink and some food."

The footman bowed, his immaculately powdered wig very white in the pale sunlight. Amalie gave her mother one last glance, then turned and happily followed Lottie and the footman.

Sam watched her child disappear into the mansion and marveled that Amalie could feel secure so quickly. She was an intrepid and outgoing child, but usually she insisted on staying close to her mother for at least the first thirty minutes in any new situation. Her behavior spoke volumes about Langston and his home.

"She certainly appears to be well on the road to recovery," he murmured, "though I am sure it will do her good to stay in the country. You made the right decision."

His deep, warm voice that was usually so cool when he spoke to her sent yet another frisson of excitement down her spine. "I made the only decision I could," she answered, knowing that in coming here she was helping her daughter but not herself. She was seeing the compassionate side of Langston more and more, and if she was not careful, she would come to care for him.

"So you did," he said, his voice becoming distant once more.

Clearing her throat, Sam said briskly, "So. When shall I see your theatre? I need to look it over so that I will have an idea of what things I will need. And have you decided on the play we will perform?"

"No," he said, starting toward the entrance. "But I shall."

He paused on the threshold while the butler held open the massive double doors. The glow of a chandelier hanging in the foyer behind him gilded the hair of his arrogantly held head. It took Sam's breath away. She fought down her trepidation about what the next two weeks held for her and followed him into the house.

THAT EVENING, Sam took one last look at herself in the full-length beveled glass on her bedroom wall. The severely cut primrose velvet became her. The low, square neckline bared her shoulders, and the spray of tiny damask roses at the high waistline accentuated the curves of her bosom.

To her pleased surprise a vase filled with her favorite roses had greeted her when she'd entered her room earlier. Now she went over to the dresser where the vase sat and removed one more bloom, which she fixed in the thick curls of her hair.

Sam was thankful she had let Lottie persuade her to buy one new evening dress. There would be many nights when the guests would gather for dinner and entertainment, and to have at least one fashionable gown would be to her advantage.

"You'll do," Lottie said, pride reddening her cheeks. "More than do, if you ask me."

Sam smiled and made a playful curtsy. "Thank you kindly, ma'am."

Lottie harrumphed as she pushed her glasses up her nose and started tidying the room, but Sam saw her grin. "Best hurry or you'll be late," the nurse said gruffly.

Instead of rushing out the door, Sam caught Lottie in a hug. "Thank you, best of all friends, for everything."

"Don't be thanking me, Miss Sam. You're the one who provides for all of us, and I know you didn't want to come here. His lordship hasn't been exactly pleasant to you in the past." Her shrewd blue eyes watched Sam's reaction. "But we couldn't do different."

Sam knew that Lottie suspected there was more than money and Amalie's health behind Sam's acceptance of Langston's offer. "Langston has done what he felt necessary. As have I." Picking up the matching long gloves and sliding them on, she added, "But you are right. I must hurry if I am to visit Amalie before dinner. Will you be coming?"

"Just as soon as I get things put away here. Tell the gel to get in bed."

"Yes, ma'am," Sam said saucily.

"Get away with you." Lottie replied, chuckling. It was good to see Miss Sam in high spirits. She rarely had reason to be.

Sam found the maze of halls and doors daunting, but with perseverance, she found the stairs to the fourth floor, where the nursery wing was. Amalie was in the third room on the right. Walking briskly, Sam counted down.

"I say, who are you?"

Sam twirled around, startled by the young voice, and saw that one of the doors she had passed was open; a tall, thin boy stood in the entrance. The candle he held cast shadows over the sharp planes of his narrow face. Bright blue eyes peered at her from beneath a shock of blue-black hair. His forehead was high and his nose straight. A handsome child, Sam thought.

"I am Mrs. Davidson, Amalie's mother," she said. "I am an actress, and Lord Langston invited me here to perform for his houseguests."

"Ah," the boy said, coming toward her. "You are the little girl's mother. You don't look like her."

Sam suppressed a smile. He spoke as though he were a grown-up and Amalie a child, but she guessed him to be close to her daughter in age. He might be all of ten, possibly eleven.

'Amalie resembles her father."

"Where is he?" the boy asked, a curious, almost bereft tone creeping into his voice.

"He died at sea a number of years ago."

"Oh. I *am* sorry." A stricken look came over his face, and he turned abruptly away. "Good night, Mrs. Davidson."

Before Sam could say anything further, he was gone, the door to his room quietly closed. She shook her head at his strange behavior, but just then, Amalie's door opened and her daughter's head popped out.

"Mama? I thought I heard your voice." She beckoned Sam in. "Were you talking to that horrid boy?"

Sam smiled as she entered Amalie's room and followed her to the cozy-looking bed with its bright blue coverlet and big feather pillows. "Why is he a horrid boy?"

Amalie climbed under the coverlet and plumped her pillows before leaning back into them. "He just is. He tried to order me about and make me play blind man's bluff when I did not wish to."

"Ah," Sam murmured, sitting on the bed and smoothing back the curling wisps that had come loose from Amalie's braid. "He must be the domineering sort."

"Exactly," Amalie said, happy to see that her mother understood. "He said that tomorrow we would go outside and play, and when I told him I would not because I've been sick, he said I had to. He said he was Viscount Taunton and his father owns this house and I had to do what I was told."

So, Sam thought, he was Langston's son. He perhaps didn't have the look of his father, but he held himself in the same arrogant way. Where was his mother?

It was a question guaranteed to make her feel decidedly peculiar. The too-familiar tightness settled in her chest, and it was an effort to remain focused on Amalie's chatter. Luckily Lottie arrived and immediately took over.

"Miss Sam," she said in shocked tones, "you're going to be late for dinner, and that will never do in a place like this. Now be off with you."

"Mama, stay—"

"Enough of that, girl," Lottie interrupted. "Your mother has a job to do. Besides, I'll be with you."

Knowing Lottie was right, Sam gave Amalie a good-night kiss and departed. She was never comfortable with strangers; she would be even more uncomfortable arriving late so that all eyes would be upon her as she entered.

As she closed the door to her daughter's room, a smile pulled at Sam's mouth. This trip was good for her daughter. And she was clearly feeling better. Look how affronted she'd been by Langston's son.

No matter what transpired, Sam owed a great deal to the Marquis of Langston.

CHAPTER NINE

WHEN SAM REACHED the salon, she told the footman she did not wish to be announced. After a flicker of surprise at her unusual request, he impassively and silently opened the door.

Sam paused on the threshold to get her bearings. The room was immense, with chairs and tables scattered about and groups of people gathered around them. The walls were five times her height, the ceiling domed and covered by cavorting nymphs and cherubs painted in rich colors. Gold trim defined matching panels on the walls.

"Mrs. Davidson," a male voice said. "I was beginning to think Langston was pulling my leg when he told me you would be present."

Sam turned to the Earl of Ravensford with a smile. His bronze hair glowed in the light from the three chandeliers.

"I am glad to know someone here," she said, giving him her hand, which he raised to his lips. He lingered over the kiss, and Sam realized he was flirting with her, but she felt nothing.

"Mrs. Davidson," another voice intruded, one that made Sam tingle. "I did not hear the announcement of your arrival. Ravensford must have been lying in wait for you by the door."

Sam withdrew her hand from Ravensford's clasp and faced Langston. Formally dressed, as she had seen him many times before, he still took her breath away. His hair gleamed like gold, and his dark eyes sparkled with an emotion she could not name.

"Langston," she murmured, keeping her hands at her sides. "I asked the footman not to announce me. I felt it would be pretentious, given my circumstances."

Only after she said the words did she realize how much they revealed: all her insecurities, and to the man she least wanted to be aware of them.

His dark gaze held her, and Sam completely forgot about the Earl of Ravensford, who seconds before had been so welcome. One hand fluttered at her throat, as though that would ease the tightness there.

"I see you are wearing my roses," Langston said, his gaze devouring her. "They become you as much here as they did in London."

With a jolt Sam realized he was referring to the mysterious roses she had found in her dressing-room the night he visited her—the night he had nearly seduced her. Crimson mounted her cheeks and butterflies swirled in her stomach. Why had he sent them?

"Perhaps Mrs. Davidson would like a glass of sherry," Ravensford's voice intruded.

She turned to smile at him. "Thank you, but I think I recognize a gentleman near the fireplace. I shall go and pay my respects."

It was a bold move, and one no proper young miss would even contemplate, Sam knew. But she was no proper young miss, or even a proper matron. She was an actress, and the outrageous was expected of her. Moreover, the tension she sensed between these two, who were supposed to be friends, made her anxious to get away. And never mind her own unbridled response to everything about Langston.

THE MARQUIS WATCHED her glide toward the fireplace, her head high and her hips swaying.

"You might have told me that you'd changed your mind," Ravensford said shortly. "It would have saved me the effort."

Langston glanced at his friend in surprise. "What are you raving about?"

"The Divine Davidson, who else?" Ravensford said, casting an appreciative glance in her direction. "If I'd known you intended to seduce her yourself, I would have found other game."

"Don't be an idiot," Langston said, fighting off his irritation at Ravensford's assumption. "Nothing is changed. I still count on you to lure her into your bed and out of Deverell's reach."

"Then you'd best stop devouring her with your eyes," Ravensford said, humor once more flavoring his words.

Unclenching the hands he had not consciously clenched, Langston said, "Don't worry. She sits by you tonight, and although it is not proper protocol, I expect you to escort her in."

"My pleasure," Ravensford said, the amusement in his voice more pronounced. "In that case, I'd best go after the lady and stake my claim."

Langston watched his friend head toward the fireplace and cursed himself for being ten times a fool. The woman was here to be bedded by Ravensford so that Deverell would not want her and not hate *him* for being the one to bed her. For if he did, he might just as well duel Dev.

He caught the butler's signal that dinner was ready, and he located his own partner, the wife of a neighboring landowner. Yet, determined as he was to ignore the actress, he could not block out his awareness of her. Even in the hushed flow of voices, he heard her husky alto with its tiny catch when she laughed. From the corner of his eyes he could see the rich primrose of her gown and the generous curve of her bosom, and the blood pounded in his temples. His response to her was as primordial as it was obsessive.

He scowled as he seated his partner at the table.

"Langston," Lady Roberts said, fluttering her fan, "whatever is the matter with you? I don't believe you've heard a word I've said, and your frown would scare off a less brave soul than I."

She said this with a smile, but Langston saw that she was indeed nervous and realized he had been allowing his preoccupation with Mrs. Davidson to affect his dealings with others. It would not do.

Flashing her a grin that had sent more accomplished flirts than she floundering in rocky waters, he said, "Pardon me. But you know how it is when a bachelor entertains."

Lady Roberts tittered. "The latest *on-dit* says that Lady Cynthia is expecting to relieve you of the burden of entertaining without a hostess."

The last thing he wanted to discuss was the rumor of his pending proposal. He was still not sure what he meant to do with regard to Cynthia. A conversational trap such as this was something he did not intend to fall into.

With a hint of chill, he murmured, "I am sure Lady Cynthia knows the value of rumors as much as I do."

Before Lady Roberts could protest, he turned to the woman seated on his left, the Dowager Countess of Ravensford, his friend's grandmother. When he and Ravensford were boys the countess had always taken their side in a scrape, saying they needed to be left alone to grow and find themselves. She was still opinionated, but now her feisty manner was generally aimed at her neighbors. Born in a different time, she did not take kindly to this one. Tonight was no exception.

Lifting her lorgnette to rheumy blue eyes, she said in the loud tone of one who is nearly deaf, "Who's the chit in the pink gown with roses in her hair? Damned fine figure of a gel. Why, she'd put the Gunning sisters to shame, and they caught a duke and a peer." She shot a shrewd glance at Langston before resuming her rude stare at Sam. "Don't tell me you asked her here for the purpose of dalliance, Langston, for I won't believe it of you."

"Then you will be happy to know I did no such thing," he snapped, finding the countess *de trop* for the first time in his life.

The countess's smug grin told him he had fallen into her trap. *Damnation.* Langston clamped his jaw shut and gave himself time to gather his wits.

He made himself smile and reply in mild tones, "Mrs. Davidson is a beautiful woman. Is it any surprise she is the toast of London?"

"So," the countess continued, "that's the Divine Davidson. No wonder you've been looking at her with bed in your eyes, my boy. Ravensford's been panting after her all evening, and the two of you always did have the same taste in chits."

Langston choked on his turtle soup. The countess was more outrageous than ever. He shot Ravensford a venomous look, but the earl shrugged it off. "She's your problem, old boy," he mouthed before grinning at Samantha Davidson, who was blushing furiously.

Sam could not believe this was happening to her. Who was this old biddy, and why was she speaking so loudly?

"My grandmother," Ravensford whispered in her ear as if reading her thoughts. "She's like this when she gets around Langston. Blames him for my never marrying. Says Langston's failure to remarry has encouraged my own reservations, so she punishes him."

"That is utterly ridiculous," Sam retorted before catching the gleam in his eyes. "Oh, you are bamming me."

He smiled. "A little, but, alas, not much."

The urge to inquire further was great, but Sam contented herself with ignoring the old lady's stare and taking a sip of her soup. Ravensford's whispered aside that the countess's bark was worse than her bite was amusing, but not comforting.

Dinner was slow and the countess's continuing comments peppered the conversation. Sam did her best to maintain her composure, as she saw Langston trying to do. But grim lines had formed around his mouth and his eyes glittered dangerously.

Well, she told herself as she sat straighter, it was his fault. He needn't have invited the old woman any more than he'd had to engage her to act for the party.

She cast him a resentful glance, which was intercepted by the countess, who began to cackle. Sam instantly regretted her lack of control as every head at the table turned towards the old woman who was rocking back and forth in her chair, the lorgnette bouncing on her scrawny bosom with each laugh.

"Well, Langston, seems you've met your match this time. This gel is no whining miss like Annabelle. No, this one will run you a merry chase."

Langston chose that moment to stand and say, "I believe dinner is over. There is tea in the drawing-room, ladies."

His dismissal came none too soon for Sam's comfort. Unfortunately the salon was no better.

The dowager countess sought her out, sitting beside her before Sam could rise and curtsy.

"Don't bother with those things, gel," she said, motioning Sam to remain seated. "Noticed you were sitting alone and thought we might talk privately."

Sam gaped at her, searching frantically for a polite way to escape. She was certain the countess wanted to talk about Langston, and she most certainly did not.

"Wanted to tell you about Langston, since 'tis obvious the boy can't take his eyes off you." She chuckled. "Thought he would never marry again after Annabelle's death, but appears I was wrong."

Sam was aghast. The woman was speaking of things that were none of Sam's business. She was not betrothed to Langston and never would be. "I am terribly sorry, Lady Ravensford, but the Marquis of Langston and I are not close."

The dowager's silver head bobbed like a bird pecking for seed as she groped for her lorgnette. "Don't believe you, gel, or don't believe you won't soon be close. I'm not one for the namby-pamby speaking and slyness that passes for manners in this age."

Sam gulped and glanced desperately around to see if there was some means of escape from this extraordinarily outspoken woman. The luxury of speaking her own mind without regard for the consequences had never been hers.

She noticed several of the other ladies were avidly watching them. No escape there. She realized she had no choice but to stick with the countess.

Putting aside any qualms, she asked, "My lady, why have you singled me out?"

The old woman chuckled again, finally succeeding in locating her lorgnette and raising it to her eyes. Two large blue orbs studied Sam. "Because I see honesty in you, gel, and courage. 'Tis not often I find that combination. Now, Langston's got them, too, as has Ravensford. But I can tell 'tis not my grandson you're interested in, although he's plainly interested in you. And I don't want his heart broken!" she admonished.

Sam was astonished. This woman was perceptive and intelligent, traits she admired as the other admired courage and honesty. "I would never hurt Lord Ravensford intentionally, or anyone else, for that matter."

"Except Langston, I wager." When Sam started to protest, the dowager put her beringed hand on her arm. "Now don't lie to me, girl. I saw the way you looked at him. The heat is mutual."

"What's mutual?" Langston's deep baritone asked from right in front of them.

Sam gave a start. The conversation with the countess had been so absorbing that for the first time since meeting Langston, she had not sensed his approach.

"None of your affair, Langston—yet," the old woman said firmly, swatting him with her closed fan. "Now I must retire. A lady of my years don't do well if she keeps late hours."

Langston made her a deep bow before helping her up. "My lady, you are as nimble of mind and spirit as you were when I first met you."

"Flirt," she said, smiling. "Were I fifty years younger, I'd give this gel a run for her money." Her blue eyes sharpened as she looked him full in the face. "And I don't want my grandson hurt, do you understand me?"

"Perfectly," Langston replied respectfully.

"Good," she said with a wink at Sam.

Without asking leave, Langston took the dowager's seat beside Sam on the gold-upholstered settee, and the room that had seemed so large when she had first entered it now seemed oppressively small. His thigh made contact with Sam's, sending shivers of heat through her body and making her treacherous mind think of his lips on hers.

She all but groaned aloud. The size of the settee they shared did not help matters. If she moved any farther away from him, she would be on the very elegant Aubusson carpet.

Langston angled his body to face her. He was so close Sam could see the shadow thrown on his high cheekbones by his thick blond lashes. She could not, however, divine the thoughts in his dark eyes.

Quite unnerved, she made to rise. His hand shot out and circled her gloved wrist. She felt the heat of his grasp through the kid leather.

"Please let me go," she said, her voice husky and soft.

"When I am finished."

His thumb was rubbing tiny, titillating circles on the inside of her wrist. Did he know that her stomach was doing somersaults? She hoped not.

"What do you want?" she asked, realizing she could not thwart him without creating a scene. "Have you decided what play we will produce?"

He didn't answer, only continued to watch her, his gaze going from the roses in her hair to the roses just below her breasts. "Are you going to break Ravensford's heart?" he finally asked, his voice harsh.

It was the last thing she expected him to say. "Of course not," she responded. "He does not love me, so his heart is not in jeopardy."

"And if he were to love you?"

She lifted her free hand to her throat, as if to still the pulse that hammered there. "Why does it matter to you?"

His eyes glittered, the pupils black pools. The scent of lemon and musk assailed her. Her breathing quickened in anticipation of his reply.

He shrugged and leaned away, breaking the spell holding her captive. "Because I do not wish to see my friend hurt as my brother has been."

So, they were back to that. Sam tamped down her anger. "Your friend and your brother are grown men. They should know that not everything they covet in life will be theirs, just as many things they desire will fall into their hands like ripe fruit."

"And rot," he finished. He rose, releasing her wrist in the process. "Would you care for a game of whist? I believe the guests are putting together some tables."

Sam got to her feet, as well. "No, thank you, my lord. I have neither the funds nor the inclination to play games of chance."

She pivoted on her heel and strode away, wondering why she had thrown her situation in his face.

"Scowling is not one of your more attractive expressions," Ravensford said, materializing at her side.

Grateful for the diversion, Sam took no offense. "I am certain that there are any number of things I do that are not attractive."

"Langston bothering you?" His eyes were the color of sherry and, she feared, more perceptive than she would have liked.

"He can be a very domineering man," she said noncommittally.

Ravensford smiled. "Yes, he does behave in that fashion when he is bent on getting his own way."

"So I have learned," Sam said dryly. She was not going to let Langston ruin what little pleasure there was to be had here. Besides, tomorrow was another day. "If you will excuse me, 'tis late."

"Allow me," Ravensford said, picking up a candelabrum without waiting for her answer.

Sam knew his ultimate intention and knew, too, that she must refuse him. She debated whether to allow him to escort her to her room and proposition her now or to decline his company and put it off for another night. The countess's words echoed in her mind, emphasized by Langston's.

"Thank you," she said.

The trip to her room was made bearable by small talk, all of it carried by Ravensford. It was actually a pleasant interlude, and Sam wished she could be friends with this interesting man, but knew better. Most men wanted only one thing from her, and

Ravensford was no different, only more charming than most in pursuing his goal.

At her door, she turned and gave him her hand. "Thank you for the entertaining company."

"The pleasure has been all mine." He took her hand and carried it to his lips. His mouth lingered, but Sam felt nothing. No sparks. No tingles. Nothing.

Ravensford's smile turned rueful and he released her, stepping back and bowing. "I see that my suit is not welcome, and I am sorry for it."

She smiled at him, surprised again by his perception. "So am I, my lord."

And she truly was. She liked and respected him. If only he were the one who made her heart beat faster.

But he was not.

LANGSTON ROSE EARLY, as was his wont. His valet, James, was bustling about the adjacent room preparing the marquis's riding habit.

Wrapping himself in a robe to ward off the room's chill, Langston crossed to the window and pulled back the brown velvet draperies. The cold from the frost-rimmed windows hit him. It had snowed during the night. That would make his ride more exhilarating.

He smiled in anticipation, but then froze. Below him, in the dormant Elizabethan herb garden, a grey-caped figure moved. He would have recognized her anywhere from the sway of her lithe body and the way she held her head. Samantha Davidson was walking in his garden, pausing every few feet to examine one of the hardier plants.

It was a jolt to realize that he liked seeing her strolling in his garden before the sun was fully up. He was certain that all his other guests were still abed, whether in their own chambers or another's, he cared not.

"My lord." James's voice came from behind him. "Everything is prepared."

Langston took one last look at the graceful figure before allowing the heavy draperies to fall back into place. Then he hurried across the thick brown-and-blue carpet to where his clothes were laid out. If he dressed quickly, he might catch her before she came back inside.

He berated himself as he removed his robe and reached for his clothes. Samantha Davidson's whereabouts were none of his affair—he'd left that to Ravensford. It was apparent his friend had not succeeded in bedding her last night, and now he found that his gut clenched at the very thought of Ravensford doing so.

"Milord," James asked in concern, "do you have an ague?"

Langston whirled around. "No. Nothing of the sort."

But he did. He had a sickness that was more than an ague, worse than anything he might have imagined. There was a need in him that grew with each passing day, a need to possess the one woman he could never have.

"Damnation!" he said, slamming his fist on a table, oblivious to his valet's startled reaction. The Wedgwood vase danced to the edge and crashed to the floor. "Double damnation!" Langston growled, shutting his eyes against the picture of her in another man's arms.

No, he decided, he would not go chasing out to the garden hoping to catch this woman before she re-entered the house. He was not at all sure he'd be able to keep his behavior circumspect.

CHAPTER TEN

THE SOUND OF THE DOOR drew Sam's attention from the puzzle she, Amalie and Stephen were working on. She had come into the nursery an hour before to visit Amalie, who was improving with each passing day, and found her daughter engaged in play with the son of the house. The sight had made her smile.

While the two children baited each other, they also shared many of the same interests. At the moment, they were getting along famously.

"Mrs. Davidson." Langston's greeting slipped over her like satin. "I did not expect to find you here."

She got to her feet and smoothed the skirt of her lemon muslin morning dress, giving herself time to compose her answer. When she spoke, her voice was not as light as she would have wished. "Good morning, my lord. Nor did I expect to see you here." She bestowed an artificially bright smile on him that said she could give as good as she got. "I came to see how Amalie was and, well, it seems I was persuaded to stay."

"Father!" Stephen yelped, jumping to his feet and racing toward Langston. The boy skidded to a halt several feet from his parent. "Pardon me, sir. I am forgetting my manners." Turning slightly to face Amalie, he said, "May I introduce Miss Amalie Davidson. My father, Marquis of Langston."

Amalie rose and did a very creditable curtsy before saying, "No need to be so formal, Stephen. I have already met his lordship and we have an understanding." She eyed Langston severely. "Do we not, my lord?"

Appalled by her daughter's lack of manners, Sam said, "Amalie, apologize to his lordship immediately."

Amalie defiantly stood her ground. "But you speak to him that way. Why can I not do the same?"

Exasperation sharpened Sam's voice. "Because you are a child, and an ill-mannered one at that."

"And very like her mother," Langston murmured, stepping between them and putting a hand on Amalie's shoulder. "But enough bickering. I did not come here to ruin everyone's fun. I came here to see Stephen."

He turned to the boy and began questioning him about his day. Sam was taken aback to hear the reserve that entered Stephen's voice as he answered his father's queries, especially after the joyful way he'd greeted him only minutes earlier. Stephen had been a trifle standoffish with her, but she could not fathom why he should be so with his father.

Perplexed, she studied the two. The boy's face really did hold little resemblance to the father's. His chin was more pointed than Langston's and his nose straighter. The mouth Sam had thought like the marquis's really was not. It was full and held the same hint of sensuality, but the lips were not as delineated nor as wide. While Langston's hair was blond, Stephen's was black as a storm and just as wild, falling in waves to just below his ears.

But the greatest contrast was the eyes. Langston's were darkly brooding, whereas Stephen's were light blue and sad somehow, making Sam wonder what had hurt him.

A tall, lanky boy, he reached Langston's shoulders. He held himself very erect, making Sam think that someday he would carry himself with the same arrogance Langston did. Meanwhile, he resembled an unhappy little boy who was trying to look aloof and haughty.

Sam's heart went out to him. What had happened to cause this?

She set herself about easing some of the tension. "Would you care to play goose with us, my lord? The children had been pestering me to do so, but I told them they were no challenge to me, not with my superior skill."

"And I might be a worthy opponent?" His eyes gleamed.

"Perhaps." She set up the board in front of the nursery window. Taking a seat and picking up the dice, she raised one inquiring eyebrow. "Well, what are you waiting for?"

In a trice the two children pulled up stools and reached for their markers, Amalie her favorite pink and Stephen black. Sam chose the yellow.

"I shall take my lucky brown," Langston said, sitting opposite Sam so that the children were between them.

Her eyes met his, and it was as though time stood still. When she realized what was happening, she pulled her gaze away.

"Now," she said, her voice husky, "as the oldest lady present, I shall go first."

"No fair!" both children chorused.

"Mama, you must throw the dice, and the person with the highest number goes first."

"That is correct," Stephen said.

Sam suppressed a smile. The two of them were united.

"Well, if you insist," she murmured, risking a glance at Langston. The smile in his eyes warmed her.

The game was an hour of fun, with each player moving forward or back as the throw of the dice dictated. At one point Langston was well ahead, and the other three joined in a wish for him to have bad luck.

"Papa," Stephen said, his voice high with excitement, "you are beating us all, and 'tis not gentlemanly for you to beat the ladies."

Langston grinned and shrugged. "They must take their chances with the rest of us."

Sam had never seen the marquis so relaxed, and she found herself liking this side of him. He was a complex man.

They would have played longer had Lottie not arrived to take Amalie to her room for a nap.

Noting the redness of Amalie's cheeks and the glitter in her eyes, Sam decided that her daughter might not be quite her usual self yet, but she was fast approaching it. This trip to the country would accomplish what she had hoped for, she was certain.

"Come along now, missie," Lottie said, taking Amalie's reluctantly held out hand.

"If you will excuse me," Sam said, rising.

Langston stood, too, followed by Stephen. "Of course." Turning to his son, he said, "Would you care to come to the stables?"

After a moment in which his face registered surprise, Stephen answered excitedly, "Yes, please, sir!"

Sam was glad that the two would be continuing their fun together even as she was perplexed by Stephen's initial surprise. Was Langston normally an ogre with his son? Somehow she could not imagine him so. However, it was not her concern, she told herself firmly as she followed Lottie and Amalie from the room.

SEVERAL HOURS LATER, Sam wandered listlessly through the ground floor of Langston's Castle. The ladies were in the parlor playing whist or embroidering, gossiping all the while. The gentlemen were either out hunting or playing billiards, a game she had never learned.

This was her third day in the country, and she was beginning to wonder if Langston really *had* hired her to supervise his guests in performing a play. So far he had said nothing further about it to her.

Melancholy was settling over her, and it was a state she abhorred. Determined to nip it in the bud, she started back to the breakfast room for a cup of tea and a bite of food from the sideboard, which was kept provisioned throughout the day.

She was about to pour herself a cup of the strong brew when the Honorable Emily Hershaw arrived and helped herself to a cucumber sandwich. Sam smiled at her.

The other woman was close to Sam in age. She was petite and pretty, with an almost girlish figure, but her blue eyes held not a hint of warmth as she stiffly returned Sam's smile.

"Those sandwiches are very good," Sam said lightly, by way of conversation. "I had several yesterday."

"I noticed." The Honorable Emily's smile widened to show white, sharp little teeth. "I remember Mama saying a lady should always be careful how much she consumes when in the presence of others."

On the surface there was nothing in her words to offend, but Sam recognized the tone all too well, and her smile froze. Before she could reply, a deep male voice said, "Emily, I have heard a great many of your mother's homilies on your lips, but I have yet to see you follow any of them."

It was Langston, and he was defending her. Sam was astonished.

The Honorable Emily turned red before turning white. "Langston. I should have known you would side with Mrs. Davidson."

It was a provocative statement, accompanied by a pointed look at both of them before the woman pivoted on her dainty heel and strode away. Langston watched her disappear from the room before turning to Sam, who was pouring more tea into her cup.

"Emily has always had a tongue that is sharper than her mind," he said. "And envy is her besetting sin."

While Sam wondered if her hearing was amiss, he helped himself to a plate of scones, cream and strawberry preserves, then poured a cup of tea to which he added two heaping teaspoons of sugar.

"You have a sweet tooth," Sam said in surprise. It was something she never would have guessed, and it made him seem more human, more approachable.

He took a healthy bite of a scone, chewed for a moment, then grinned. "My mother says 'tis *my* besetting sin, and if I am not careful, I shall rue the day I ever saw a sweet."

Sam found herself grinning foolishly at him, any animosity they'd felt forgotten as they both enjoyed their repast. She knew it was temporary, however, and could not help wondering what had brought him into the breakfast room at just this moment.

Langston watched her deliberately sip her tea, to which she'd added no sugar, he noted. They were opposites in so many ways, and he wondered why he was so drawn to her.

Setting down his empty plate, he said, "Mrs. Davidson, would you care to take this opportunity to look over the theatre with me? I thought you could perhaps tell me what is needed before we start to organize the guests and assign roles."

She took a last sip of her tea and set the saucer and cup down before looking at him. She searched his face for a long moment before replying, "I was beginning to wonder if the play was all a sham. That you invited me here only to ensure that I am away from London when Lord Deverell returns from the Continent."

Langston flushed. "Nonsense. Dev won't be back from the Continent for months." But she was right about one thing—the play *had* been merely an excuse to get her here. Damn, but she was perceptive. He had better give her the name of a play to perform, and he would—as soon as he thought of something appropriate. And had she guessed about Ravensford? Had he already approached her?

The notion infuriated him, and he set his cup down rather sharply on the sideboard, causing the tea that remained to splash over the rim. He was a thousand times a fool. He had expressly asked Ravensford to seduce the woman. Of course he hoped his friend succeeded.

"Then let us be off," he said coldly. "I am sure there are many things that will need doing, since the theatre has rarely been in use since I inherited the castle."

He grimaced as he remembered the last time. Annabelle had been in the early stages of her pregnancy, and she had insisted that a group of neighbors come for a fortnight and put on a play for one another's enjoyment. She had loved such things. He had closed the theatre after her death.

Silently they made their way through the labyrinth of corridors that led to the small wing where the theatre had been built. Langston had brought a candelabrum with him, and paused long enough to light its three candles before opening the door.

The smell of mildew and dust assailed them.

"It has been almost ten years since it was last used," he said. "The play I would like you to do is *The Taming of the Shrew*. Do you think the place is suitable?"

She stepped past him into the large room. "Well, yes. But we shall have our work cut out for us."

Her rich voice played over him, arousing part of him he did not want aroused. And her willingness to shoulder the responsibility for setting the theatre to rights was yet another aspect of her he could not help but admire.

He took a deep breath before replying, ''I am afraid so.''

Together they walked to the stage and she examined the props to see which ones were usable, then checked the curtain to see if it could still be lowered. Langston was almost mesmerized by her graceful movements. She picked her way through the clutter, brushing at cobwebs and layers of dust with a matter-of-factness he found intriguing. Most women of his acquaintance would be disgusted and calling for servants. But then, she was not like any woman he'd ever known.

At last she turned to him and smiled. ''I shall have it ready for use in two days, if you will provide me with several strong men to lift and cart, and several girls to scrub.''

The yellow candlelight burnished her perfect complexion and lent interesting angles to her features. The excitement in her lovely eyes ignited a powerful response in him.

He wanted her. God help him, he wanted her.

How had he ever thought he could allow another man to touch her, to encourage it, even? Asking her here had been a mistake, for he was the one who wanted to touch her—and knew he must not....

He reached for her, and she came into his arms.

Exultation rushed through him as her mouth melded with his. Blood pounded in his ears, and it was all he could do not to lower her to the floor and take her then and there.

He tangled his fingers in her hair, luxuriating in the rich texture and sensual sliding of the strands against his skin. A soft moan escaped her lips, only to be swallowed by his.

"Oh, Sam," he murmured, separating enough from her to look down into her slumbrous eyes, "I want you."

"I know," she said, her voice a husky whisper. "I know."

"I want to feel you against me. Your skin on my skin."

"I do, too," she breathed, her eyes telling him she spoke the truth. Unquenched passion sparked in her dilated pupils.

A distant part of his brain listened to their love talk and marveled that he could so forget himself as to go this far with her. But his body was beyond his mind's control. His body was a slave to the desire she evoked.

Sam gazed up at him, longing for his mouth to cover hers. Her breasts tingled where they pressed into his chest, and her loins ached where they nestled against his response to her. He wanted her in the most elemental way possible.

The precious minutes in her dressing-room had been like this—heated and demanding and exciting. How had this happened? What had come over them?

He nipped her lower lip, making her gasp in pleasure. Who cared how it had happened? It just had, and she felt light-headed and reckless. She felt wonderful.

His hands roved up and down her back, stopping to massage the muscles on either side of her spine. His lips glided over her skin, along the curve of her jaw and down her slender neck. Shivers of delight coursed through her.

"Langston." She made his name sound almost like a prayer.

"Jon," he said against her heated flesh.

"Jon," she echoed as his mouth moved lower, following the modest cut of her gown. His lips were just above the swell of her breasts. If he went a fraction lower, his mouth would be directly on her breasts, and...

"More," she cried, arching her back.

More.

The word reverberated through Langston's desire-taut body. More. Annabelle had always demanded more when their lovemaking was peaking. She had been insatiable, and he had always reveled in it—until her betrayal.

More.

The word was like a sword slashing down between him and Samantha. His ardor faded, the ache in his flesh not quite abating, yet no longer beyond his ability to control.

He pulled away, staring down at her passion-darkened eyes, and cursed himself. And cursed her.

"Damn you for the temptation you are," he growled, releasing her.

Shocked, Sam reached for something to steady herself with. Her hand gripped a rickety chair and clung to it like a lifeline on a storm-tossed ocean. He stood several feet from her now, his shoulders stiff, his hands clenched at his sides. Tension radiated from him in waves.

It was all she could do not to let the tears building in her eyes spill down her cheeks. The last thing she wanted was for him to know how much his rejection hurt, if hurt was the word for the emotion swamping her. She did not know. She did not even know what she felt for him. It could be hatred or—she shuddered—it could be love.

Either way, she could no longer stay here, humiliated by her weakness, by her need for him. Before he could turn on her and vent the anger she sensed in him, she fled.

Langston heard her go and resisted the urge to stop her. He had come so close. For the second time, he had nearly seduced her. He had wanted her and the consequences be damned.

Heaven help him.

LANGSTON STARED BLEAKLY into the fire, his feet propped on an ottoman and his hands holding a snifter of brandy. Outside, snow fell in a white curtain that obscured the view from the library window. It was midnight, and his guests were either playing cards or billiards, or had gone to bed. Samantha Davidson had retired hours ago.

He imagined she was alone, but perhaps she was not. Perhaps Ravensford was with her. Pain shot through his chest.

He took a swig of brandy. After all, he had wanted Ravensford to seduce her. Deverell would not hate Ravensford for life, as he would hate his brother.

But it was no good. Deny it as he might, he wanted the damn woman. He wanted her with a hunger that made his bones ache and his body throb.

He could still feel her in his arms, her luxuriant hair freed from the chignon and tangling in his fingers. He could still feel her need for him.

He groaned and took another gulp of the fiery liquor.

"So, this is where you are hiding," Ravensford said quietly, coming in and closing the door. "I wondered why you were not playing the attentive host tonight." He lowered himself into the large leather chair beside Langston's. "Must be because Mrs. Davidson is no longer up."

So she was in bed alone. Relief flooded Langston, and then he scowled at his reaction.

"Care for some brandy?" he asked in an effort to sidetrack his friend.

"Don't mind if I do," Ravensford said, stretching his long legs out in front of him. "And seeing as 'tis conveniently located on the table between us, you won't have to get up to serve me."

Langston snorted. "You are in my home too much for me to wait on you. 'Tis lucky for *you* the drink is close."

Ravensford did, however, have to get up and go to the sideboard for a snifter. He splashed brandy into it and took an appreciative sip. "French. Very good."

"It was laid down by my father twenty years ago, before the wars made it impossible to get without smuggling."

In a serious tone Ravensford said, "You are trying to change the subject, but I won't allow it. I have seen the way you watch her. What are you going to do?"

Unease moved down Langston's spine. But there was no sense in pretending he did not understand. He and Ravensford had been friends for too long and had had few secrets between them.

He sighed. "I don't know."

"Make her your mistress and be done with it," Ravensford suggested bluntly. "Dev won't be back for many months, what with Napoleon escaping Elba, so you don't have to worry about what he will do. By the time he returns, you and Mrs. Davidson will doubtless no longer be a pair."

The urge to get up and pace the floor was extreme, but Langston held himself in check. "My mother will be here soon," he said, instead.

"Bringing Cynthia, no doubt," Ravensford added.

"Exactly."

"Well, Langston, you are in a tight spot. 'Tis not quite the thing to have your mistress under the same roof as your mother and future wife."

"Particularly my mother. I have not committed myself to Cynthia yet." He knew it was splitting hairs, but once again he felt a need to make that fact absolutely clear.

Ravensford swirled the amber liquid, seeming intent on the changing colors flickering in its depths.

"You will have to forget Annabelle's treachery someday. Cynthia would be a good place to start."

"Perhaps," Langston said.

"She will make a good, complaisant wife." Ravensford glanced at his friend. "You won't have to worry about her cuckolding you."

"That is why I chose her."

But nor would she give him the passion that Samantha Davidson did. Making love to Cynthia would be like making love to a marionette—stiff and mechanical, and for the sole purpose of begetting heirs.

"Damnation," he muttered, gulping the last of his brandy.

"She will also be a good mother to Stephen."

Langston poured himself another drink, denying the knowledge that Samantha Davidson would also make a good mother to Stephen. She was a good mother to Amalie.

Bloody hell! What was he thinking? Samantha Davidson was the woman his youngest brother believed he was in love with. And she was an *actress*. Perhaps he could make love to her, but he most certainly could never marry her.

The thought of making love to her brought a deep ache to his loins and a flush to his skin that had nothing to do with the liquor he had consumed. He reached again for the decanter.

"You can always drink yourself into oblivion," Ravensford said, sensing his friend's denial.

"So I can," Langston muttered, pushing the hair back from his forehead and frowning. "But that would change nothing."

"No, it would not." Ravensford put his glass on the table and stood. "Someday, my friend, you will have to risk your heart again."

Langston did not reply, only waited for the sound of the door opening and closing. Ravensford was astute as always, but it did not make it any easier to know he was right.

CHAPTER ELEVEN

SAM RODE THE MARE at a leisurely pace, her horsemanship being less than expert. The groom trailed behind and to her left. She wished him gone, but knew to tell him so would scandalize him. And besides, she did not know her way around Langston's estate.

Overhead the sun struggled through heavy clouds. The snow had melted in the night, but it looked as though the warming would be short-lived. She pulled the collar of her burgundy wool jacket up around her neck and almost regretted the impulse that had set her on this course.

Her nerves had been raw since yesterday—ever since her passionate encounter with Langston in the theatre. He had haunted her dreams, evoking sensations that left her feeling hot and unfulfilled.

"Ma'am," the groom said, interrupting her disturbing reverie, "we be leavin' his lordship's land. And I know he wouldn't like yer bein' here."

Sam gave him a curious look from under the burgundy feather that sat jauntily in her tilted hat.

It was an expensive affectation she had purchased especially for this trip, knowing that the aristocracy was horse-mad and that at some point in her stay she would be asked to ride.

"I thought he got on well with all his neighbors."

"That be the case...mostly, ma'am." He glanced nervously around as though any second he expected an ogre to jump from the forest. "But this is Mr. Huntly's property."

"Huntly!" Sam's voice squeaked as it rose an octave. "Huntly lives next to Lord Langston?"

"Yes, ma'am. And..." His words trailed off and he looked sheepishly at her. "It ain't none o' my business to speak o' his lordship. Only it ain't good fer us to be here."

Sam began to shiver, and chided herself for thinking her sudden chill was caused by anything besides the cold. Why, the groom's nose was red with the wind, and the heavy clouds hinted of snow.

A shot rang out. Bark sprayed from a beech tree not more than ten feet from them. Sam's mare reared up. With a shriek, she fell to the ground, the horse dancing away until the groom caught the reins.

"Ma'am, are ye all right?" he asked, swinging down from his mount.

Sam sat up, feeling dazed and wondering why the trees seemed to be hopping about. At last her eyesight cleared, and she remembered the cause.

"Who shot at us?"

"Huntly's gamekeeper, most like. His master don't like trespassers, and he tells his people to shoot."

"Well!" Sam said indignantly, standing and attempting to brush the dirt and frost from her skirts and jacket, "What if he had hit one of us?"

The groom shrugged. "We was trespassing."

She gaped at him, not believing his calm acceptance of so violent an act. "Trespassing is no reason to shoot someone."

"They hang people for poaching."

It was true. Sighing, Sam took her reins from the groom's outstretched hand and prepared to let him give her a hand up.

"Stay where you are!" a man's voice commanded.

Sam froze, wondering if this was the gamekeeper come to finish what his bullet had started. Twisting her head around, she searched the trees. When she glanced at the groom, she saw that his face was as white as a ghost.

A man dressed in dark brown hunting clothes emerged from the north side of the woods. One hand held his horse's reins, the other held a smoking pistol.

It was Huntly. He smiled and Sam's stomach seemed to sink to her feet. It was not a pleasant smile.

"Why, Mrs. Davidson, how delightful to find you on my property. Have you finally grown tired of Langston and come to seek my company?" he drawled, moving until he was within mere feet of her.

The cold had whipped color into his normally pale cheeks, and his brown hair hung over his forehead. His hands were covered by leather gloves, and his boots were muddy, as though he had been walking for some time.

He looked deadly, and Sam wished Langston was here to protect her from him. There was no mistaking his malevolent intent, for the gleam in his eyes as they raked over her form made it abundantly clear. She could not expect the groom to help her, when to do so would be his death sentence. If only the man could slip away and go for assistance!

The groom must have read her mind, for while Huntly feasted on her with his eyes, he quietly took himself off on his horse. Now it was up to her. She was an actress, and a damned good one: good enough to keep Huntly at bay.

Huntly took a step toward her, and she took a step back. "Mr. Huntly," she said, swallowing the fear rising in her throat, "I did not know you lived nearby. Langston did not mention it."

He sneered. "He would not. Langston and I are not on the best of terms, as you may have guessed."

"Yes." She giggled, despising herself for the hysteria bubbling up despite her resolve. "I gathered that. I understand you are both running for Member of Parliament from this county."

"That and more," Huntly said darkly. "The only reason he wants you is because I do." He watched her avidly. "You know that, don't you?"

It was on the tip of her tongue to tell him about Lord Deverell, but she did not wish to betray the young man's emotions to this scoundrel. Instead, she murmured, "Langston does not want me for himself, sir. He asked me here to help entertain his house guests."

"Hah! By 'want' I mean desire, madam. Langston desires you. I have seen it in his eyes when he watches you."

Sam's fingers twitched nervously, and she wondered fleetingly if she could somehow mount her mare and be away before Huntly could stop her. One glance at his watchful eyes and tightly clenched muscles told her the answer. She would have to brazen this out by trying to persuade him that she found him attractive, but this was neither the time nor the place for dalliance.

She took a calming breath. "You are mistaken. Langston is paying me a handsome sum to put on a Shakespearean production. *The Taming of the Shrew*. His guests are vastly amused."

It was no good. Huntly's mouth thinned into a cruel smile, and he closed the distance between them. The gun fell from his fingers as he reached for her. Sam sidestepped him.

"Sir! Pray control yourself!"

She tried to put her mare between them, but just as she made a dash for the other side of the animal, he seized her wrist and yanked her to him, wrenching her back and shoulder. She forgot the pain instantly as his hands pinioned her to his chest.

His breath was hot on her cheek. She twisted her head away, only to feel his breath on her neck, an even more intimate horror. He held her hands trapped between their chests, and her efforts to push him away were futile.

He was so close she could see the pores of his skin and the tiny lines around his mouth. She stifled the scream rising in her throat. Fighting him would get her nowhere, except beneath him and hurt.

She sighed, long and soft, drawing on all her reserves of skill and control. "Really, Huntly, you do not have to maul me. I would enjoy your ca-

resses—'' she cast a critical eye around the clearing
''—only not here. 'Tis too dismal and cold by
half.''

His eyes narrowed and his grip tightened, but he
paused in his assault. ''You would?''

Sam fluttered her lashes and kept her eyes
averted, knowing that she could not look him in the
eye and continue this charade. ''Of course, but not
here. Not like this.'' She lowered her voice, inject-
ing warmth and seductiveness into it. ''Perhaps we
can meet somewhere else, somewhere closer to your
home?''

One of his hands began to move up and down the
arm it had been so brutally gripping. Sam took this
as a sign that her ploy was beginning to work—but
she was not out of trouble yet.

''I have a small hunting lodge not more than a
fifteen-minute ride from here,'' he said, the cruel
curve of his mouth starting to soften. ''We could
enjoy each other there.''

Sam sensed this was a test, and to refuse would
be to destroy what little progress she had made. Yet
she did not intend to leave this clearing with him.
The groom would bring help here.

Licking cold, dry lips, she murmured in a voice
she prayed was seductive, ''I have always found
that anticipation sweetens the pleasure. Surely you
can wait until this evening.''

The hand that had been moving up and down her arm caught her wrist in a crushing grip. "I have waited as long as I intend to. Come with me now or I shall take you right here."

Sam again stifled a scream. There was no one to hear her. She had to do something drastic, something that would convince him of her sincerity. Taking a deep breath to hold her nausea at bay, she leaned into Huntly and pressed her lips to his.

He responded instantly, his mouth grinding into hers, his tongue thrusting between her lips. He put one hand on her upper back and the other on her buttocks, clamping her relentlessly against his body.

Sam moaned against him, wishing for the first time in her life that she would faint. It would be a blessing of sorts, she thought, feeling his arousal hard against her stomach. And then it seemed she might get her wish, for blackness rose up before her.

Vaguely she heard the crack of underbrush and the thunder of horses' hooves. But it was in the background, as the world disintegrated around her. Huntly used one hand to rip open her jacket and blouse with a vicious yank—

"Damn you to hell! Release her or I will shoot you dead."

Coming back from near oblivion, Sam recognized Langston's voice. She opened her eyes and saw he had a pistol aimed at Huntly. She offered a fervent payer of thanks heavenward. The groom had reached him in time.

Instead of letting her go, however, Huntly moved enough to show Langston her shredded clothing while managing to keep one arm hooked around her waist so that she could not get away from his hateful touch. With freedom so close, Sam twisted frantically in an attempt to break his hold. He caught both her wrists in one hand so easily that she knew it was futile to continue.

Instead, she focused on Langston, begging him with her eyes to end this torture. But his gaze was not on her face, it was on her chest, and it was filled with anger—at her.

Sam gasped and blood rushed to her face as she realized that Huntly had exposed her breasts. She struggled to free her hands from his grip, but it was useless. She shook her head in an attempt to completely dislodge her chignon, which Huntly's man-handling had already started tumbling down. A few heavy locks of hair fell over her breasts, partly concealing them from Langston's furious scrutiny.

Langston saw red pulsating waves. Never in his life had he been so angry. Never. Not even at An-nabelle's betrayal.

Samantha Davidson stood half-naked in Hunt-ly's embrace, her full, firm breasts exposed for

Huntly's caress. When he'd been crashing through the trees, still some distance away, he had seen her lean into the man's arms and press her lips to his. She was the bastard's mistress and they had planned this meeting, no matter what the groom had told him. There was no other explanation for her behavior.

"Oh, please, Langston," she said, her beautiful face contorted with an emotion Langston found disturbingly like fear. "Make him release me!"

Langston looked from one to the other. Huntly's eyes were a brittle blue. Hers were a bruised green, dark circles accentuating their haunting beauty. Could she be an unwilling victim? The idea formed in his mind only to be quickly denied. She *had* leaned into his kiss. She *had* seemed to beg for his touch.

And yet...

Jaw tight, Langston ordered, "Release her, Huntly."

Huntly did as told this time, but slowly, provocatively. "She wanted me, Langston. I think you know that."

Huntly's oily voice grated on Langston's raw nerves. And a glance at Samantha Davidson's exposed charms only made his blood boil. Watching her fumble with the torn fabric of her shirt and jacket enraged him anew.

He averted his gaze. "Move away from her."

Huntly smiled knowingly. "She wanted me, Langston. Are you too blind to see that?" His voice lowered, became sinister. "Or does that knowledge excite you?"

Langston clamped down on the urge to split Huntly's face open. "Damn you, Huntly. Get away from her or I will make it my concern to see that you do."

Huntly sneered, but moved until there was a space between him and Sam. "Is she worth that much to you, Langston, that you would risk your political career by attacking me? She is nothing but an actress. A slut."

Langston heard the words, realized they were nothing he had not said about her, and then realized it did not matter. Raw fury drove him now. Fury at the man who had exposed her and fury at her for drawing such intense emotion from him.

"Get away from him," Langston said to her, his voice deadly. "I don't want you near him if I have to shoot."

He saw her swallow of fear before doing as he ordered. It did nothing to ease the demons driving him. Nor did her frantic attempts to cover herself with her torn clothing.

"You may have her for now, Langston," Huntly said as he edged toward his waiting horse, "but there is always the future. And I am very good at biding my time, something you would do well to remember.''

Langston resisted the urge to shoot Huntly right then and there. "Get out of here before I decide the best way to deal with your sort is to do away with you.''

"Tut, tut, Langston," Huntly drawled. "You are forgetting who owns this land.''

"No, I am not. I am letting you live for another day," Langston said, his tone brooking no further argument.

With a leer at Samantha, Huntly bounded into the saddle. Langston noted with satisfaction that the bastard sat more stiffly than necessary, as though anticipating a bullet between the shoulder blades.

"I am not like you, Huntly," he said loudly and clearly. "I won't shoot you in the back.''

Huntly did not look around as he kicked his mount into a gallop, making for the protection of the trees. Only then did Langston look again at Samantha Davidson.

She stood near her mare, her eyes wide and wary, clutching her shredded lapels about her bosom.

"What are you staring at?" he demanded, striding to her and yanking off his jacket as he went. He tossed it to her. "Here. Wear this. Your lover won't return."

Her mouth opened in shock. Before she could say a word, he grabbed her by the waist and hoisted her roughly onto her saddle. She landed with a thud.

"Oh! You are no better than he!" she exclaimed, grasping the mare's mane to keep from falling off.

Without a word, Langston took the reins and led her horse to his stallion, where he mounted. Then, he set a brisk pace toward his own property.

She had been in Huntly's arms. She had kissed him.

He had to regain control of his emotions.

"Where are we going?" she asked, her voice catching on the last word. "This is not the way to the stables."

"No, it is not."

Up ahead lay a small cabin, nothing more than a main room and a tiny sleeping alcove. Normally it was used by his gamekeeper. Today it would be for him.

Reaching the stone-and-wattle hut, he dismounted and tethered his horse. As she watched him with apprehension, he strode to her and pulled her down. She fell onto him, her hands landing on his shoulders. It was an embrace he had not planned, and it acted like a match to tinder.

His intention had been to berate her, rail at her, call her all manner of names. Or had he always intended to take her, to quench the fire she never failed to ignite in him?

God help him, he did not know.

He crushed her to him, reveling in the feel of her lush curves pressed to him, the scent of damask rose that still clung to her. His rational mind took flight. He had to taste her, had to consume her before she drove him beyond all reason.

His lips crushed hers. She tasted of wind and cold and wet. His hands roamed her back, fitting her to his hardness.

"Please," she said against his moving lips, "please, don't. Not like this."

He kissed her more fiercely. His hands found her hips and adjusted them to his aching loins.

Panting, barely cognizant of what he did, he said, "You were in his arms. I saw you kiss him. Now kiss me."

"He forced me," she gasped, the words barely audible. "You saved me."

He groaned and crushed her to him. He buried his face in her wind-tossed hair and murmured, "You are mine. Heaven help me, but you are."

Her head fell back against his supporting arm, her chestnut tresses cascading like a satin waterfall. Her eyes, heavy with desire, gazed at him. She licked her mouth, which was soft and moist from his kisses. His kisses, not Huntly's.

"I am going to make love to you," he said, exultation coursing through him like a river raging through wilderness.

"Why? You don't care for me."

Her whispered words inflamed him. "I don't know. You bewitch me, and I must have you."

Before she could protest, he took her lips again. More gently this time, but no less demandingly. The part of him that ruled when he was sane exploded in a desire he could no more stop than he could stop breathing.

He slipped his hand beneath the wool lapels of the jacket he had given her, and his fingers closed on the hard nipple of one breast. He massaged it and caressed it, mesmerized by the silken feel of her and the strength of her response.

A moan escaped her; her chest rose and fell against him. It was the beginning of the end.

Desperate for her, desperate to ease this agony of desire she created in him, Langston swept her into his arms. He kicked open the wooden door of the hut and strode inside, kicking the door shut behind him. Against the far wall was a rustic bed barely big enough for one.

He set her down on it, his mouth never leaving hers. Her arms twined around his neck, and her back arched so that her breasts pressed into him and sent heated darts to the center of his desire.

She was his! Reveling in the knowledge, he slipped his jacket off her to expose her flesh for his sight alone.

"Beautiful," he murmured, tearing his lips from hers to gaze at her form. "I knew you would look like this."

With shaking fingers, he touched first one creamy orb and then the other. He ached to suckle her. Leaning down, he skimmed his teeth across her flesh, making her nipples harden in response. He felt her fingers tangle in his hair and hold him to her.

"Jon." Sam breathed his Christian name in wonder as he made her feel sensations she had never imagined possible. Part of her knew that what they were doing was a mistake, that they would both regret it, but in this instant out of time it did not matter. All that mattered was that he continue what he was doing. That he make love to her.

Eagerly he slipped her torn jacket and blouse from her shoulders. Her breasts rose majestically above her chemise and stays. He cupped each mound in turn, marveling at the feel of her.

"You are like the finest satin," he whispered, his fingers kneading her fullness as he gazed down at her. In her eyes, he saw her acceptance of what he was doing to her—with her.

Moving with a sureness born of need, he took her mouth again and slid his hands down her ribs, over the fine muslin of her chemise. Quickly he divested her of clothing. He stroked the creamy skin of her abdomen, and then his fingers trailed downward to the heat of her passion.

He murmured against her open lips. "You are ready for me."

She nodded, her tongue dancing with his as she reached for him. Shock jolted through him when her fingers moved against his engorged flesh. He felt her fumbling with the buttons of his breeches, and then she was holding him.

He sucked in hard, his entire body going rigid. "Sam!"

"I know," she crooned, her low voice stoking the fire within him.

He could stand no more. Swiftly he slid between her thighs. "Wrap your legs around me," he ordered, looking deeply into her eyes and seeing the hunger she made no effort to hide. "Take me inside you."

As her thighs moved against his flanks, he thrust into her. They were one.

With eyes half-shut in ecstasy, he watched her eyes reveal the same delight as he moved within her. Tiny gasping whimpers came from her, exciting him beyond belief. Never had a woman aroused him as she did.

He increased his pace, feeling her contract around him. Soon. Very soon.

Her back arched and he knew. His mouth swooped down on hers, and he captured her cry of release with his kiss as he joined her in oblivion.

He lay over her for what seemed an eternity, blanketing her hot flesh with his body. She was like a furnace that had consumed him. And heaven help him, he wanted her again. He moved inside her, questioning even as he demanded.

Her eyes opened. She looked sated, with swollen lips and heavy lids. Her hair fanned out beneath her, a smooth, dark contrast to the rough yellow muslin of the sheet they lay on.

"Join with me again," he murmured, leaning down to nibble her bottom lip.

A smile curved her mouth and lit her eyes. "I thought we were already joined."

Her hips undulated beneath him and he found himself moving with her, delighting in her sensuality. It would not be long before he exploded into her once more.

Until then, he would not think, but simply feel.

CHAPTER TWELVE

ONLY LATER, as she attempted to make some semblance of decency out of her torn blouse and jacket, did she attempt to speak to him about Huntly.

"Jon...Langston," she corrected when he stared coldly at her. "The incident with Huntly...it was not what you think."

He tucked his shirt into the waistband of his breeches. "Are you saying you did not kiss him?"

Anger began to percolate in her. "I did not do so willingly."

He pushed his feet into the muddy Hessians he had kicked off an hour ago. "It appeared that way to me."

"You are wrong." She threw his jacket onto the dusty floor and stomped on it in her frustration. "I was trying to keep him from raping me. Surely your groom told you his intentions."

"He said you were in danger. But he does not know your past relationship with Huntly."

She drew back in shock and pain. "I have no past relationship with that odious man. What have I done to make you believe these things of me?"

He dusted off his jacket and held it out to her. Taking a step toward her, he pinned her with his gaze. "You have bewitched me. You have made me forsake my honor to be with you. It seems that nothing matters except holding you and making love to you." His mouth twisted bitterly. "And heaven help me, I want to make love to you again even now."

Cold seeped into Sam's bones and she began to shake. "I have taken nothing from you but abuse. 'Twas you who seduced me. 'Twas you who brought us here and made love to me. I did not hold a gun to your head or whip you into ardor. You did that yourself." Her voice became scornful. "Now you blame me for what you wrought. You are no better than Huntly, only more self-righteous."

He glared at her before pivoting on his heel and heading outside to untie the horses.

They rode back to Langston Castle in silence, the bitter words they had shared forming an unbreachable wall between them. Yet even with pain lodged in her heart and tears threatening to seep from her eyes, Sam could not deny what she felt. His passion had seared her, and burned away the veil of confusion she had felt about him.

She knew now that she loved him.

It should not have come as a surprise. Against her will, she had begun to respect him, then to like him, and coloring it all had been the passion. Love was inevitable.

A sigh of despair escaped her, and she huddled deeper into the warmth of his jacket. The memory of his lips on hers, his body in hers, and his tenderness toward her suffused her with emotions so strong that she reached for him across the space separating their horses.

"Jon—" she said, needing to make him understand her feelings "—what we did…what I did with you, I did not do lightly."

He glanced at her coldly and said nothing.

Pain at his rejection constricted her chest. Humiliation at her weakness drained the blood from her face.

When Langston Castle came into sight, he stopped. "The best we can hope for now is to get you inside without anyone seeing your state of *déshabillé*."

His voice was tinged with disgust, whether at himself or her, Sam did not know and no longer cared. Still, she knew it would not do for them to be seen like this. Her blouse was shredded, Langston having finished in passion what Huntly had started in lust, and her hair tumbled down her back in tangles. Servants—and Quality—talked.

"You are right," she muttered, looking at him.

What she saw in his eyes as they feasted on her made the breath catch in her throat. Ardor and hunger blazed from him, calling to her. After all the anger and cruel words, he still wanted her.

"You are beautiful," he said, his voice deep.

She clutched the reins with fingers that shook, and her mare sidestepped nervously in response. "Please, Langston, do not do this to us. One second you hate me, the next you desire me. I cannot take much more of this."

"Nor I," he said, breaking the spell and jumping down from his horse. "You are a witch," he muttered, coming towards her.

He reached for her, his hands closing around her waist, and she slipped along the hard muscles of his chest and thighs until she stood on her feet, cradled between his legs.

She felt his heart beating. Need flooded her, as fresh and raw as though they had never loved before. She saw the same emotion in his eyes.

Her face, her body, must have given her away, for he bent and covered her mouth with his. She leaned into him, grateful for the support he gave her weakened legs. He was everything she wanted, and his passion was greater than anything she had ever experienced.

When he put her from him, his breathing was hard and his eyes were dark. "Enough, or I shall forget where we are and do something we will both regret."

Nodding, she followed his lead. Moving cautiously from bush to tree, to statue, they made it to the back of the mansion unseen.

Putting a finger to her lips, he whispered, "Wait here while I take the horses round to the stable. I shall return and show you the back way up to your room."

She watched until he was out of sight, then leaned her head against the cold, damp wall of the house, feeling the grit of limestone press into her forehead. Tears seeped between her lashes and trickled down her cheeks. Never, not even when her husband deserted her, had she felt such despair.

She loved Langston, and she knew it was a mistake. But she could no more change her heart than she could change what had happened between them today.

She took a deep breath of the cold air. Lifting her head, she straightened her shoulders. Whatever her feelings, she would survive, and she would not let him see what he had done to her.

The crunch of footsteps on the gravel pathway warned her of his return. She wiped at her cheeks.

"Quickly," he said, scowling at her, all traces of passion erased from his features as though it had never been. "Luncheon will be served soon, and it will look strange if we are both absent."

He was right. His guests had already been watching them with knowing smirks. Sam followed him through the side door. The smell of meat cooking told Sam they were near the kitchen. Langston led the way up a narrow set of stairs the servants used when traveling to and from the different floors. The steps were steep, and she was thankful for the presence of a handrail.

They climbed two stories before Langston stopped at the landing and opened the door a crack. After making sure no one was in the hall, he let her out.

"Don't be late or people will wonder what is going on," he warned her.

Sam moved quickly down the hall and into her room.

Langston stood where he was for a moment, marveling at her poise after everything that had happened. Then he strode into the hall and around several corners until he was in the opposite wing of the house. Entering his darkened suite, he was suddenly tired, tired to the bone.

After telling James he would not require his services until dinnertime, Langston sank onto the mattress. His mouth twisted in self-derision. He was supposed to protect Dev from the woman, but who was going to protect *him?*

Just the thought of Samantha Davidson made the blood rush in his ears and his body tense. The urge to possess her was frighteningly intense.

He jumped to his feet and strode to the window, where he yanked the draperies aside and stood staring at the barren landscape. He pressed his forehead to the frosted glass in an attempt to cool his overheated blood. It was no use. He stalked across the room and willed himself to think of something else.

"Damn her!" he said, ripping off his shirt and washing himself with the cold water in the basin. If Dev learned of this, he would never speak to him again.

A harsh bark of laughter escaped him. The final laugh was on him. He had certainly made sure that his brother would never take Samantha Davidson to wife.

WHEN SAMANTHA did not appear for luncheon, Langston discreetly sent a footman to find her, only to learn she had gone to the nursery wing. An hour later, he opened the nursery door and was met by the startled faces of Stephen's nurse, Mary, and Mistress Lottie.

"My lord," Mary said, jumping up and bobbing a curtsy.

Lottie was slower to rise. "My lord."

"We was just having a bit of tea," Mary said, her plump face red.

Langston forced himself to smile. He was not irritated with these two. "The last time I consulted the housekeeper, it was quite all right for my servants to have tea. I am looking for Mrs. Davidson and the children. Do you know where they are?"

Mary wiped her hands on the starched front of her apron, but before she could speak, Lottie said calmly, "Miss Sam and the children are at the theatre. She came to get them over an hour ago."

"Thank you," he said, pivoting on his heel and striding out.

When he arrived at the theatre, he hung back in the shadows of the entry. His first intention had been to berate Sam for not coming to luncheon, but of course she did not have to be at every gathering. Once more, he was being unreasonable.

Running his fingers through his hair, he propped himself against the door jamb and watched the activity on the stage in silence. The skylight above the stage was undraped, and weak winter sun filtered down to the wooden boards. Dust motes danced in the air as the two footmen he had assigned to cleaning duty swept and dusted. Sam was in a corner, opening boxes and taking out their contents. Amalie was dancing around with a black domino over her head and shoulders, the ends trailing on the floor like a train. Stephen was not more than ten feet from Sam, piling boxes on top of one another.

Such were the acoustics of the theatre that when Sam told Stephen to be careful, Langston heard every word. The boy stacked one more wooden box on top of the two he had already positioned, then started climbing. Reaching the top, he spread both arms for balance and started to stand. The bottom box cracked. Stephen flailed his arms in an attempt to keep from falling the five feet to the floor.

"Oh, my God!" Langston said, his heart lurching. He rushed toward his son.

"Stephen!" Sam's shout blended with Langston's as she dropped the vase she was examining and darted toward Stephen's swaying body. She got below him just before he hit the floor.

Stephen's yelp of fear was cut off as he landed on Sam with a jolt that sent them both sprawling in a tangle of limbs. By now Langston had reached them. Gently he lifted Stephen off Sam and laid him down flat on his back.

But Stephen sat up instantly and said breathlessly, "I'm fine. How's Mrs. Davidson?"

Amalie hurried over and knelt beside her mother, her face white. "Mama, are you all right?"

Sam grinned at her daughter. "Just had the air knocked out of me." Rolling over, she got onto her knees in front of Stephen. "You're sure you are not hurt?"

Langston looked at her, noting the streak of dirt on one cheek that accentuated the pallor of her complexion. "I think he is more frightened than hurt. You did cushion the blow for him." He stood and gave her his hand. "How are you?"

Ignoring Langston's query and the hand he extended to her, Sam smoothed the black hair back from Stephen's forehead. "Perhaps this will teach you not to climb on a pile of boxes when a ladder could work better." She softened her words with a smile.

He nodded sheepishly. "I hope I did not harm you," he said, his bottom lip trembling.

"Oh, Stephen," Sam said gently, puling him into her arms. "I'm fine."

Langston watched his son and his mistress comfort one another. When Amalie wriggled into the embrace, he stepped back. Knowing that there was nothing further for him to do and that everyone was none the worse for wear, he turned without a word and left. Suddenly he felt very much alone.

LANGSTON DRESSED for dinner, knowing that he needed to thank Samantha for catching Stephen. If she had not been there, the boy would have been badly hurt. He remembered the fear, his hands clenching. He rarely felt completely comfortable around Stephen, but this afternoon had shown him how deeply he cared for the child.

Waving his valet away, Langston shrugged into his jacket and took a deep breath. Minutes later, he knocked on Samantha Davidson's door. He heard Lottie grumbling about visitors at inappropriate times just before she yanked open the door.

"Your lordship," she said, surprise lifting her eyebrows.

"Good evening, Mistress Lottie," he said, amused by the disapproval that rapidly replaced her astonishment. "I wish to speak with Mrs. Davidson."

Lottie reluctantly stood aside for him to pass.

"Thank you, Lottie," Sam said. When the nurse did not leave, she added, "That will be all."

With a snort, Lottie left, but not without one last glare at Langston, to which he paid no heed. His attention was on Samantha. She wore the same evening gown she always wore, as well as the damask roses he had sent to her room every day. The pleasure he felt at her silent acknowledgment of his gift tightened his gut.

"You are stunning, as usual," he said, taking a step toward her before catching himself. He was here to thank her, not seduce her.

Her smile was tentative and her voice husky when she said, "Thank you. But why are you here?"

He cleared his throat. "I have come to escort you to dinner."

"I would prefer to go alone," she said quietly.

Langston's cheeks flushed in annoyance. He had not expected her to refuse. "I wish to speak with you in private. We can do so here, or on the way to the drawing-room."

Her lips tightened. "Gallant as always." She picked up her Paisley shawl and draped it over her bare shoulders.

"And your sarcasm is as endearing as always," he said, reaching for her, intending to adjust her shawl.

She stepped away and he saw her chest rise in a deep breath. He knew exactly how she felt. A touch would be his undoing. He moved back and formally held his arm out to her. She rested her fingers lightly on the crook of his elbow.

Silently they entered the wide hallway, its dimensions built to accommodate the voluminous skirts of earlier times. Wall sconces filled with beeswax candles provided a modicum of light.

They did not get far before Langston stopped and turned to face her. "Thank you for saving Stephen. If you had not taken the brunt of the fall, he might have been seriously injured."

As solemn as he, she replied, "I only did what anyone would. Stephen is a delightful child, and I care greatly for him."

"Perhaps anyone *would*," he murmured, "but you *did*. I am in your debt."

She cocked her head to one side and gazed thoughtfully at him. "I do not want you in my debt, Langston. I do not want anything from you that you do not give willingly."

He opened his mouth, intending to tell her that she had no say in the matter, but she silenced him with a single finger to his lips. Where her flesh met his, he felt as though a brand seared him.

She let her hand drop. "But I would ask a favor for your son."

He drew back, frowning. "That is the last thing I would expect of you."

Her eyes flashed. "Why am I not surprised that you think me so shallow?"

"You mistake my meaning, Samantha. Only, Stephen is not your concern."

She sighed. "I know, but he is such a lonely little boy. And he longs so for your affection."

Langston stiffened. "Has he said so?"

"No," she said quietly. "But I can see it in his eyes whenever you are near. He worships you, but something has happened...or not happened." She took a deep breath and the next words come out in a rush. "Why don't you love him?"

Langston's anger flared. "I did not come to talk to you about Stephen and myself. 'Tis none of your concern."

Even in the flickering light, he could see her face pale. She lowered her lashes to hide the fury he knew she felt.

"You are right, my lord," she said in a voice that was mocking, as well as sad. "Your son's happiness is none of my concern." Drawing herself up, she turned away from him. "Shall we continue to the drawing-room? I find that I am famished."

Once more, he held out his arm to her, and once more she rested her fingers lightly on the sleeve of his coat. No further word passed between them, but Langston felt her disdain in the tenseness of her body, so near to his. And, much as he disliked it, he had to admit to himself that she was right.

Stephen was a child who had had too little love in his life. And it was Langston's fault.

THAT NIGHT, Samantha lay in the large Elizabethan bed and stared out the window. She had left the draperies open so that she could gaze out at the moon-drenched gardens; she knew sleep would not come easily tonight. A light snow was falling, and the trees appeared to be shrouded in gauze. The distant hills were almost completely obscured.

Restlessness seized her and she rose, wrapping her worn green robe about herself and donning slippers. She paced the room, tempted to light the fire for warmth. She paused by a table and picked up the book she had found in Langston's library. It was by Jane Austen, and she knew it would be light and entertaining, portraying a society she could never enter. She set it down unopened.

She had been shocked when Langston came to her door before dinner. Her rescue of Stephen had been instinctive, and she had not expected thanks from the marquis. Nor had she anticipated telling Langston how she felt about his treatment of his son. He had not taken it well.

She sighed.

Life was so complicated. Before she had met Langston, all she wanted was to act and provide for her daughter. Her life had been full—or almost full. She had hoped someday to find a man she could love and marry. Now she loved a man who lusted for her but did not love her, and she cared also for his child, who had obviously seen little happiness in his short life.

They were heavy burdens she had never expected to bear, and there was nothing she could do to ease their weight.

All evening she had resisted the urge to look at Langston, but it would have been easier to cut out her eyes. He had been debonair and charming to everyone, while staying far away from her. Yet whenever her gaze *had* strayed to him, he was watching her. She could almost have deluded herself into thinking he suffered as she did.

Her musings were interrupted by a soft rap on the door. Her heart skipped a beat. It could be only one person, and she had two choices: open the door or pretend to be sleeping.

Fingers shaking, she opened the door a crack.

His face was ravaged and his breath smelled of brandy. "I could not stay away."

It was a statement of need and desire that matched her own raging emotions. They came together in a passion that swept them deeply and inexorably into its abyss. Their hunger was beyond control, beyond rational thought.

Her mind spun as his lips and hands moved over her, molding her to his hardened body. She never knew how they reached her bed, nor when their clothes fell away. All that mattered, all she wanted, was his body pressed to hers, his skin slick and hot against hers.

When at last he was poised above her, she opened for him with a cry of surrender.

Langston held her tightly as he possessed and was possessed by her. His response was beyond his comprehension, his need for her beyond reason. For this moment in eternity, nothing mattered but the feel of her under him and the tightness of her around him.

He would worry about the consequences of their actions later. Much later.

He stayed through the night, desperately trying to quench his body's thirst for her. And when he tired, she roused him to greater strength. He could not get enough of her, nor she of him.

In the coldest part of the night, just before dawn, he left, slinking through the halls of his own house like a thief. It left a bitter taste in his mouth.

And still, as the devil was his witness, he wanted her.

CHAPTER THIRTEEN

SAM AWOKE LATE, her body exhausted. When she rose on one elbow and pushed the hair back from her face, she saw that he was gone. She fell back into the pillows and covered her eyes with one arm. What would happen now?

He had her heart, but did he want it? She did not think so.

"Sleeping late?" Lottie's gruff voice asked.

Sam jolted upright, embarrassment staining her cheeks as she saw the shambles of the room. Her nightclothes were strewn across the floor in a trail leading from the door to the bed. Langston's spicy scent clung to the rumpled sheets. The erotic musk of lovemaking hung in the air.

One glance at Lottie's averted eyes told Sam that the nurse knew.

"Best be rising, Miss Sam. Amalie is already up and wondering where you are. I wouldn't be surprised if she barges in here any second now."

Sam dressed hastily and hurried upstairs. As she approached the door to the nursery, she heard childish voices and then the deep, rich sound of a man's laughter. It took her a moment to recognize Langston's voice, for he had never really laughed in her presence.

That realization was overshadowed by apprehension. How could she face him so soon after their night of lovemaking, and with the children watching? She was afraid there would be a difference in the way she behaved toward him, a look on her face or a movement of her body that would give them away. Amalie would sense romance and expect marriage, and Sam knew that was impossible.

She could not go into that room. Yet how could she disappoint her child? Amalie did not deserve to suffer because of what was occurring between her mother and the man her mother loved. Nor did Stephen.

Lifting her head and squaring her shoulders, Sam took on the greatest role of her life: a woman who could calmly, dispassionately, face the man who had changed her life. For the children's sake, she would succeed.

She knocked briefly and entered. "Good morning," she said brightly.

The three of them were eating breakfast at a round table by the window. Sam made herself smile and move casually toward them, her attention seemingly focused on Amalie's happy face, even though she was achingly aware of Langston with every fiber of her being.

"Mama!" Amalie said, jumping up and running to embrace Sam. "I thought you would never come, but Lord Langston said to give you time. We saved a place for you."

"How generous," Sam said lightly, putting her arm around Amalie's shoulders. "And thank you, Langston, for suggesting it."

The look he gave her was hooded, his thoughts unfathomable. Did he regret yesterday and last night? Apprehension clawed at her before she could push it away.

"Mrs. Davidson." Stephen's polite voice stopped her agonizing thoughts. "Amalie and I were hoping you would join us on a ride into the village. Amalie wants to see the pig that lives on the green, and Papa says he will take us."

Sam looked at Langston and prayed he would not know how much she wanted to be with him. To spend time with him and to be with the children simultaneously would be wonderful and painful, and something she would remember always.

When he returned her silent query with seeming indifference, she bit her lip. Perhaps he did not at all care for her company on this little jaunt into the village. But then, he obviously had had no qualm about her joining him here in the nursery. Dear heaven, it was so confusing! Why was he sitting here now looking so stone-faced?

"What about the other guests?" she asked. "Shouldn't they be included?"

Stephen frowned. "No. We want it to be just the four of us. Right, Amalie?"

"Yes, please," Amalie said, her mouth full of toast.

Sam glanced at Langston, whose face still gave nothing away. "The other guests will relish being left to their own devices for an afternoon," he said coolly. "I heard several muttering that all their time was scheduled."

Picking up a cold piece of toast and slathering it with preserves, Sam spoke warmly for the children's sake. "In that case, I would be delighted to go with you. But Amalie must change to a warmer dress and wear a heavy cape and mittens. She may be better now, but the doctor warned me that once a person has an inflammation of the lungs, that person is always susceptible afterward."

Both children jumped up, and Amalie flung her arms around Sam's neck. Stephen took Sam's hand and squeezed it, saying, "Thank you so very much, ma'am. You don't know how awful it is to be constantly cooped up in this house."

Their response brought tears to Sam's eyes. She had realized that Stephen was becoming comfort-

able with her, but she had not thought he was secure enough or cared enough to take her hand of his
own accord.

AN HOUR OR SO LATER all four were ensconced in
one of Langston's closed carriages and bouncing
along the rutted road that led to Langston Village.
Amalie gripped the leather strap hanging from the
ceiling and eyed the marquis critically. "Does everything have to have your name? Are you that important?"

Instead of displaying irritation at the impertinent question, Langston chuckled. "It would seem
so. Actually, the house and village were named after my great grandfather when he was the marquis."

"Oh, then that is all right," Amalie said. "I was
beginning to think you were too puffed up with
your own consequence."

Sam choked. "Amalie!"

"'Tis quite all right," Langston said. "I am not
so puffed up with my own consequence that I take
offense. Amalie has a genuine curiosity about who
I am."

And so do I, Sam thought. She was only beginning to see the many facets of his personality.

"Father," Stephen said in his solemn voice, "do you think we might go to the sweetshop? I would like Amalie to try the ginger candies."

Langston smiled. "I think that can be arranged."

The children grinned at each other, and for the remainder of the trip Amalie chattered like a magpie. For his part, Stephen was quiet and kept a watchful eye on his father, despite some slight lessening of reserve.

Suddenly the carriage hit a deep rut and Sam flew forward, landing against Langston. His arms clamped around her so that she was cushioned against his chest. She could feel his heart beating and smell his musky scent. Her body tingled and her breathing quickened.

"Pardon me," she said huskily as she attempted to pull away.

"Of course," he murmured.

Without ceremony, he set her back on the seat opposite him. Sam pressed her back into the green velvet squabs and angled her legs so that they did not touch his. She was not at all sure she could bear another encounter, even so innocent a one. It tore her apart to be confined in this small space with him, to see every nuance of his expression, to inhale the familiar scent of him, and know she meant nothing to him.

To her disgust, she saw that her hand was shaking when she grasped the leather strap to keep from bouncing into his lap again. She had to get control of herself. She was not a slave to her desires and never had been, not even when she had run away with Charles Davidson. She had been infatuated with an older man who seemed to have all the polish she lacked, and who truly seemed to care for her. When she looked back on that marriage now, she could see that she had married Charles to escape her stepfather's cold harshness and unreasonable strictures.

Her husband had never made her feel the way Langston did. She had never felt this trembling need that started deep within and expanded outward until it consumed her. It was heady, and it was frightening.

The carriage rolled to a stop and the children clambered out before the footman could lower the step. Their exuberance was contagious, chasing away Sam's melancholy.

She looked around as she took the hand the footman offered. She noted the sweetshop, a tavern and a greengrocer prominently placed in the center. There were a number of other small business establishments, suggesting prosperity. A smattering of people hurried about their affairs. A man passing by recognized the marquis and pulled his forelock in respect.

"Good day, Samuels," Langston said, smiling at the man.

When a young woman with two small children in tow passed by, Langston grinned. "It seems you have your hands full, Mrs. Potter." The mother smiled and nodded.

Sam watched the byplay, not really surprised by his ease with the people, but intrigued by their ease with him. She would expect Langston to know his tenants—he was that type of man—but she had also expected him to be more aloof.

Meanwhile, the children disappeared into the sweetshop, and knowing Amalie's penchant for anything with sugar in it, Sam hurried after them.

A couple of hours later, Sam shook her head at Amalie's plea to remain longer in the village. "You will have a stomach-ache tonight from all the candy, as it is. And Lord Langston is ready to leave."

"But, Mama—"

"Amalie," Stephen said firmly, "your mother is right. We should go now. We can return another day."

Sam smiled at the boy, appreciating his intervention. When Amalie grudgingly acquiesced, Sam was amazed. She eyed her daughter with fresh interest and realized that she looked up to the boy. It seemed, in fact, that the admiration was mutual, and Sam was touched. But despite the children's growing affection for each other, this trip would soon be only a memory to pull out and relive on cold winter nights.

It was a sad thought, and she pushed it away as she helped the children back into the coach. Amalie was popping the last sweet into her mouth and simultaneously trying to smooth her crumpled skirts when Sam felt a tug on her skirt. Looking around, Sam found herself staring into the haunted eyes of an old man.

"Spare a ha'penny, m'lady?" he asked, still clutching her skirt. A fleck of spittle fell from one side of his mouth, and his sallow cheeks were covered in several days' growth of grizzled beard. His clothes were threadbare.

"Of course," Sam said, sympathy for the man's plight misting her eyes. She dug into her reticule, coming up with several shillings, which she pressed into his bony hand.

"What are you doing?" Langston asked, coming up behind the old man.

The beggar's eyes widened with fear, and he shuffled back from the marquis. "Nothin', m'lord."

Langston shook his head. "John, you never learn. Now give the lady's money back and get on home."

A lone tear fell from the old man's eye as he held his hand out, the silver shillings gleaming in his palm.

"No!" Sam declared. "You must keep the money. 'Tis nothing." She stepped back, stumbling against the coach. Catching her balance, she scowled at Langston. "He needs the shillings more than I do."

"*He* lives with the vicar and wants for nothing. Don't you, John?"

The old man's eyes shifted from the marquis's to Sam's. "Yes'm," he mumbled. Still, his fingers closed around the coins and he shuffled sideways, increasing the distance between himself and the marquis. Suddenly he turned and darted off.

"You have lost your money," Langston said to Sam in a flat voice. Then, quirking one dark brow, he asked, "Why did you insist? John is well cared for. Those clothes are last winter's set. He will not let the vicar get rid of them."

Sam lifted her chin. "I gave him the money because he needed it more than I do." Instead of again telling Langston that she was not the avaricious woman he took her to be, she got into the carriage and turned her head to look out the window. She did not want to see the derision she knew would be on his face.

Langston climbed in behind her. Both children dozed off after the carriage was rolling, and the trip home was made in silence. When they pulled up in front of Langston Castle, the children were still asleep and Langston had to summon a footman to help carry them inside. From the corner of her eye, Sam glimpsed a traveling carriage, its massive cargo of luggage still being unloaded. Briefly she wondered who had arrived for what appeared to be an extended visit. She had thought all the guests were here, and consequently had assigned everyone their part in the play.

Still, she was cold and hungry and her body ached from lack of sleep. She would meet the new guest soon enough. Right now she needed a nap to put herself to rights.

ALICIA, Duchess of Rundell let the heavy crimson draperies fall back into place. She had seen enough. Crossing to the fireplace, she pulled hard on the bell rope to summon a servant, whom she sent to Langston with a message.

When her oldest son arrived, Alicia went to him with open arms. "Jon, 'tis so good to be here."

Langston grinned and hugged his mother. Stepping back, he said, "I am glad to have you here.

You have no idea of the trouble it is to give a house party and not have a hostess.''

She returned his grin, leading him to one of the two gold damask chairs grouped around the roaring fire. Sitting, she asked, ''Can I interest you in scones or tea?''

He cocked his head to one side and studied her before answering. ''You know you can, but that is not the reason you summoned me.''

She had the grace to blush, her porcelain skin made more attractive by the hint of color. Ladling two heaping spoonfuls of sugar into his cup, she said, ''As usual you come right to the point, Jon. That is what makes you so formidable in the Commons.''

He sat down and bowed his head in acknowledgment. ''I prefer to think it is my superior grasp of government, and my willingness to compromise.''

''That, too.'' She handed him a plate with two scones and generous portions of clotted cream and strawberry preserves.

''Well?'' he asked as he spread cream and jam on one of the scones.

Alicia took a deliberate sip of her tea before setting the cup and saucer down and fixing him with her silver-grey eyes. ''The actress. I saw her getting out of a carriage with you, Stephen and a little girl.

Why is she here, and why was she with you and your son?''

Langston held his mother's gaze while he thought about just how much he should tell her. Certainly not that he and Samantha Davidson were lovers.

''She is here to produce a play for my house guests. She was also invited so that Ravensford would seduce her and make it impossible for Dev to continue wanting to marry her.'' He took a large bite of his scone.

Alicia's eyes narrowed as she studied her son. Of all her sons, he was the most unlike her. Where she was impulsive and loved to enjoy life, Jonathan was controlled, and had dedicated his life to the betterment of those less fortunate. He would make an excellent Duke of Rundell, but she was not sure he was happy. Today there was a brooding look in his eyes, as though something troubled him greatly.

''Has Ravensford's suit been successful?'' she asked, watching him closely.

The urge to glance away from his mother's probing gaze was strong, but Langston resisted it. He had never lied to his mother, and he was not about to start now—especially not because of Samantha Davidson.

''No, it was not.'' He let out the air he had been holding and took a sip of tea, wishing the brew was stronger. ''She turned him down. Meanwhile, Napoleon has chosen this time to escape Elba. I received a missive saying Dev's stay in Brussels will be indefinite. The allies are gathering in Brussels, but according to the message, no one really thinks Napoleon will attack.''

Instantly alarmed, Alicia asked, ''Is Deverell in danger?''

Langston took a deep breath and let it out slowly. ''I do not think so. I pray he is not. Napoleon would be mad to think he could gain power again. His troops are beaten and dispersed. He will never be able to assemble an army.''

''I see,'' Alicia said. ''This message came after you had already arrived here?''

''No,'' Langston said, putting worry for Deverell to the back of his mind, knowing his mother was just starting her inquisition. ''It came while I was still in London. However, at some point Dev must return. I thought it better if his inamorata was another man's mistress when he returned.''

''Ah, very thorough. But what will you do now that she has refused Ravensford?''

''Hope that Dev will not return for some time.''

Even now, sitting across from his mother and knowing she wanted to hear something more definite, he could not bring himself to tell her all. A man did not discuss his mistresses with his mother.

But it was more than that. Something had happened to him. Samantha Davidson was his secret vice, his obsession. He did not want to admit his fascination with her to anyone, no matter how it might ease his mother's mind to know that he was bedding the actress. And, for some reason he did not care to study, he did not want to increase his mother's already strong distaste for Samantha.

"Mrs. Davidson is not the money-hungry woman I took her for. Nor is she the type of actress I thought." He took a deep breath. "She cares for people. She gave money to John the Beggar today, and when I told her he did not need it, she replied that he needed it more than she." Langston slowly released the breath he had been holding. "And she loves her daughter with an intensity that is... warming."

"Ah, yes. The little girl in the carriage. Do you think it wise for her to be playing with Stephen?"

Anger, unexpected and strong, burst in Langston, and when he spoke, it was an effort not to show it in his voice. "Amalie is a child, Mother. I will not condemn her for the sins of her mother—if indeed sins there are."

Alicia's mouth thinned, and she asked very softly, "Does Mrs. Davidson mean more to you than you have let on?"

There it was. The question he had been hoping to avoid. "She is a very beautiful woman and an accomplished actress."

"And nothing more?"

Langston found his renowned calm deserting him.

The duchess took pity on her son. "I already know, Jon. Servants are very observant, often more so than their employers would wish. My maid knew within minutes of our arrival."

He should have known. His valet would have been aware that he had not returned to his own room until the wee hours of the previous night.

Still, his anger returned at her duplicity. "Then why have you put me through this inquisition?"

She sighed and leaned forward to take both his hands in hers. "Because you are my son, and because I had hoped it was not true. But listening to you, I know it is." She squeezed his hands. "Are you going to offer her marriage?"

The question took Langston aback. "I had not considered it," he said stiffly.

She nodded and reminded him softly, "Cynthia is with me." Her eyes searched his for some reaction at the mention of the woman to whom he was almost betrothed. There was none.

His face was shuttered, keeping all his thoughts from her, as usual. The only time she had ever seen him reveal his emotions was when Annabelle died, and just moments ago—when he spoke of Samantha Davidson.

A chill of impending disaster snaked down Alicia's spine, and she knew she had to do something to divert her oldest son from the path he was heading down. Although he denied any tenderness for the actress, she sensed he would change his mind, and marriage to an actress would be only slightly less damaging for Langston than for Deverell. Langston, at least, did not need to marry an heiress, but his reputation, and the shame...

Releasing his hands, she sat back in her chair. "Cynthia said she is looking forward to talking with you this evening."

Langston sensed that his mother had reached some sort of decision, but he did not know what it was. Regardless, he was grateful to her for changing the subject. He was not ready to consider his next step with Samantha Davidson.

"Then I had best leave, Mother. There is much to be done before we meet for dinner." He rose and took the hand she extended to him, then left her room.

Alicia remained in her chair long after Langston left, her mind churning with possibilities. But she knew in her heart that there was only one course of action open to her. Just as she had asked Langston to intervene to save Deverell from the actress, so must *she* intervene to save Langston from that infernal woman.

And there was no time like the present, she decided, standing and crossing to a small Louis XIV desk. She took a seat and pulled out a sheet of thick cream-colored paper, embossed with the Duke of Rundell's crest and kept here for her personal use. In her delicate black script, Alicia invited Mrs. Samantha Davidson to take tea with her before dinner that evening.

CHAPTER FOURTEEN

SAM STOPPED outside the Duchess of Rundell's suite and wished there had been some way to refuse the graciously worded invitation, which had really been a command. She could guess what the duchess wanted, and the knowledge was not comforting.

Her palms were moist inside their black evening gloves, and she nervously touched the rose nestled in her hair, its familiar scent giving her a modicum of calm.

At least she looked her best. Lottie had seen to that, fussing over her like a mother hen. She straightened her shoulders and knocked.

"Come in," a deep alto voice commanded.

Sam entered and closed the door behind her. Vaguely she noted that the room was magnificent, done in tones of crimson and gold, a massive fireplace ringed in marble dominating it. But it was the woman seated on a gold damask settee who caught and held her attention.

No longer in the first blush of youth, she was nonetheless a very handsome woman. Her coal-black hair was done in the latest fashion, with a diamond tiara holding the thick tresses from her shoulders. Curls cascaded around her face, accenting grey eyes of startling clarity and brilliance. Her figure was slim, almost like that of a young girl, not a matron with three grown children.

Suddenly Sam noticed Stephen, sitting over by the window. His presence took her momentarily by surprise, but when he turned his face in her direction and she saw the ease there, she realized that he and the duchess were close. After all, she was his grandmother.

"Your Grace," Sam said, sinking into a deep curtsy.

"Thank you for coming, Mrs. Davidson," the duchess replied, motioning Sam to a high-backed chair opposite her.

"Mrs. Davidson," Stephen said, jumping up and crossing to her. "I did not know you were going to take tea with Grandmother." He smiled broadly, distributing his charm equally between both women. "I do hope you like each other."

In a cool voice, the duchess said, "Stephen, 'tis time for you to be going. Mrs. Davidson and I have some matters to discuss."

Sam knew that Stephen's hope was most unlikely. It was obvious that his grandmother shared none of his affection for her.

"Yes, ma'am," he said, bowing to both before proceeding from the room with all the maturity he could muster.

"Do you take milk and sugar in your tea?" the duchess asked, not smiling.

"Milk only," Sam said, watching the woman pour steaming tea into a pair of delicate cups decorated with the Langston crest. A very effective reminder of the difference in their stations, Sam thought. Nevertheless, she was determined not to let the duchess intimidate her.

"A sandwich?"

"No, thank you," Sam said.

Alicia took a sip of her tea, then put the cup and saucer down with a clack. "There is no sense in continuing this flummery, Mrs. Davidson. We are both mature women, both mothers, so I will pay you the highest compliment I know by going right to the point."

Sam again felt the moisture on her palms. The tea she was drinking seemed too hot. She set it down and sat a little straighter. Her gaze did not waver from the duchess's solemn countenance.

"I know that my youngest son, Lord Deverell, has asked you to marry him. Apparently you refused." The duchess's eyes were as cold as a winter lake. "But now I arrive at Langston Castle and find you ensconced here in the guise of helping my eldest son produce a play for his guests."

When Sam remained silent, the duchess's mouth tightened at the corners. "I see that you do not intend to offer a comment. You are a very wise woman, Mrs. Davidson." She leaned forward, her eyes pinning Sam. "But you are not the woman for either of my sons."

The duchess knew, Sam thought, trying desperately not to betray her emotions. Nothing she could say would change anything.

"So, you are still not speaking," the duchess said, her voice cold. "Well, no need. I want you to leave Langston Castle immediately. I will pay you twice whatever Langston has offered."

Sam spoke now, her tone uninflected, her words measured. "Langston has already paid me for organizing the play. It is sufficient for what I did. And I will be leaving as soon as it has been performed, which I believe is to be the last night of the party."

The duchess rose and moved to the mantel before turning back to face Sam. "Langston's engagement is to be announced that evening."

Langston engaged! Sam licked suddenly dry lips and fought the darkness closing in on her. Had she been standing, she would have fallen. As it was, she gripped the sides of the chair with both hands.

Swallowing hard, she managed a polite smile. "How nice for him. I am sure he is delighted."

"My offer still stands," the duchess said quietly, almost gently.

Sam made herself concentrate on the other woman. She could almost see pity in the duchess's face. Almost.

"Why?" Sam asked, rising and smoothing her skirts. "I am no threat to your family."

The duchess's beautiful mouth turned down. "I fear you are, Mrs. Davidson. Langston's first marriage was a disaster. He deserves this one to be a success. Your presence will keep that from happening."

A bitter laugh escaped Sam. All her vaunted skill as an actress was not enough to keep at bay the pain caused by Langston's engagement to another woman. She was a fool.

"I fail to see how that can be. Langston does not even like me." She smiled sadly. "No, Your Grace, you overestimate my importance."

The duchess stared long and hard at Sam, her face thoughtful. "Perhaps you are right. Perhaps that is why Langston told me about you."

Sam's eyes widened in shock. Then she gathered her wits and said, unable to keep a note of sarcasm from her tone, "How pleasant for you to know."

Sam willed herself not to collapse. If she could survive just a little longer, this interview would be over. Then she would return to her room. She would pack her bags and have Lottie pack Amalie's. She would leave Langston Castle and never return.

Just a little longer.

"It was certainly informative," the duchess said with a slight smile that did not reach her eyes. "Will you take my money?"

Sam pulled herself up and returned the duchess's gaze. "No, thank you. I will not take your money to leave Langston's vicinity any more than I would take Langston's money to leave Lord Deverell's vicinity. I am not a woman who can be paid off, because I am not a woman who would do something to make it necessary to be paid off. Whatever you may think of me, Your Grace, I am not a whore and never have been."

There, Sam thought. The words were out. She had faced down the most powerful duchess in England. But she felt as weak as a newborn kitten, and when she sank into a curtsy, it took all her strength to pull herself out of it.

"If you will excuse me, Your Grace," she said. It was impertinent of her to ask to leave, and she could see that the duchess was surprised by her temerity.

"You may go," the duchess said, turning her back.

Sam went out, closing the door behind herself and almost dropped to the hall floor. With a supreme effort, she made her feet move, one in front of the other, along the corridor, around a corner, down a flight of stairs and down yet another hall. Only when she reached the sanctuary of her own room did she allow herself to collapse.

Thank goodness Lottie was with Amalie, Sam thought fleetingly. She lay on the bed, staring with tear-filled eyes at the cavorting cherubs and lascivious fauns on the ceiling. There was no reason for this misery. A wife would make no difference to what was between Langston and her. Very likely he never even intended to see her again after this house party was over. Their coming together had been chance. Nothing more.

The sound of the door opening made her jump off the bed and wipe her gloved hands across her eyes. She did not want Lottie to see her this way.

"Lordy, Miss Sam!" Lottie exclaimed, bustling into the darkened room. "Why are you here, instead of downstairs with all the other guests?"

Reaching a side table, she lit a candle and peered at Sam, who sniffed and met her gaze defiantly.

"I do not feel well enough for such a large dinner," Sam said. "Indigestion."

Lottie pushed her spectacles up the bridge of her nose and moved closer. "You've been crying," she said accusingly. "What has his lordship done?" She took a quick look around the room, as though expecting to find Langston lurking in some shadowed corner.

Sam turned her back to Lottie and crossed to the dresser to rummage in a drawer for a handkerchief. "Langston has done nothing. I told you, I do not feel well."

"Harrumph! More likely you heard the rumors."

Sam paused in the process of bringing the handkerchief to her nose. "Rumors?"

"You can't fool me," Lottie said in a nononsense tone. "You heard about Lady Cynthia, his as-good-as-betrothed. According to James, his lordship's valet, it's been a long time coming, too."

"His first marriage was ill-fated," Sam muttered into the handkerchief just before blowing her nose.

"That's what James says." Lottie bustled about lighting a brace of candles and picking up the shawl that had fallen from Sam's shoulders when she had rushed into the room. "I'm thinking you should go down, missy. You're stronger than this, and you don't want his lordship thinking you're embarrassed by the presence of his betrothed."

Sam stiffened. Trust Lottie to put a different slant on things—and be right. After their outing today, Langston would never believe she was unwell. He would know her absence was because of Lady Cynthia, and Sam refused to give him that satisfaction.

Lifting her chin, she said, "Thank you, Lottie. Never let it be said that I am a coward—for I am not."

"That's my girl," Lottie said, draping the shawl over Sam's shoulders. "You never let your stepfather cow you, nor that good-for-nothing husband of yours, neither, so don't start with this man. Train 'em as you intend to go on, I always say."

Sam looked at herself in the beveled glass. Her cheeks were flushed and her eyes were bright, but there was no puffiness and her nose was not red from crying. Her appearance was excellent. She kept that in mind as she descended to the first floor, even going so far as to let the footman announce her. There was a general shifting of heads and several pairs of raised eyebrows as she paused in the entrance.

She saw him standing near the fireplace in the midst of a small group of people, including the duchess, all of whom were laughing. On his right arm was a young woman—a striking young woman. Tall and elegant, with hair the color of ripe corn and lips the shade of cherries, she was dressed in cream muslin so finely woven it appeared nearly translucent.

Sam's heart plummeted. Lady Cynthia, for she had no doubt of the lady's identity, was everything a man like Langston would want in a wife: stunningly beautiful, well-bred and well-connected, at ease in the circles in which the marquis moved.

"Mrs. Davidson." Ravensford's deep baritone was welcome and comforting. "You have joined us, after all. I was beginning to think you were ill."

Sam made herself smile into the earl's knowing, but kindly eyes. "I was a trifle tired from an afternoon outing, that is all."

He extended his arm to her and she gladly took it, grateful for his presence in a group of people suddenly grown cold and distant. She felt everyone's attention on her and wondered for the first time if they all knew about her liaison with Langston. Until now, she had not noticed such avid curiosity.

"Let me introduce you to Langston's newest guests."

Sam kept her smile in place and forced herself
not to flee the room. She could and would meet the
two women who were causing her heart to break.

When they reached the small group, Sam sank
into an automatic curtsy, although it was not as
deep as the one she had performed earlier in the
day. She felt rebellious.

"Your Grace," Ravensford said, lifting Sam
from her shallow obeisance, "let me introduce Mrs.
Davidson, the Divine Davidson, I might add, and
the toast of the *ton*."

The Duchess of Rundell inclined her head graciously, not letting on that she had already made
Sam's acquaintance. "How do you do, Mrs. Davidson," she said in a clear voice. "I understand
that you are here to orchestrate a play for Langston's guests."

It was all Sam could do to act as though there
were no undercurrents to this meeting. She was fast
finding that her skills as a thespian were nothing
compared to those of the duchess and her oldest
son, both of whom watched her with bland coun-
tenances.

"And," Ravensford interjected into the silence,
"this is Lady Cynthia Clyde. She arrived with the
duchess today."

Sam turned to the woman who would soon marry
the man she loved. Lady Cynthia was as beautiful

close up as she had been from afar. Her complexion was that of the typical English rose, and her eyes were more brilliant than emeralds. She exhibited no haughtiness when she extended her hand to Sam and smiled graciously.

Sam returned her smile and, somehow, survived the meal and the ensuing socializing. However, she did not remain long after the men rejoined the women. She could not bear to see Langston hang on Lady Cynthia's every word and devour the girl with his eyes. Ravensford's entertaining anecdotes during dinner and prompt attention afterward did little to ameliorate her agony.

Upstairs, she paced her room and worried about how best to flee this untenable situation. Perhaps Lottie could speak to someone in the household staff and arrange for a carriage. The three of them could be gone before anyone awoke tomorrow.

With a sigh of resignation, Sam sank into a chair and buried her face in her hands. She could not leave. She could not repay Langston the money he had already given her. She and Amalie and Lottie would need it for the year ahead, especially as most of her savings had been wiped out by the doctor's bills. Besides, she could not be sure Amalie wouldn't contract an inflammation of the lungs again, and then where would she be?

And it was not as though she even had a reason for her devastation. Langston did not love her and had never hinted that he did. As for marriage, it was an impossibility and always had been. Men of Langston's station married their own kind and kept actresses as their mistresses.

So be it. She would stay.

The room cooled and still she sat, thoughts turning over and over in her mind as she sought a way to ease the pain of remaining. She knew that every time she saw Lady Cynthia it would turn the knife in her heart, but she also knew she had to stay for her child's sake.

She rose and went to the fireplace, where she took a poker and agitated the coals to flames. They danced up the chimney and cast shadows on the unlit recesses of the room.

A light tap on the door made her look up. She knew it must be Langston.

He did not wait for her answer before entering. He moved toward her in the dimly lit room, not stopping until he was close enough for her to see the darkness in his eyes.

The orange glow of the flames cast his face into relief, making it appear sinister. His blond hair was disheveled, falling onto his high brow in waves that she longed to push back. His shirt was open at the neck, his immaculate cravat gone. He looked rakish and devilish and driven.

"Why did you leave?" he asked, his voice deep and velvety, accusing in its intensity.

Sam shrugged and looked away, once more concentrating on the fire. She poked at the coals in jerky motions that sent sparks flying.

"Answer me," he demanded, reaching for her.

Sam stared into his eyes and did not know what to think of the passion and denial she saw there. She let the poker slip from her slack fingers. It landed on the floor with a clang that neither heeded.

"I am not yours to command," she said in a whisper.

"You are my folly," he said, his voice so deep it was nearer a growl.

Still holding her shoulders, he bent forward and took her lips. His mouth ravished her, his tongue demanding entrance that she could no more deny than she could deny her love for him. He kissed her until she clutched the edges of his shirt to keep from sinking to the floor.

His hands began to move up and down her arms until they slid the sleeves of her evening gown down and exposed her chemise-covered bosom to his gaze and his kiss. His lips suckled her through the gossamer cotton, sending tingles throughout her body. All her pain evaporated in the heat of his passion.

Her will to resist him was nonexistent, her desire for him all-consuming.

He scooped her up and carried her to the bed, where he set her gently down. "I cannot get enough of you," he murmured, his voice tortured as he hastily began to undo the buttons of his shirt.

The sudden chill she felt as he let go of her was enough to restore her senses. She slipped from the bed and stood facing him, one hand clutching the bodice of her gown to her breasts in an attempt to cover her near nakedness. Her voice was tight with suppressed anger and hurt.

"Why are you here, Langston? Your betrothed is in this house, and your mother. Your mother!" Her voice rose. "You told her about us. No doubt you told her to summon me and make it plain that our dalliance meant...means nothing to you. That I am nothing but a whore in your eyes. Just as you made me in your mother's."

He stared at her, and to his everlasting shame, he wanted her more than he ever had.

"You have stolen my honor and now accuse me of making you a whore?" he said coldly, suppressing the urge to throw her to the floor and drown in the release she alone could give him. "For wanting you, I have committed an act that will earn me my brother's undying hatred, and I have abused the trust of the woman I am almost engaged to. It is I who am debased!''

"How dare you!" She took a step toward him. "You blame me for your own weakness!"

His laugh was a bitter crack in the deathly silence. "And your response to me is no weakness? You want me as badly as I want you."

Her head dropped and her voice was a whisper. "Yes, I do, but not like this. Not as your whore. Not when you have a woman who is soon to be your wife. Not when your mother's condemning eyes follow me because you told her about me."

His mouth curled bitterly. "There is no other way, and both of us know it."

She *was* nothing but his mistress, with all the shame and pain that entailed. She could take no more. "Get out," she said harshly, quietly. "Get out and leave me alone."

He cast her one hard, fulminating glare and left.

As the door closed behind him, she sank to the floor, oblivious to the cold, oblivious to anything but the breaking of her heart and the devastation of all her dreams.

But she could not have acted differently.

CHAPTER FIFTEEN

SAMANTHA LINKED hands with the other cast members and bowed to the small, select audience seated in the Langston Castle theatre. She was pleased with the performance and with her part in bringing it about.

The morning after Langston left her bedroom for the last time, she had approached Lady Cynthia and offered her the part of Kate, the role Sam had intended to play to Langston's Petruchio. Lady Cynthia had willingly agreed and worked hard to learn her lines for this evening. With Sam directing, Lady Cynthia and all the cast members had done superbly.

Now they were all going to their rooms and dressing for the ball that was to follow and which would be attended by all the local people who had not been invited to the play. Sam had been invited, but was not going. She planned to use the time to pack. She, Amalie and Lottie would leave before daybreak tomorrow.

Rising from her bow, Sam smiled, taking genuine pleasure in the success. "Congratulations on your first leading role," she said to Lady Cynthia, who was on her right. "If you should ever need to earn your living, I am sure you could do so on the stage." It was a bold statement to make to one of the Quality, but Sam felt comfortable enough with Lady Cynthia to do so.

The blond beauty laughed. "Thank you, Mrs. Davidson. I shall be sure to keep that in mind."

Sam ignored Langston's frown as he watched the two of them from his vantage point on Lady Cynthia's right. He had been scowling at Sam every day for the past week. When she visited the children and he was there, he would leave immediately, and Stephen and Amalie had begun to comment on his rude behavior. Stephen seemed quieter than usual, which hurt her to see, but there was nothing she could do except to care for him while she was here. He was not her child.

"We had best cut this short," Langston said, his deep voice full of irritation as he stepped between the two women.

Even now, Sam found her pulse racing at his nearness and the scent of spice and musk that drifted from him. He still had the power to make her want him—no, more: to love him.

Turning from him and Lady Cynthia, Sam made her way to the back of the stage and down the stairs, careful to stay away from groups of people where she might be drawn into conversation.

In her room, she finished packing and paused to gaze at the large four-poster bed, the bed where Langston had slept with her and made love to her. If she tried hard enough, she could imagine him sprawled across it, his face inches from hers and his warm breath caressing her skin. In that small space, she had experienced ecstasy and pain such as she had never known.

She pivoted abruptly away. It was time to see that Amalie was packed and tucked into bed. She also wanted to say goodbye to Stephen.

She met Lottie outside Amalie's bedchamber. "She's asleep," the servant said, "but the young master is not." She nodded in the direction of the nursery. "He's in there waiting to say goodbye to you, Miss Sam."

Tears misted Sam's eyes. She would miss Stephen. He was a boy floundering in an adult world where he was not sure of his welcome. Langston's treatment of his son was the one area where Sam found the marquis to be less than compassionate, and it wrenched her heart to see it. Stephen needed love, lots of love and caring and time.

Easing open the door, Sam stepped inside. Stephen was sitting quietly by the window staring out at the winter night.

"Stephen," she said softly.

His head swiveled sharply and he leapt to his feet. "Mrs. Davidson!"

Seeing the joy on his face brought a lump to Sam's throat. She hoped Lady Cynthia would grow to love him and become the mother he so desperately needed.

"I wanted to say goodbye to you," she said, going to him and holding out her arms.

He came into her embrace and hugged her fiercely. "Please don't leave," he said, hiccuping.

Sam held him to her and knew he was struggling not to cry. If only she could take him with her... But that was a ludicrous idea. Someday he would be a duke, and she would not even be a memory to him.

She stroked back his thick, black hair and let him hug her as long as he wished. At last he released her, and she made herself smile at him, instead of gathering him back in her arms.

"I have to go, Stephen. You know that. My stay was only temporary." She swallowed around the lump in her throat. "But I want you to know that I will never forget you. You are a brave and kind boy, and some day you will make a splendid duke." She smiled gently. "Amalie will miss you sorely."

He nodded, his face solemn. "I will miss her. She is a good sport."

Sam grinned. Leave it to a boy to admire a girl because she's a good sport. "And she thinks the same of you."

"I know," he mumbled. "She told me." He looked away for a second and then pinned her with the intensity of his blue eyes. "Will you come back?"

Sam's chest hurt, and it was on the tip of her tongue to tell him what he wanted to hear. But she could not. She respected and cared for him too much to lie. She shook her head.

"No, Stephen. I am sorry." She took a deep breath and chose her words carefully. "Your father hired me for the play only. I shall return to London and to the Drury Lane Theatre. This time at your home was only a holiday."

Stephen twisted away and went to the seat by the window. "I don't want you to go," he said in the imperious voice he sometimes used when he knew he was not going to get what he wanted. Sam had been pleased to notice that he had used it less and less while she and Amalie had been here.

She went to him, taking the chair beside him and grasping his hands. "I know, sweetheart, and I wish we did not have to go. But we must.'' She squeezed gently so that he looked at her. "We will write."

"Perhaps," he said, freeing one hand to wipe at his eyes. "Can Amalie write?"

"I taught her."

He turned his face away, and Sam knew he was hiding tears. She wanted to take him in her arms and comfort him, but realized that he was old enough to find the strength within himself.

"My father does not like me," he murmured.

Sam almost did not hear the words, and when their meaning sank in, she wished she had not. "Oh, Stephen, I am sure he does." Even as she refuted his statement, doubt gnawed at her.

He turned back to her. "No, he does not. He has done more things with me these past two weeks than ever before. 'Twas because of you and Amalie... and... and when you leave he will stop. Soon he will return to London, and I shall stay here with my tutor. No, my father does not love me at all."

The last was said in a voice so devoid of hope Sam's heart contracted. Poor little boy. But there was nothing she could do, nothing in the world. Blinking back tears of her own, she reached for him, no longer caring if she offended his sensibilities.

For the second time that night, he clung to her.

Later she put him to bed, wishing with all her heart that he would find some measure of acceptance and happiness in his life. And when she went to her own room and climbed into bed, she prayed for him and for herself. The man who had broken her heart was doing the same to Stephen.

Her limbs felt leaden and her eyes ached with unshed tears. The brief moments she had shared with Langston would have to last her a lifetime. If she was lucky the pain would fade with time.

Sam scrunched up her pillow and buried her face in its feathery embrace. The room was cold and her body stiff with suppressed anguish. She had shed enough tears to last her an eternity, and she would not cry now.

AN HOUR BEFORE dawn pinked the sky, Sam, Amalie and Lottie climbed into Langston's traveling carriage. Glancing out the vehicle's window, she saw a lone male figure standing between the parted curtains in the library.

Sam turned to Amalie, who was cuddled against her, and kissed her daughter's tousled hair. The love of her life was beyond her reach, but she had her child, a gift that would bring her joy for the rest of her life.

It was enough. It would have to be.

LANGSTON WATCHED the coach pull out of the drive.

He had looked in on Stephen after the ball and seen that his son had cried himself to sleep. He knew it was because Samantha and Amalie Davidson were leaving. He knew, too, how Stephen felt.

Langston sighed and dropped the curtain.

He had not wanted to become involved with the woman, but he had. He had compromised his integrity for her, and he would do it again. He would lose his brother for her.

The realization was appalling.

Crossing to the dead fire, he picked up the poker and jabbed at the coals, then dropped the instrument and threw himself into a leather wing-chair.

Samantha Davidson had come into his life, and he knew he would never be the same. Watching her over the days had shown him how the love of a mother for her child could brighten any day. Her fierce protectiveness of Amalie had gained his respect. She had even dared to lecture him about Stephen, and in the process had shown him that he could no longer fear the son because of the mother. Samantha Davidson had shown him the power of love.

She had also shown him the power of desire, a yearning so great that everything paled in comparison. Her past, his brother, his dreams for the future seemed as nothing when he was with her.

He was beginning to perceive how his mother might have been able to leave her family for a man she thought she loved. He was even beginning to understand why Annabelle had risked everything. Even betraying him by having another man's child, if she was captive to desire and thought herself in love.

Now the woman who had enlightened him was gone, and he could have stopped her by telling her he loved her, but he did not love her. He desired her beyond anything, but that was not enough to risk marrying a woman who would completely alienate his friends and family.

Scowling, he rose and paced back to the window, where he opened the draperies again and stared at the now empty drive. The carriage was gone, the sound of its wheels on the gravel but a memory.

She was gone from his life. He glanced at the message that had arrived yesterday evening from Winkly. The Bow Street Runner said he was now investigating the death of Samantha Davidson's husband. He hinted at suspicious circumstances, but did not elaborate.

Langston crumpled up the message and tossed it into the dead fire. The information no longer mattered to him.

CHAPTER SIXTEEN

Sam gazed out the window at the street where a light dusting of snow fell to the cobbles and quickly melted. It had been a freak snowstorm just as the trees were beginning to bud.

She had spent the past weeks watching the newspapers for notice of Langston's engagement. She must have missed it, but that was no consolation for the pain of knowing he was marrying another.

She crossed to the fireplace and held out her hands to the meager warmth of the small blaze there. Since her return to London, she had been frugal in heating every room but Amalie's. But even that had not been enough to keep her small reserve of funds from being eaten away.

She sank into a chair and stared at nothing, trying unsuccessfully to make her mind a blank. Langston's image would not be banished.

Someday she would forget the agony of watching him with another woman. Someday she would forget the ecstasy she'd found in his arms and his tenderness towards her daughter. Someday she would be able to see a tall man with blond hair and not instantly hope he was Langston.

Someday. But not yet.

"Miss Sam," Lottie said, bustling into the room, "a message was delivered for you earlier, but I forgot, what with Amalie's play and all."

"Of course," Sam said, smiling as she rose to take the paper.

Without another word, Lottie left to go to the kitchen, where the preparations for dinner waited. Sam sank back into her chair and broke the wax seal on the note. Holding it so as to get more illumination from the fire, she read the contents:

> Meet me at the main entrance to Hyde Park at twelve today. I have news concerning your dead husband that may interest you.
>
> Huntly

Her husband? Sam's hands began to shake. What sort of information could Huntly have? Charles had drowned at sea when Amalie was a baby.

She took a deep breath, crumpling the paper into a ball before throwing it into the fire, where it crackled and disappeared. She did not want to meet Huntly at any time, and particularly not after the incident at Langston Castle. But what if he really did have some new information?

It was only ten-thirty. She could easily be at the main entrance to Hyde Park by twelve. She would take her pistol, and if she was careful, surely there was nothing Huntly could do to her in so public a place.

She would learn what he knew—or said he knew.

Sam fetched her reticule, donned a grey spencer and told Lottie she would return in time for rehearsal.

She decided to enter the Park at an entrance some distance from the main one. The fashionable members of the *ton* were not yet about, but their servants, nannies and children were. Sam smiled at several harried young women who pushed or pulled their young charges along the paths.

When she saw the main gates to Hyde Park, she stopped and took the pistol from her reticule. Holding her hand in her skirts so that the weapon was hidden from view, but easily accessible to her should she need it, she strolled up to the gates and waited.

New grass poked up from the soil in light green waves, and the trees were covered with buds that presaged a canopy of leaves. The gentle breeze was laden with the scent of growing things.

At last she heard Huntly's oily voice. "Samantha," he said. "I knew you would not disappoint me."

He had come from the street just outside the Park. Sam turned to face him, her hand gripping the pistol for reassurance. Langston would not save her this time.

"I do not recall giving you permission to use my Christian name," she said, bravado strengthened by ire at his overfamiliarity.

His cold eyes grew hard. "I don't require your permission. I can call you a whore if the mood takes me."

The color drained from her face. He was on the attack. "In that case, I don't have to stand here and listen to you, do I? But then, if you did not want to tell me something, you would not have sent the note."

The muscle on the side of his mouth twitched, and he took a step toward her. " 'Tis for your own good."

She raised one eyebrow in doubt. "Somehow I find that hard to believe."

He took another step toward her, and she backed away, the hand clutching the pistol beginning to perspire. She needed to moderate her anger so as not to provoke him to violence.

His mouth curved into a cruel smirk. "What if I told you your husband is not dead?"

It was the last thing she had expected. Her mind reeled. Once that had been her fantasy, but no longer. Charles had been an avaricious man; he would take everything she had worked so hard to gain. He would take Amalie's future from her.

"I would not believe you. His death was verified."

"Did they find his body?"

Sam gulped hard on the rising uncertainty. "Of course not. He was in the middle of the Atlantic Ocean."

His smirk widened. "Then you cannot be certain."

Her rigidly held muscles began to ache. "Why are you doing this? What do you hope to accomplish?"

"I want you for my mistress."

There it was: the answer to all this madness. But how did it fit? "How could I be your mistress if Charlies is still alive?"

"A husband is no hindrance. Particularly if he is not in the country."

"What do you mean?"

"I have found your husband, Samantha. He is living in America, in New Orleans. If you don't consent to become my mistress, I will contact him and tell him how successful you are, how wealthy you are—"

"That is a lie and you know it!" she interrupted him, her pulse pounding.

He shrugged. "He won't know that. You are the toast of the London stage. I will have him brought back, and from what I have learned of him, he is a profligate. I don't think you want him around. But if you become my mistress, I will forget his existence."

Sam stared at Huntly, frantically trying to control her confusion. In a calmer voice, she said, "You are mad. Charles is not alive." She took a deep breath. "And I would never become your whore."

He sneered. "You are already Langston's. What matter if there is another man in your bed?"

Attack upon attack. But this one was more painful than the first. The tightness in her chest was extreme—and so familiar. Sam told herself she was beyond this torment. She was not Langston's mistress, had never really been. Not in the accepted sense of the words. But still, the hurt was there.

"I am no man's whore, Huntly."

Without waiting for him to say anything further, she spun on her heel and hurried back through the Park, the pistol gripped in shaking fingers.

LANGSTON READ Deverell's short note and knew he would have to tell his brother the truth. Dev was bringing a courier packet from the Duke of Wellington to the Home Office and would be in Lon-

don for two days. He intended to see Mrs.
Davidson during that time and would brook no in-
terference from Langston.

Langston shoved his fingers through his hair,
ruining the fashionable Brutus style his valet had
labored over.

"Damnation," he muttered, striding across the
library and then retracing his steps. What if she
agreed to Deverell's offer this time? She had
Amalie's health and future to worry about, for he
had no doubt that Samantha Davidson would do
whatever it took to provide for her child. That
much he had learned when she accepted his offer to
come to Langston Castle. She was a proud woman,
and he knew her well enough to realize she would
not have come to his home if she had not believed
it was the only way to help Amalie.

He raised his head and stared unseeingly out the
window. Perhaps it would be better to let Deverell
marry the woman. She had many admirable qualities and in many respects would make a good wife,
better than some chits of the *ton*.

His mouth twisted wryly at the tightening in his
gut. It was time he stopped trying to fool himself.

He still wanted Samantha Davidson.

She was the reason he had not asked Lady Cynthia to marry him. She was the reason he searched
every room of every function he attended, unable

to relax until he was sure she was not present. She was the reason he no longer slept and had lost so much weight his valet demanded that he get a new wardrobe.

Sam would never break Deverell's heart by telling him about her affair with Langston, but nor would she deny the importance of what had happened between them. She, after all, was more honest than he, and he could no longer condemn her for actions they had both committed.

But his mother would tell Deverell. She had her own memories of a marriage that had once been less than perfect. The Duchess of Rundell would do whatever was necessary to keep her youngest son from a marriage she considered a mistake.

Tired of wrestling with his thoughts, Langston left the room, saying to Peter, "Have my gelding saddled and brought round immediately." He needed to ride, to get away from his thoughts.

Peter, his blue-and-gold livery sparkling, hastened to do the marquis's bidding. Something was wrong. His lordship rarely ordered his servants about; he was unfailingly courteous. But not today. Not, in fact, since he had returned from Langston Castle.

In short order, Langston was mounted and on his way.

He kept the spirited animal in check until they turned into Hyde Park, then he gave the horse its head. The stretch of dirt road was completely empty at the moment and so was perfect for both animal and rider to release the devils driving them.

The woman came out of nowhere, stepping into the horse's path.

Langston pulled hard on the reins. The startled horse's forelegs lifted off the ground, and man and beast tumbled to the dirt. Langston managed to pull his feet from the stirrups at the last second and roll free. The horse clambered to his feet and pranced away.

The woman stood frozen, her eyes wide, her mouth an O of horror.

"Samantha!" Langston rushed to her, noting that his heart still lurched at the sight of her. "What the hell were you trying to do? Get yourself killed?"

She stared at him as though he were a ghost, her wonderful roses-and-cream complexion white with shock. Her beautiful eyes were full of terror. Dirt dusted the hem of her plain woolen gown and smudged one side of her nose.

She was stunning.

He ached to hold her, but instead, he seized her shoulders and shook her. He wanted to throttle her for being so careless of her safety, yet when her hair came loose from its pins and floated in satin tendrils to her shoulders he wanted to bury his hands in its luxuriant length. God! He didn't know what he wanted.

He released her and stepped back, taking deep breaths to calm himself. He was not going to let her nearness overpower his self-control again.

She blinked and her eyes focused on him. "You almost ran me down," she said, her rich alto sending shivers of longing through him.

"You stepped right in front of me. Didn't you hear the hoofbeats?" Disgust at his weakness for her tinged his words.

It was an effort not to catch her hand when she combed her fingers through the loose strands of hair framing her face. He wanted her, wanted her so much it was as though the weeks that had elapsed since he'd last held her hadn't occurred. He had missed her.

Her gaze shifted from his, and she bit her bottom lip. Then she straightened her shoulders and looked at him, as though she had come to some sort of decision. "I believe I owe you congratulations on your betrothal to Lady Cynthia."

He stared hard at her. It did not answer his question, and it was a subject from out of thin air. Or was it? Two spots of hectic color rode her otherwise pale cheeks, and her eyes challenged him.

Quietly, not taking his eyes from her, he said, "I am not betrothed to Lady Cynthia."

He watched her gulp and the spots of color on her face recede. "You are not? Your mother said you would be. At the ball. After the play."

He took an involuntary step toward her. "My mother did what she felt necessary. So did I. I am not engaged to Lady Cynthia."

Her gaze slid away. "Oh."

"You left without a word."

She looked up at him. "You allowed the coachman to bring us back to London. You knew."

"Yes, but I would never stop you by telling the servant not to do your bidding." He took a deep breath and added, "Not after you told me to leave you alone."

She tilted her head to one side. "And you did. It was better that way. That is why we left after the play. I knew it was best for all of us. My presence must have been awkward for you."

How to tell her that it had been torture, especially after she had told him to leave her? Suddenly he wanted to change the subject; this one was too close to the pain in his heart.

"Stephen was distraught," he said.

Her fingers played with the fabric of her skirt. "I spoke with him before leaving. It was all I could do."

He had not known that. Stephen hadn't told him. Langston studied her, wanting to know what she felt for the boy he called his son. "Why did you bother? He is no concern of yours."

Her eyes flashed. "He is a lonely little boy, with no mother... and no father to speak of."

She could have slapped him and done no more damage. But he knew it was deserved.

"You are right. But he's not the only one who is lonely."

Her eyes searched his face. "What do you mean?"

Langston did not know what he meant, or what he wanted from her. He only knew he had missed her. He took another step toward her until they were less than two feet apart, and he could clearly see every nuance of her expression.

"I... I missed you, Sam."

She swallowed hard and he longed to reach for her, to kiss the soft skin of her throat. Instead, he kept the small distance between them, waiting for her to bridge it.

"What about Lady Cynthia?"

"What about her?" he asked, not caring at the moment if Lady Cynthia disappeared from the face of the earth.

"You will eventually be betrothed to her, I know. You will marry her. What will happen then?"

He shrugged. "It will mean nothing to us. You and me. Men of my world marry for heirs, not... desire."

Her mouth tightened and her eyes darkened. She appeared to be in pain, but surely she understood. It was the way of the *ton*.

What he did not tell her, did not understand himself, was that he was not sure he *would* marry Lady Cynthia. The reasons for doing so were becoming less and less convincing.

"You want me for your mistress." Her voice was flat.

"Is that not enough?"

The corners of her mouth drooped. "You are no different from Huntly. He offers the same arrangement. But I do not want to live as any man's mistress. I will not subject myself or my child to that."

Langston felt as though someone were squeezing his chest. The urge to smash something was close to overwhelming. "Huntly? Is he the reason you are here? Is he still importuning you?"

"No more than you are, my lord."

Before he could reply, she turned and walked away. His first inclination was to pursue her, but in his heart he realized that would only postpone the inevitable. Her rejection of his offer was obvious, whether she voiced the words or not. She would not become his mistress, and he would not ask her to become his wife.

He gathered the gelding's reins and vaulted into the saddle. It was time to put aside his foolishness and ask Lady Cynthia to marry him. She would accept. It was time he got on with his life—if he could.

A WEEK LATER Deverell found his brother sitting in the library, a half-empty decanter of liquor on the table beside him and a glass of whiskey in his hand. Something was seriously wrong.

"Langston," Dev said, striding farther into the room. "Wellington's papers are safe at the Home Office, and Mother is her usual self." He moved to stand directly in front of Langston. "She told me to come to see you."

The marquis did not bother to look up. "Why am I not surprised? She did exactly what I expected."

"I know about your having Sam at Langston Castle," Deverell said, "and I demand to know why." He frowned as Langston took a long swallow of whiskey. "But I did not expect to see you three sheets to the wind."

Langston's mouth curled as he held the glass to catch the light from a nearby candle. He studied the glowing amber liquid. "Mother did not tell you?"

Deverell snorted. "She said something about acting and a play. None of it made sense. You know how she is when there is something she wants to say but is thinking better of it."

Langston turned his dispassionate gaze on Deverell. Drunkenness had given him a modicum of numbness. His brother looked older. There were lines on his face that had not been there before and a weary cast to his eyes.

"You know why I had her there, Dev. You just don't want to admit it."

Deverell scowled. "Because of me? Or..." He didn't finish. "What happened?"

Langston downed the last of his drink and poured another. "Why don't you call me out again and be done with it, Dev?"

Langston knew he was behaving perversely, but could not stop himself. This was the meeting he had been dreading since the first time he had made love to Samantha Davidson. It had been long in coming, but ultimately not long enough.

Dev's hands curled into fists. The blood drained from his face, leaving him haggard. "You bedded her, didn't you?'' He ground his teeth. ''How could you?''

Langston laughed, an ugly sound that seemed to echo off the walls before fading into bitterness. There was no reason to deny the truth and every reason to admit it. Still, it was not easy.

''How could I not?''

''Damn you! Did it make you feel big to seduce her, to make sure that she would never accept my offer?''

More weary than he could ever remember being, Langston took a swallow of whiskey. ''It made me feel wonderful and magical . . . and deceitful. I sacrificed my honor on the altar of passion, and I would do it again.''

Deverell stared at his brother, noting the haunted cast to his eyes and the cynical twist to his lips. Then it hit him. ''You love her! You love her and won't admit it!''

Langston set his glass down and stood, moving to the desk, away from the liquor. ''I want her. I desire her. I even need her—but love her?'' He shrugged. ''I don't know.''

The fury that had driven Deverell for the past hours began to dissipate. His brother's misery was so intense that Deverell began to feel sorry for him, even to understand. God knew he had felt all of those things for Samantha Davidson. But to the degree Langston did? Witness to his brother's destructive drinking, he began to doubt it.

In fact, there had been times in Brussels when he had not even thought about Sam. He had been too busy with Wellington and the portents of war. And if he were honest, there had been the women of easy virtue to occupy his nights. No, Sam had not consumed him as she had obviously consumed Langston.

With the understanding came a lessening in his resolve to berate his brother.

"Did she come to you willingly?" he asked, both dreading and anticipating the answer, but needing to know for his own peace of mind.

"Yes."

It took all of Deverell's strength of character to say, "Then she loves you, too. Sam is not the type of woman to go to bed with you willingly otherwise."

Langston smiled, a bare curve of lips that had nothing of pleasure in it. "Then why won't she become my mistress?"

"It has gone that far, has it?" Dev could not believe his normally astute older brother's stupidity. "She won't sell herself to you, Jon. If you want her, you will have to offer your heart, and for Sam that means marriage.''

"I know.''

"Then what keeps you from it?''

"Everything,'' Langston thundered. "You. Cynthia. My heritage.''

"Don't let me stop you.'' Dev caught the sarcasm in his tone and paused. He owed it to Sam to be glad for her. She'd never been anything but honest with him. On a more even note, he added, "I may want her myself, but she wants you. I care enough for her not to stand in the way. I...I shall even endeavor to be happy for you.'' And even as he said the words, Deverell knew they were true. He would try; it was not in his nature to do otherwise. "And 'tis not as if you are engaged to Cynthia. 'Tis an understanding only, and one that I think she will let you cry off.'' He grinned roguishly. "Since her come-out, I would wager that her interest has shifted elsewhere. As for your heritage, you would not be the first man of rank to marry an actress. Nor, likely, the last.''

Langston gripped Dev's shoulder and squeezed, an old sign of affection that had fallen by the wayside during the past months. "Thank you, Dev. I do not know that your blessing makes what I did all right, but it makes it easier to know that you do not hate me for it.''

Dev covered his brother's hand with his and gripped it hard. "Then you will ask her?"

Langston stared past Deverell's shoulder. " 'Tis the only way she will take me. And heaven help me, I must have her.''

CHAPTER SEVENTEEN

SAM SHIVERED in the small confines of her Drury Lane dressing-room. For the thousandth time she wished there was a fireplace; but she knew it was not the cold that made her tremble. Langston had been in the audience tonight.

She stripped off the dress she had worn for her performance and donned the primrose evening gown she had bought for Langston's house party. The hooks were beyond her ability to reach, and she cursed herself for even bothering. She had forgotten that she'd needed Lottie to help her fasten the dress at Langston Castle. Normally she did not change clothes for the after-play gathering, but tonight she had needed the confidence the evening gown gave her.

A knock made her jump, the gown falling off her shoulders. "Who is it?"

Even as she asked, she knew. She could sense it in the tingling sensation that moved over her skin.

"Let me in, Sam. We must talk." Langston's deep voice made goose-flesh break out on her arms.

"There is nothing to discuss," she said, fumbling with the folds of the gown's bodice, knowing that Langston would not take no for an answer. She did not want him to see her like this. "Please go away," she added, jamming her arms back into the sleeves and yanking the dress over her shoulders.

The doorknob turned, and Sam cursed herself for failing to have a lock installed after Langston's last visit so long ago. With one hand behind her back, holding the dress together at her waist, and the other pushing away the heavy strands of hair that had fallen into her face, she stood her ground as he entered and closed the door behind him.

She felt alternately hot and cold, and the small dressing-room seemed to shrink with Langston's presence.

"What do you want?" she asked in a husky voice.

"You."

It was a bald statement that brooked no discussion. It sent chills down Sam's spine and made hope burst in her chest.

"Me?"

He strode toward her, not stopping until he was close enough for her to see the lines around his eyes. He looked haggard and had lost weight, but his impact on her was still devastating. She felt the heat of his body and sensed his tension.

"Heaven help me, Sam, but I cannot stay away. Ever since you left Langston Castle I have wanted you back. I thought I could deny it, but our near collision in Hyde Park showed me 'tis impossible."

The agony in his eyes told her he meant every word, and her body was leaning towards him before she even realized it. The urge to be in his arms was overwhelming. He was all she wanted, all she would ever want. Somehow she kept her sanity and pulled away from the inferno that was his desire for her.

"I won't be your mistress," she said, her voice hoarse with the strain of denying him what she wanted as badly. If only he wanted her for his wife.

He gripped her shoulders and drew her to him. "Marry me."

"What?" The word came out in a gasp. Her hand fell away from the back edges of her gown as she leaned into his clasp and searched his face. "Do not play this cruel joke on me, Langston."

His mouth twisted. "The cruel joke is on me. I am asking you to marry me."

Even in her shock, she understood what he meant. He did not want to marry her, did not think she was good enough to marry.

"But you do not want to."

He stared down at her. "No, I do not want to, but I must. 'Tis the only way to have you. I know that."

It was true. As much as she loved him, she would not raise her daughter under any other circumstances. Sam had never had a normal family, her real father dying while she was a baby and her mother's second husband treating her like an unpaid servant. Still, she believed in the importance of family ties and she wanted Amalie to believe in it, too.

"You would never be happy as my mistress," he said. "You would resent me and eventually grow to hate me. I do not want that."

Once more Sam was amazed at his perceptiveness, but immediately realized she should not be. It was his gift, what made him so effective in the Commons and so well liked by his constituents. It was part of him.

But she could never marry him. He did not love her, he simply desired her, and there was a world of difference between the two.

"Please, leave," she said. "I'm sorry. I cannot, will not, marry you."

"Damnation!" he said, yanking her to him. "I'll be damned if I let you go."

His mouth crushed hers. It seemed an eternity since he had kissed her. Bliss made Sam's knees weak and her body pliant as she sank into his embrace.

His tongue delved deeply into her mouth. His hands roamed her back, slipping to her hips to pull her close to his arousal. Sam clung to the lapels of his jacket, her mind spinning, her body tingling. This was ecstasy. Denying it was hell.

Feebly at first, then with more force, she pushed against him, twisting her head to free her mouth from his. "Stop, Jon. We must stop this madness."

Her hands slids from the folds of his jacket, down his arms to his wrists and tried to pull his fingers from their mesmerizing ministrations to her back and hips.

"I will not marry you. No matter how you make me want you." She gasped as his mouth traced the curve of her neck.

"How can you deny this?" he murmured, kissing the hollow near her throat.

"Because I must," Sam replied, straining to escape him.

His mouth roamed lower, and Sam thought she was losing her mind in the pleasure he gave her, despite all her resolve to resist him.

A knock at the door made them leap apart. Langston's eyes were darkly brilliant as he continued to gaze at her. Sam realized the bodice of her gown had fallen to her waist and that he was feasting on the swell of her breasts, so evident beneath the thin veil of her chemise.

"Who is it?" she managed to ask.

"Sam. Samantha, 'tis me. Deverell."

The sharp intake of Langston's breath drew Sam's attention. He was pale and drawn, as though a sword had been thrust between his ribs and all the blood drained from his body. Sam had to do something to ease his devastation.

"Lord Deverell, I...I am not dressed. Please come back later." She looked frantically around the room for her robe. It lay where she had left it, across a rickety, straight-backed chair. She grabbed it up and thrust her arms into the sleeves. "Or better yet, I shall meet you in the back room. Later."

"Are you all right, Sam?" Deverell's worried voice filtered through the door. "You don't sound like yourself."

Sam glanced at Langston and quickly away. "Yes. Yes, I am fine. I am just tired from the play."

She waited until she could no longer hear his footsteps receding before speaking to Langston. "You must go. I do not think either one of us wants your brother to find you here."

Langston ran his fingers through his hair, pushing it back from his forehead. "He already knows about us."

"What? You told him?" It was too much. "First your mother and now your brother? You...you bastard. Get out."

His eyes narrowed and a muscle twitched in his jaw, but he said nothing before striding from the room. Sam watched with tear-filled eyes and cursed herself for a fool. But there was no time for weakness. She had told Lord Deverell she would meet him, and she would. She had given her word.

She managed to get one of the other actresses to hook the dress. Before leaving the room, she took a rosebud from the vase of flowers that had been sent to her room and secured it in her hair.

Minutes later she paused at the doorway to the crowded room and studied the occupants, looking for Lord Deverell. She had no wish to be accosted by some other buck and caught in the social whirl that would keep her here later than she wanted. Then she saw him. Deverell was leaning against the wall on the opposite side of the room, his attention on the glass of champagne in his hand.

Sam pasted a smile on her face and threaded her way through the milling dandies, bucks, actresses and actors. When someone tried to engage her in conversation, she simply widened her smile and kept moving.

"Lord Deverell," she finally said, feeling as though she had run through a barricade of lances. "I did not know you were back from Brussels."

He grinned at her, but Sam saw the sadness in his eyes. "I brought a courier packet from Wellington to the Home Office." He paused, his gaze roving over her. "You look well, Sam."

She forced herself to return his smile and hoped her eyes were not as revealing as his. "Thank you. So do you."

He chuckled, but it was not a happy sound. "Brussels agrees with me. It is exciting and momentous. History is being made there." He paused and his face became serious. "I must return tomorrow. That is why I wanted to speak with you tonight."

Sam nodded, looking away from his penetrating perusal. Her inclination was to excuse herself, but somehow, in some odd way, she felt she owed him this chance to end things.

"I . . . I know you won't accept my offer of marriage," he said. "And in spite of the ring, I think I gave up when I left for Brussels. You are not the sort of woman to be bought by money and position, and I respect you for it." His mouth twisted wryly. "Although I could wish you different for my own benefit."

Sam sensed rather than saw the curiosity of the people around them. Lord Deverell's pursuit of her had never been discreet. Putting a hand on his arm, she suggested, "Why don't you escort me home? It will be more private."

He nodded his agreement.

Outside, he offered her his arm, and by mutual consent they began walking in the direction of her house. The night was brisk, the moon a brilliant sickle. Spring was still only a teasing whiff of warm air during the daylight hours.

He was the first to speak. "Will you marry Jon?"

She tripped, but his arm beneath hers kept her from falling. "Marry Langston?"

"Don't come the innocent with me, Sam. You see, I know Jon loves you. He spoke with me."

Sam caught her breath. "He told you he loves me?"

"Not in so many words," Deverell said softly. "He loves you, Sam, although he does not realize it. His first wife betrayed him with another man. Stephen is not Jon's son, and Jon has never forgotten that."

Sam stopped and turned to face Deverell, shock making her cold. "Not his son? How could she do such a thing to him, to both of them?" Bemusement made her mind whirl. "That explains a great deal."

Dev shrugged. "How can anyone betray another? I don't know. But she did, and it has affected Jon's whole life."

"Poor Stephen...and Jon," she murmured, her heart breaking for the little boy with no father and the man with a son who was not his own. A son who would always remind him of his wife's betrayal.

"It has been difficult for the entire family," Dev said with feeling. "Jon has suffered a great deal. That is why I had to talk to you." He put his hands on her shoulders, and his eyes held hers. "When he asks you to marry him, Sam, accept."

She stared at Deverell, seeing the sincerity in his eyes. "I... He already has. I... I refused him."

"What!"

Sam turned away. "I cannot marry him. I know he needs a wife, that Stephen needs a mother, but I am not that woman." She took a deep breath to still the rapid beat of her heart. "I do not believe that Langston loves me. A marriage between us would only sow discontent and pain. For both of us. For our children. I cannot."

Dev gently shook her. "You are wrong. I know it. Jon loves you. Otherwise he never would have betrayed me. You have to understand the kind of man he is."

Anger began to course through Sam, her defense against the argument Deverell presented so well. "He does not. He lusts after me—" she shook her head "—but he does not love me. And I will not condemn us both to a marriage without love, because sooner or later lust will burn itself out and there will be nothing left." She twisted from his grasp. "No. Better to let it go now than pay for an indiscretion the rest of our lives."

"Give him a chance."

Sam smiled wanly at him. "Thank you, Lord Deverell, but I don't think there is any more to discuss. Although . . . I am curious about why you are suddenly supporting him."

Deverell shrugged. "Because he is my brother and I love him. Because he loves you and I think you feel the same for him. Because you don't love me."

"I see." And she did. Lord Deverell had matured from the devil-may-care rake who had sought her out just months before. He was beginning to consider other people's needs and desires before his own.

When they reached her door, Lord Deverell took her hand and said, "Please, think about what we have said." When she opened her mouth to protest, he stopped her by putting a finger to her lips. "I have learned much in the past months. I have seen men and women play at love, and...have participated myself. I have watched people destroy themselves. But I have also seen the power of love in the rebuilding of my parents' marriage. Don't turn your back on Jon."

Helpless at his entreaty, Sam forbore further denial. Sadly she watched him leave, his boots ringing on the cobblestones.

The next day was no easier than the night before. At noon a messenger delivered a dozen red damask roses to Sam's door. The accompanying note said they were from Langston. Sam told the man there would be no reply, then closed the door and buried her face in the fragrant blooms.

A KNOCK on the library door interrupted Langston from his work on his Poor Laws bill. It had not yet passed the Lords, and worrying that it might not, he was making notes regarding further revisions.

"Who is it?" he said sharply.

The door opened a crack. "'Tis I, Papa," Stephen said hesitantly. "May I talk to you? Please?"

Langston set down his quill and ran his fingers through his hair. He had been on edge all week, and his temper was short, yet he did not have the heart to deny his son's request. Stephen asked very little of him. And he was determined to be a better father.

As Stephen approached, Langston studied him, the boy who was his heir and yet not of his body. He could no longer deny the tenderness he felt for the child, had always felt.

"Papa," Stephen began, sitting stiffly in a chair in front of the desk and wringing his hands as he spoke, "I know you are busy, but...I miss Mrs. Davidson. I miss Amalie."

Langston felt as though the boy had hit him over the head with a brick. He had to choose his words with care.

"I can understand that you miss them. Amalie was a playmate and Mrs. Davidson often joined the two of you. But, after all, you only knew them for a fortnight, Stephen."

The boy looked solemnly at his father, his eyes older than his years. "But you were nicer then. You spent more time with me when they were there. Now you are busy all day."

Langston sighed. "I brought you here to London with me, didn't I?"

"Yes, but I might as well be at Langston Castle for all I see of you." He paused, then blurted, "Why don't you love me?"

Taken aback, Langston realized that he should have seen the question coming. Stephen rarely came to talk with him, and never about the amount of time they spent together. Noting the disillusionment and need in Stephen's eyes, Langston knew he had to tell the boy the truth. It would not be easy.

He rose and walked around the desk and pulled up a chair to sit beside Stephen. He reached for the boy's hand. A wariness entered Stephen's eyes, but he remained silent.

"Stephen," Langston said, picking his words carefully, "I have something to tell you, something that you were not old enough to understand before. But I think you are now."

Before Langston could continue, Stephen said, "I am not your son, am I?"

Oh, God! The pain in the child's eyes, the anguish in his voice, were beyond anything Langston had imagined. He shook his head. "No, you are not, but your mother was my wife, so in the eyes of the world you are my son."

Stephen's thin shoulders began to shake, and his narrow face crumpled. It was more than Langston could stand. With a muttered curse, he pulled the boy onto his lap and into his arms.

Long minutes later, when Stephen's hiccuping sobs became sporadic, Langston drew a handkerchief from his pocket and handed it to him. After the boy blew his nose with a loud, defiant honk, Langston asked gently, "Who told you?"

"No one, really. 'Twas gossip. Spec-speculation by the servants. They say I don't look at all like you." Stephen shrugged, his shoulders rising and falling in fatal resignation. "And you never...never seemed to want to be with me. Not as Mrs. Davidson wanted to be with Amalie."

It was the truth. Oh, Lord, what had he done? For all his concern for the less fortunate of the world, he had allowed his dead wife's betrayal to cause him to close his heart to a small boy who needed him more than anyone. He had so feared another betrayal that he hadn't allowed himself to love another man's son.

And it had taken Samantha Davidson's visit to his home for this child to realize what was missing. Remorse twisted his gut as he hugged Stephen to him.

"Stephen, the circumstances of your birth will never come between us again. Please forgive me...son."

CHAPTER EIGHTEEN

ALICIA, Duchess of Rundell, contemplated what her grandson had just told her. During the past ten years, she had become the child's confidante and in the process had grown to love him fiercely, as though he truly were her flesh and blood.

"Please, Grandmother," Stephen pleaded, "you know he was different. He..." It took great courage for the boy to continue, to admit that his own father did not love him. "He was nicer to me when she was with us, although he is trying now. I thought he might even be starting to care for me...a little."

"Oh, Stephen, my dear. Come here," Alicia said, holding out her arms. When he came closer but declined the embrace, she smiled. He was at the age when little boys no longer wanted to be coddled by a grandparent. "If you will not let me hold you, then sit here beside me."

He took the seat, close enough to touch her but distant enough to feel adult. "Grandmother, please help me find her. Father said he asked her to marry him." His blue eyes round and big with longing, he whispered, "She refused. I did not think anyone would refuse him anything."

The shock took Alicia's breath away. Langston had asked the actress to marry him? What was happening? It was an effort to hide her reaction from Stephen; he was so sensitive.

"When did he ask her?"

"I don't know. He told me yesterday." He shook his head in bewilderment. "I really want her to become my mother. She is kind. And she spends time with me."

Alicia's heart was wrenched by his misery. She had always known Stephen's life had little love in it, and whenever possible she had tried to be a mother to him, as well as a grandparent. Evidently she had not been as successful as she had hoped.

Against his will, she gathered him to her, and to her astonishment, he allowed it. That alone told her how tormented he was.

Smoothing the ebony hair from his forehead, she said, "I will speak with him, dear. I will do what I can."

And she would. She loved her son, and he must truly care for the Davidson woman if he had asked her to marry him. But did the actress care for Langston? Perhaps not. She had refused him. Alicia sighed.

She loved this child. He was the light of her life, even though he was more often in the country at Langston Castle than in Town with her. He was not responsible for the fact of his birth. And Stephen was right. At Langston Castle, Jon *had* been more approachable and *had* spent more time with the boy.

If Mrs. Davidson would ease Stephen's pain, then surely that was more important than her profession or her past.

LANGSTON COMMITTED Winkly's most recent missive to memory before throwing it into the fire. The vicar of the parish where Samantha claimed to have been wedded did not remember marrying Mr. and Mrs. Charles Davidson. And the register did not mention their union. A Mr. Josiah Thomas was the vicar who signed the church's record that day, a man no one in the community claimed to know anything about. Winkly was looking for Mr. Thomas. Langston's return message to the Bow Street Runner was to find the acting troupe Charles Davidson had been with and the identity of the other party investigating Charles Davidson's whereabouts.

Langston frowned as he paced to the window and gazed out at the garden that was beginning to come out of its winter sleep. Who else could be concerned with Charles Davidson? The man was legally dead—that was the first thing Winkly had confirmed.

A knock on the door interrupted his reverie. "Excuse me, my lord," the footman said, "but a note has just arrived from the Duchess of Rundell, and she requests an answer be sent back with the messenger."

Her note was short and terse. She wanted him to call on her immediately, and she didn't give any reason.

"Tell the messenger that I shall be there shortly. Have the phaeton brought round."

It was a quick ride, the air brisk and the sun bright. The streets were crowded as usual, but no challenge to the skills of a member of the Four-in-Hand Club. On the way, Langston refused to dwell on why his mother had summoned him, for he knew from experience that the reason could be anything.

When he arrived, the butler informed him that she was in the morning-room.

"Langston," Alicia said in reply to her son's peremptory knock. "Thank you for coming so promptly." She smiled at him, determined to start as she meant to go on. "Have a seat."

He did so. The morning-room, which faced east, gathered the early sun, so it was bright and cheerful. It was where his mother handled the household accounts and her personal correspondence. In one corner was a delicate Sheraton desk, in another an embroidery frame. He eyed her warily.

Her smile widened. She knew he would be more apt to speak openly if he was unsure what this was all about and had not had time to prepare an answer. She knew how persuasive and downright evasive he could be when he chose.

"Tea?"

"No, thank you, Mother." He lounged back in the overstuffed chintz chair, his legs sprawled in front of him. "Don't try to distract me. 'Tis not every day you send an urgent message."

Realizing that he was going to be direct, Alicia said, "No, 'tis not. But nor 'tis every day that Stephen tells me his father has proposed marriage to an actress."

Langston's eyes narrowed. "I should have known he'd tell you after spending the night here."

She smiled gently. "Yes, you should have, dear. Will you please tell me now?"

He pushed out of the chair and strode to the window and back again. "There is not much to tell. I want her. Marriage is the only way."

Bald words, spoken harshly and quickly. They told Alicia more than any speech. There was an air of tension about her son that was not normal. In fact, the last time she had seen him in this state had been at Langston Castle when he'd first told her about his relationship with the actress.

"But she has refused."

"Yes." He held Alicia's gaze. "She turned me down. I know Stephen wants her for a mother, but I cannot make her have me."

"What about Deverell?" Alicia knew it was beside the point, but she did not understand what it was about the actress that made her so irresistible to two of her sons.

Langston shrugged, the gesture belying the tightness of his body. "Dev understands. He wanted her, too."

Alicia nodded, not understanding anything. "Why don't you take her for your mistress, as you suggested Deverell do?"

"For the same reason he would not do it. She refuses. And she has a small daughter whom she would die to protect and for whom she will not set a less than normal example." He shook his head. "No, Samantha Davidson will never become any man's kept woman. She would not want that stigma for her child." He took a deep breath.

More confused than ever, Alicia nevertheless recognized the pain her son felt. Something had happened to Langston. He had always been her sensible, pragmatic child. Now he was as emotional as Deverell.

"What are you going to do?"

He ran his fingers through his hair. "I don't know. Pursue her, I guess."

The next question had to be asked. "What will you do about Cynthia? She expects an offer from you. Her parents expect it."

His mouth twisted in a smile that held no humor. "I know, but somehow I doubt that Cynthia will be devastated. Much as I like and respect her and her parents, I know that our marriage would have been one of convenience for both of us. In fact, many times I felt that Cynthia's interest lay elsewhere, but that in deference to her parents she intended to accept me." He shrugged. "I chose her from friendship, not love. And I already have my heir, so if she had strayed it would not have been a catastrophe."

"You may be correct," Alicia said, remembering Cynthia's covert glances at the Earl of Ravensford, glances to which the earl seemed oblivious.

Langston sank back into the chair. "So there you have it, Mother. It explains nothing, but that is the way it is."

She smiled tenderly at him. "I cannot lie to you and say I am glad, but I do understand."

He returned her smile. "I think you do. Your marriage has not been an easy one."

"No, but your father and I have managed to stay together and find love with each other. 'Tis more than most people ever have." She paused. "And if you truly love Samantha Davidson, then I will not stand in your way—and I will see to it that your father does not, either."

His smile disappeared. "Thank you, Mother. But I do not know whether I love her, only that I must have her and marriage is the only way."

TWO DAYS LATER the Duchess of Rundell looked down at her grandson's carefully brushed hair. Stephen sat close to her in the Rundell carriage, his gloved hands fiddling with the hem of his coat. He was almost as nervous as she was.

"Grandmother, do you think she will see us? She has refused to see Father." Worry puckered his face.

Alicia smiled with a confidence she did not feel. While she had no doubt the actress would see them, she was not sure the woman would believe them and agree to accept Langston. But she had done much thinking and watching in the past several days, and she could no longer bear the sight of Langston's suffering, much less Stephen's.

"She will see us, dear. And she will do what we ask." She put an arm around Stephen, as much to comfort herself as him, she admitted wryly. "We shall persuade her to marry your father."

A sigh of relief escaped her grandson. "I knew you would make everything all right, Grandmother."

A cold frisson of anxiety skated down Alicia's spine. Stephen put such faith in her that there were times when it alarmed her. She prayed she was not about to disappoint him.

Instead of sending her servant to knock on the door, Alicia bade her to stay in the carriage with Stephen and went to the door herself. She sensed that coming here as the mighty Duchess of Rundell would not accomplish her goal. She would have to come as a mother concerned about the happiness of her son.

Lottie answered the door and gaped. She knew Quality when she saw it. Real Quality, not the likes of the trumped-up men and women who pretended to be more than they were. This lady was Quality from the top of her fashionable ostrich-feather-trimmed hat to the soles of her expensive kid slippers.

When Alicia introduced herself, Lottie pushed her spectacles back up the bridge of her nose to make sure she was seeing clearly and said, "Begging your pardon, Your Grace, but you must have the wrong house.''

Alicia smiled. "Is this the residence of Mrs. Davidson?''

Lottie nodded in mute shock.

"Then I am at the right place. May I come in, and will you please summon your mistress?''

The words were phrased as a request, but Lottie recognized an order when she heard one, no matter how graciously it was couched. "Come this way,'' she said, ushering the regal lady into the parlor. "I'll get Miss Sam right away, I will.''

Lottie rushed into the kitchen where Sam was baking bread. Amalie was sitting on a stool nearby.

"Lottie, what—'' Sam began.

"Miss Sam, come quick. Take off your apron and wipe your hands. The Duchess of Rundell is in the parlor. Waiting for you.''

The spate of words was another indicator of Lottie's excitement. Sam was tempted to tease her old servant, but thought better of it, seeing the anxiety in Lottie's eyes. That, and the feeling of butterflies dancing in her own stomach.

"Mama,'' Amalie piped up, "may I go and see her, too?''

Gently but firmly Sam said, "No, dear. You stay here with Lottie. I shall go see Her Grace and ask why she has troubled to call.'' Although she already knew. The duchess was here to tell her to stay away from Langston.

Sam wiped her flour-covered hands as best she could and removed the apron from her black kerseymere dress. She tucked several stray strands of hair behind her ears and shrugged. The duchess had not announced her intent and therefore would have to take Sam as she was.

When she reached the closed door to the parlor, Sam hesitated. But she could not turn back. She was no coward. Throwing her shoulders back and lifting her chin, Sam sailed into the room.

"Mrs. Davidson." Alicia moved away from the window where she had been keeping an eye on her carriage. "Thank you for seeing me."

Sam inclined her head graciously and suppressed a wry smile. Like her son, the duchess would not have taken no for an answer even if Lottie had refused her admittance.

"What did you wish to see me about, Your Grace?"

"May I sit?"

Sam's eyes narrowed. "Of course. I did not realize we had anything to say to each other that would require more than a moment's time."

"We do," the duchess said, sinking into one of the lumpy, faded chairs, "but you could not know that."

Sam sat, also, but she was unable to match the duchess's calm.

"Mrs. Davidson, why did you refuse Langston's offer of marriage?" Alicia asked in a reasonable tone.

It was the last question Sam expected. It took all her will-power to keep her eyes on the other woman's face and not look away from her intense scrutiny.

"I do not believe that is any of your concern, Your Grace."

"I can see that the events of Langston Castle have predisposed you badly toward me." Alicia sighed. "I did what I felt I had to. You have a child, Mrs. Davidson. Put yourself in my position. I was afraid that you would ruin Langston's chance of happiness with Lady Cynthia." More softly she added, "He has not had an easy time in his relations with women. He was in love with his first wife, you see . . ."

Sam kept her attention on the other woman, trying desperately to ignore the pain caused by the mention of Langston's love for another woman. She should be past that by now.

"She betrayed him with another man." The skin around the duchess's mouth tightened. "She died giving birth to Langston's heir, but Stephen is not Langston's son."

Knowing it would do no good to tell the duchess that Lord Deverell had already imparted this information to her, Sam merely said, "That explains a great deal."

"Yes, it does."

"But why are you telling me this? It has nothing to do with me."

Alicia smiled sadly. "I wish it did not." Her smile twisted. "I will not lie to you and pretend that I am glad to be here, but I will be honest and tell you that my son's happiness depends on you."

"Wha-what do you mean?"

"Langston does not realize it, but he is in love with you."

Sam gave a tiny gasp. The duchess's statement made her tremble with all her suppressed hopes and dreams. But love was too great a gift for it to be possible. "I find that hard to believe."

The duchess shrugged. "If I did not believe the truth of it, I would not be here asking you to accept his proposal of marriage."

Sam's fingers pleated the skirts of her gown, too overwhelmed to speak.

In matter-of-fact tones, the duchess said, "As the Marchioness of Langston, you would be wealthy, able to provide anything for your child. You would never have to worry about money. You would have a position of power and influence, although your past career as an actress would bar you from the more strict drawing-rooms of the *ton*.'' She waved her hand in airy dismissal. ''But that is of little import. And one day you would be the Duchess of Rundell, wife to the most powerful nobleman in England.''

Sam's disbelief was rapidly turning to anger at the duchess's assumption that the material gains mattered. In a tightly controlled voice, she said, ''You do not understand, Your Grace. Your son does *not* love me. And I will not compromise my values. As soon as he tires of me, he will regret the passion that drove him to marriage. Then where will we be?''

''But I do understand,'' the duchess said compassionately. ''The duke did not marry me for love—he married me for my dowry and convenience. Over the years we have been through some hard times, but we stayed together, and today we are in love.'' A faraway look filled her beautiful grey eyes. ''It was not easy, and there was great pain, but there has also been great joy. And if I could do it over again, I would not change a thing. It was all necessary.''

Sam refused to be moved. Rising, she said, ''Thank you for coming, Your Grace, but I do not believe there is anything you can say to convince me.''

Alicia rose, as well, her concentration centered on the stubborn woman before her. "If you will not listen to me, then perhaps you will listen to someone else."

Alicia strode from the room while Sam watched in bewilderment. Minutes later she returned with Stephen.

"Stephen!"

"Hello, Mrs. Davidson," the boy said almost shyly.

Sam looked from child to grandparent. "Why?"

The duchess released Stephen's hand, saying, "I shall let him explain."

"Please, Mrs. Davidson," he said, his young voice cracking. "Please marry my father."

Stephen's eyes pleaded with Sam, and it was nearly impossible to deny him. He had suffered so much for sins that were not his own.

Before she told him no and extinguished the hope in his eyes, the sort of hope she well understood, she asked, "Why, Stephen? What difference would it make to you?"

He expelled a lungful of air in relief. "Because he was nicer to me when you were around. He did things with me, with us. I . . ." He looked away, as though what he had to say was too hard, as though he could not bear to see her expression when he said it. "I began to think he might grow to love me."

The last sentence was a tortured whisper, a cry from a lonely boy's heart. It broke Sam's.

She gathered him to her and held him tightly, realizing that he was sobbing. When at last his tears subsided, the duchess extended a handkerchief, which Sam used to wipe the moisture from Stephen's face.

He stepped back slightly and gave her a wavering smile. "I am sorry. I didn't mean to blubber and embarrass you."

"Oh, Stephen," Sam said softly, "you did not embarrass me. You could never do that."

The duchess said, "You could do much for him and yourself, Mrs. Davidson. And I think you could also help my son."

Sam did not know what to do or say. It was all so impossible. Langston did not love her. He could not. And yet...

She took a calming breath. "I shall have to think about what you have said. I did not know that my presence had made such a difference in his treatment of Stephen, and I thought that Lady Cynthia would make Stephen a good mother. This is all very confusing."

"Langston will never wed Lady Cynthia," the duchess said. "She was his choice of bride for a marriage of convenience. Then you came along." A tinge of bitterness entered her words. "No, Lady Cynthia is no longer a possibility."

"I see," Sam said quietly. "But I need time to think."

LONG AFTER the duchess and Stephen had left, Sam sat in the lumpy chintz chair and stared into the blackened grate of the fireplace.

She knew Langston desired her, and she knew Stephen cared greatly for her. She had not expected a woman of the duchess's ilk to accept her, and yet that seemed to have happened. Perhaps there was some validity in what the woman and her grandchild had said.

Perhaps Langston did care for her.

It was a bitter-sweet consideration, and yet... And yet, if it was true, then her greatest happiness was within reach.

And there were the children to consider. Amalie would never want for anything, and Stephen believed that there was a chance his father would grow to love him. Amalie's gains were a sure thing, Stephen's were a possibility born of hope. Did she have the right to take that hope from him? Did she want to?

Her eyes ached and her shoulders were on fire. She had to decide. She had to risk everything to gain all.

She had to accept Langston's proposal.

CHAPTER NINETEEN

DÉJÀ VU, Langston thought as he knocked on the door of Samantha Davidson's Covent Garden home. Only this time, he was responding to her request for a meeting. The note had arrived early this morning, explaining nothing, only asking him to come to her. Was she going to tell him to stop pursuing her? Or accept his proposal of marriage?

His gut clenched.

In the crowded street behind Langston, his groom walked the stallion, careful to avoid the wagons full of vendors' produce on their way to Covent Garden market. Women stood on their doorsteps shaking out rugs or exchanging gossip. It was a friendly scene, reminiscent of life in Langston Village.

It did nothing to ease Langston's tension. Just when he was beginning to think that the note must have been a cruel prank, Lottie opened the door. She studied him with a jaundiced eye before saying, "Miss Sam is waiting for you."

He entered and handed her his beaver hat and gold-tipped cane before going to the parlor. Sam stood by the window, gazing at the busy street with her hands clasped behind her back. She was in profile, and he could see how pale her cheek was and the anxiety in the curve of her full lower lip.

"Sam," he said quietly, moving to her. "I am here."

Her hands fell to her sides as she turned to face him. "Thank you for coming," she murmured.

Her husky voice made him long to reach for her. She was pain and pleasure to him, a heady mix of desire and denial.

"I cannot think what you may want of me," he said, "but of course I would not refuse your summons."

Her honey-green eyes sparked before she veiled them with her long lashes. In a voice only slightly tinged with exasperation, she said, "You cannot think why I would ask you here? Both your mother and your son have called on me."

His eyes narrowed as her words sank in. "You want me to tell them to leave you alone."

She sighed and turned away. "No," she whispered.

Barely able to hear her, he reached for her shoulders and turned her to face him again. "Then what do you want?" he asked, holding himself in check even as the blood began to pound in his temples.

"I... I want to accept your proposal of marriage."

Exultation crashed through him. The urge to crush her to him, to make her his, was intense. His fingers tightened on her shoulders, drew her closer. But much as he wanted her, suspicion kept him from kissing her.

"What did my mother and son say to you?"

She turned her head from his narrow-eyed scrutiny. "They..." A sigh escaped her. "They asked me to marry you—for Stephen's sake."

He stared at her, seeing the truth of her words, and yet sensing that she withheld something. "What else?"

She brought her gaze back to his face and swallowed. His grip intensified.

"Your mother said you love me, but do not realize it."

"What!" He released her, almost flinging her from him in his anger. "She had no right to say that. Just as she had no right to come here in the first place."

"But she did. They both did." Her chin was held high and she met his ire defiantly. "I did not beg them to come to me, and I did not tell them what I would do. I leave that between us—something you have not always done."

He glared at her, recognizing her reference to his mother's tampering while they had been at Langston Castle. "So you have decided to wed me because of my son."

She held herself in such a way that her very bearing was a challenge. "Yes. Should I be marrying you for love?"

He knew she was trying to provoke him. She wanted him to say he loved her, but he could not. He pivoted abruptly and strode to the door. Then he stopped and faced her. "No. You should be marrying for the benefits it will give you and your daughter. You should be accepting me because it is the only way you will come to me, although we both know that marriage is the last thing I want."

Before she could answer, before he could see the hurt inflicted by his words, he left. Slamming the front door behind, Langston signaled to his groom. He vaulted into the saddle and set off at a pace dangerously fast for the traffic in the streets.

But he did not care. Nothing mattered except that Samantha Davidson had accepted his offer. Soon she would be his marchioness, and the devil take the consequences.

THE MORNING WEDDING was held in the magnificent ballroom in the Duke of Rundell's Town
house. The ceilings were two stories high and
painted and molded in a baroque style. Cream
wallpaper with gold-embossed roses covered the
walls between floor-to-ceiling mirrors. The floors
were polished mahogany on which the candlelight
from three massive chandeliers shone like moonlight off a lake.

And when the vicar performing the marriage
spoke, his voice echoed in the nearly empty room.
The only persons present were the Duke and
Duchess of Rundell, Lord Deverell, Stephen,
Amalie and Lottie. Langston's brother Alaistair
and his wife, Liza, were still in Brussels, because
they had not been given enough notice of the wedding to return in time.

The reception was not much larger. The Earl of
Ravensford, a few theatre people and several of
Langston's political cronies attended. Ravensford
approached Sam while the others were filling their
plates with breakfast foods.

"Congratulations," he said. "If you ever tire of
Langston, don't forget me."

"Thank you, Lord Ravensford," she said, her
eyes skimming the room for her husband. Husband.

"Excuse me," Lord Deverell interrupted. "If you don't mind, Ravensford, I would like to speak to the bride in private. After all, I *am* the one who found her."

Ravensford made an exaggerated bow and left. "*Au revoir,* Lady Langston."

For a second, Sam did not know to whom he spoke. Then it hit her. She was not only Langston's wife, she was a marchioness!'

"Don't let Ravensford fluster you, Sam," Deverell said, taking her arm and steering her from the reception and into an adjacent room that was smaller and cozier. Instantly he released her and put a little distance between them.

"What do you wish to speak with me about?" she asked. In the back of her mind was a niggling worry that if Langston found them like this, he would think the worst.

He looked at her, his chin stubborn. "I obtained permission to return just for this occasion." When he paused, Sam nodded her head to encourage him. "I wanted to tell you...to let you know... Oh, dash it all. This is not as easy as I thought," he said vehemently.

Sam smiled gently, her apprehensions evaporating in the face of Deverell's extreme discomfort. "'Tis all right, Lord Deverell. I am not going to snap at you."

He grinned sheepishly. "'Tis Dev now. You are part of the family, and that is what I wanted to talk about. I am glad. That is, I wish you had married me, but Jon needs you more. And I hope there will not be an awkwardness between us."

"That is very kind of you."

His grin became lopsided. "No, 'tis not. But I see that it is necessary, because you love him."

So simply spoken, and so true. But how many people knew her secret? "Why do you say that?"

He came and took both her hands in his and raised them to his lips. "Because I know you well enough to know you would not marry otherwise."

Sam squeezed Deverell's fingers and stood on tiptoe to kiss his cheek. "You have matured."

"I have lived through a lot," he said solemnly.

"Haven't we all," Langston's deep voice said quietly from the doorway.

Sam and Deverell sprang apart. Chills chased down Sam's spine as she waited tensely for her husband's next words. Deverell spoke first.

"Glad you could join us, brother. I was just telling Sam that she will be good for you."

Sam glanced at her brother-in-law, worried that he was trying to provoke her husband. The roguish grin on Deverell's face reassured her.

Langston strode into the room and put his arm around Sam's waist, drawing her to him. "Thank you, Dev," he said softly. "I can think of no better wedding gift than your blessing."

"You have it, Jon." His grin widened. "Just name your first-born after me."

"What if 'tis a girl?" Sam said lightly, relief at the affection between the brothers making her giddy.

"Your first-born son, then," Deverell said. "Now 'tis time I went and talked to that Miss Julie. Your understudy is a very attractive young woman." He left with a wicked glint in his hazel eyes.

Langston chuckled. "Perhaps Dev has not matured all that much, after all. He seems back to his old self."

And what about you? Sam wanted to ask, but knew it would not ease the strain between them. She could feel the tensile strength in his arm around her and hear the sharp intake of his breath. He was as uncomfortable with their new relationship as she was.

It had not been an easy road to this destination.

Softly she asked, "And where are we, my lord?"

He stared at her for long minutes without speaking, then shrugged. "I am not sure."

If only he would mention love, Sam thought wistfully. Unable to continue this painful line of thought, she sighed and changed the subject.

"Have you looked further into what Huntly said about Charles?" The knowledge that the man might still be alive had preyed on her mind.

He turned from her to throw himself into a shadowed chair. "Yes. I think he is bluffing, but I do have someone on the case."

She moved closer in order to better see his face. "Perhaps we should wait for definite confirmation before making our marriage public."

He scowled. "Why? Are you afraid that marriage to me will dampen your success at Drury Lane?"

Sam made a moue. "Nothing of the sort, and you know it. 'Tis you who will not benefit from our union. 'Tis you who will be made fun of by your peers, not me." She smiled sardonically. "All the people I know will think I have pulled off the coup of the century." Wistfully she added, "And I have arranged to retire from the stage at the end of next month. I would leave sooner, but feel obligated. It was made clear to me that if I left precipitately the theatre would lose money this season."

He studied her. "You know the *ton* will never accept you. The men will lust after you, and their wives will never let you inside their hallowed circles. Being my marchioness will not give you respectability—though some may come round in time."

Sam swallowed her gasp of hurt. "Do you think I married you for respectability?"

He sighed. "No. You married me for security. For Amalie." Quietly he added, "And for Stephen. I have no illusions about us."

"Convenience, not love," she muttered, turning from him and going to a side table, where she picked up a small Dresden shepherdess. In the dim light, she could just make out a hairline crack, which had been mended by an expert.

"Never love," he murmured, rising and going to her. Gently he took the porcelain figure from her and replaced it on the table. "My father threw this against the wall when he learned my mother had run away with another man."

"What?" Sam turned into the warmth of his body.

"Yes," he said, the corners of his mouth rising in an expression that was not really a smile. "Mother wanted love, and another man offered it. She went with him."

Sam felt the blood drain from her face as understanding dawned. "Your wife *and* your mother."

"And all for love."

"What happened?" she asked quietly, knowing he had to tell her these things before he could come to her as a husband.

"My brother, Alaistair, caught up with my mother. He horsewhipped her lover and left him for dead." His lips twisted. "My father was so shocked by mother's act that he re-evaluated what he felt for her. After three children and twenty-seven years of marriage, he realized he was in love with her."

"A happy ending," Sam said softly.

"So it appears," he said, nodding his head slightly.

"And what about us?" she asked. "Do you think we will have a happy ending?"

He gazed down at her, hunger in his eyes and in his body. "I don't know. I hope so. I sincerely hope so."

It was enough, Sam told herself. It had to be enough. She rose to meet his kiss.

CHAPTER TWENTY

"SAM, WHAT ARE YOU doing?" Langston's sleep-laden voice asked from the depths of the satin-wood four-poster bed they shared.

Clutching her wool robe tighter to her chest to ward off the early-morning chill, Sam said, "Lighting the fire. Spring may be upon us, but it has not made it to this room."

"Let the servants do that, Sam, and come back to bed." His voice lowered, taking on a provocative tone. "I have other requirements that only you can meet."

Sam smiled in mixed pleasure. There had been moments in the past weeks when Langston's purely physical delight in their union had made her despair of the possibility of his caring for her as a person. But she would not lie to herself by denying her own enjoyment of their lovemaking, just as she would not quash the hope lying banked in her heart that her husband might love her, too—if only a little.

She gave the embers one last poke and swish and returned to bed.

SEVERAL HOURS LATER, Sam lay sated and lethargic beside her husband.

"What are your plans for the day?" Langston asked, running his forefinger down the flank of her left leg, which was sprawled across his own.

The light caress tingled along her skin and warmed her heart. Charles Davidson had always left right after having intimate relations with her, his own urges sated and her needs ignored. But Langston was a caring man; if only she could help him to purge the bitterness in his heart. She would try.

Catching his hand and bringing it to her lips, she said, "I promised the children I would take them to the Tower of London today. They long to see the wild animals. Amalie never tires of going."

"I have a speech in the Commons, but will try to meet you there."

The tiny seed of hope in Sam's heart sent out its first tentative tendril. "That will be a treat for all of us, but don't do it at the expense of your work. That is important, too."

Sighing, he rolled away and got out of bed. "I know, but we have run into opposition. Huntly's cohorts are fighting me in the Commons, and Stoneway is contesting Ravensford in the Lords.''

Sam nodded, keeping her attention on their conversation in spite of the magnificent picture Langston's nudity presented. She never tired of his beauty. Broad shoulders banded in muscle and a taut belly that rippled before blending into sleek flanks and long legs. The sight always thrilled her.

''Is there anything I can do to help?'' she asked.

He grinned at her, a wicked glint entering his dark eyes. ''Emulate the Duchess of Devonshire and give all the Members of Parliament a kiss for their vote.''

Sam laughed, glad that he was able to see some humor in this discouraging situation. ''If I remember my scandals correctly, she kissed Charles James Fox's constituents, not his opponents in Parliament.''

''True,'' Langston said, tying the belt on his robe. ''But it would not hurt.''

''I shall see what I can do,'' she promised, rising and donning her own robe. ''But if I do not leave our room soon, James will be scandalized when he comes to dress you.''

The laughter left Langston's face. ''No, he is becoming inured to our unfashionable marriage.''

Sam's happiness faded. Unintentionally she had reminded her husband of the obsessive passion between them that had led him to propose marriage in the first place. With a wan smile, she left.

Langston felt like kicking himself. The comment about his valet's feelings had been uncalled-for and only increased the strain that underlay their marriage. He had wanted to wed Sam, and he had done so. Now he had to do his best to make this union work. The many positive things it provided should help. The physical attraction between them was strong, and she was wonderful with Stephen; the boy was blossoming under her care.

But love . . . he was not sure he could ever allow himself to love a woman again. It made a man too vulnerable, too open to betrayal.

As usual, the Tower of London was milling with children and their nannies, out to see the wild animals. Sam kept a watchful eye on her two charges as they scampered from cage to cage, their oohs and ahs making her smile.

Yet even as she enjoyed their antics, the skin between her shoulder blades pricked as though someone watched her. She had felt the sensation for the past hour, and no amount of glancing over her shoulder and seeing nothing had eased her apprehension.

"Mama," Amalie said, "when will Lord Langston arrive?"

"Yes," Stephen added, "we are almost done."

Sam smiled and pushed the unease to the back of her mind. "I don't know. I told you before that he might not be able to meet us."

Stephen's face fell, and the sight tugged at Sam's heart. Langston had been spending more time with his son, with all of them, now that they were a family. At least it was more than the boy had had before.

Langston arrived just as they were leaving.

"Almost didn't make it," he said, smiling at both children. "How would you like to go to Gunter's for ices?"

"Yes!" both children shouted simultaneously, beaming with anticipation.

Sam reached for Langston's hand and squeezed it. "You certainly know the way to a child's heart."

He returned her smile. "'Tis past time I made an effort with my son."

They reached Berkeley Square quickly and piled out of the cabriolet, the children rushing into Gunter's. Langston ordered the coveted ices for everyone while they found seats.

"Perhaps we should go back to the carriage," Sam murmured, noticing three ladies of Quality doing just that. "The waiters will bring your order."

"You are with me, and we have the children," Langston said. "If you were alone or with another woman, you might wish to."

While they spoke, a woman sitting nearby cast several less-than-covert glances their way before speaking to the man at her side.

"Isn't that *her?*" The woman's voice was pitched to carry.

The man's face reddened as he nodded.

"And with children," the woman continued.

Anger at the woman's rudeness and intent to hurt stiffened Sam's spine. "Who is she?" Sam asked Langston.

He looked over his shoulder at the couple. "No one of importance," he replied, his voice also loud enough to carry. "Certainly no one we would invite to our home."

Now it was the woman's turn to redden while her escort paled. Sam gave Langston a warm smile. He had supported her in the best way possible. The rest of their stay at Gunter's was much more comfortable.

They arrived home exhausted but happy, the children still excited about their afternoon. Langston excused himself to work on his bill, saying he would have dinner with her. Happiness at his continued attempts to be with her and the children warmed Sam's heart.

She was still smiling when Hampton, the butler, said, "My lady, a message came for you."

Sam took the note from the silver salver he held out to her. Inserting a fingernail under the wax seal, she opened the sheet and read the contents. Her blood froze.

My dearest wife,
I know you have been eagerly awaiting my return from the dead. Meet me at Green Park tonight at ten if you value your current bigamous marriage.

                                                    Charles

With hands that shook, she held the paper in the last rays of the afternoon sun and studied the black script. It did not look familiar, but then, the only time she had seen Charles's writing was when he had signed his name on the church register after they were married.

"Sam." Stephen's worried voice interrupted her awful thoughts. "Is it bad news?"

Sam made herself smile reassuringly at him. "No, nothing of the sort, dear. 'Tis only a message from ... from an old friend."

Comforted, Stephen grabbed Amalie's hand and tugged her in the direction of the kitchen, where warm milk and scones waited. The sound of their good-natured bickering floated behind them.

"Pardon me, my lady," Hampton said in a deferential tone, "but if I may be so bold, I would like to tell your ladyship that you have made a great difference in Viscount Taunton's life. The staff and I would like to thank you."

The unexpected praise eased the worry gnawing at her. "Why, thank you, Hampton. 'Tis very generous of you to say so."

He flushed to the roots of his white hair and he made her a respectful bow. It was a comfort for her to know that the servants accepted her.

Sam frowned at the sheet of paper as she mounted the stairs to her rooms. What was she going to do about this? She did not believe Charles was alive, and she and Langston had discussed Huntly's threat, deciding it was only a ploy of Huntly's to make her his mistress.

Sinking into one of the several moss-green velvet chairs in her room, Sam decided to show the note to Langston. To do otherwise would only give him reason to mistrust her, and to ignore the missive completely might create large problems for them both.

Shadows were spreading their dark tendrils about the room by the time Langston arrived. Entering through the connecting door, he paused to let his eyes adjust to the dimness. A solitary candle spilled a puddle of golden light over the table beside Sam's chair, illuminating a folded sheet of paper on the rich wood surface.

Sam sat motionless, her face shaded by the fall of her thick hair, her expression unreadable. He thought she was asleep until he saw one of her hands reach for the paper.

"Are you sickening?" he asked, concern roughening his voice as he moved towards her.

"No," she said quietly, rising to meet him halfway. Her coming to him like this never failed to warm him. It was a feeling he refused to examine too closely.

Taking her into the crook of his arm, he noted she was wearing her serviceable kerseymere gown in spite of all his efforts to convince her to spend his money on a wardrobe more befitting a marchioness. "You have not changed since your visit to the Tower. What is wrong?"

"How do you know that?" she asked, her voice tired.

"Because I recognize that old wool gown." He grinned. "You would, too, if you knew the way Stephen describes it. He calls it your 'old-lady dress.'"

She chuckled. "Like his father, he is very conscious of fashion and has mentioned several times that I should dress as befits my new station."

The throaty richness of her laugh filled him with contentment, a contentment bolstered by her likening him to the boy he was only now truly allowing himself to think of as his son. He knew he owed this contentment and acceptance to her. It was a humbling thought.

Resting her head against his shoulder, she said, "Let's sit down. I have something to show you."

After he had read the note and examined it carefully, then summoned Hampton to learn that a street urchin had delivered it, Langston burned it.

"Huntly is behind this," he said flatly. "He has not ceased to want you, damn his eyes."

"But what if 'tis true?" Sam asked in a horrified whisper, her eyes round with despair. "What if Charles really is alive? Then we . . . you and I are not married."

Langston stiffened. "I don't believe it. Furthermore, I have a Bow Street Runner looking into this matter. He cannot find the clergyman who married you, nor can he find any record of the ceremony ever taking place."

She stared at him, her mouth an O of surprise. "That is impossible. I *know* I was married."

Langston frowned at her certainty. His intuition was that the marriage had been a hoax, but even if he was wrong, he would never let her go. The small changes she had already wrought in his life were tiny miracles. They made his obsession with her more acceptable.

"First, Charles being alive is a lie. Second, if the marriage truly did take place, you will divorce him."

Sam drew away to stare at him. "I cannot do that. It would require an act of Parliament. It would ruin your political life."

"To hell with it," he said, his words out before he realized what he was saying. And only after hearing them echo in the quiet room did he realize he meant them. When had it happened? When had she begun to mean more to him than the work to which he had devoted all his adult life?

God, what was happening to him?

"Jon!" Sam gasped. "You do not mean that. Your work is your life. You have too much to offer. Your Poor Laws!"

He groaned and released her to stand and pace the room, away from her disturbing closeness that always seemed to sap his intelligence. He stopped and gazed into the fire, where the ashes of the message seemed to mock him with their reminder of his obsession with his wife. The thought of losing her to another man was intolerable.

"Get your cape," he said, making his decision. "We shall both go to meet the sender of that note."

While she did as he ordered, Langston returned to his room and went to the wall safe where he kept a matched pair of Manton dueling pistols. Each weapon held a single shot, but together they would be sufficient for his needs, should tonight's events come to violence.

At nine-forty-five, Langston instructed the driver to stop the carriage under an overhang of trees. Green Park was deserted at this hour and dark enough to mask almost anything. The coach's lanterns were the only light.

Sam sat beside him, her body pressed to his, the shivers that racked her discernible even through the layers of clothing. "Everything will go smoothly," he assured her. "But you will have to meet him, not I."

She nodded. "I know. Whoever he is, he will not be expecting you, and if he sees you, he might not show himself. We have to confront him. We must stop this before it ruins you."

He squeezed her. "Shh," he ordered. "Charles is dead, and this is just another of Huntly's ploys to win you and ruin me. It will not work."

But what if it were true? Sam thought.

She sighed and turned her head away so that he could not see her expression in the faint glow from the inside lamps. She was worried and she was frightened. Not even the Marquis of Langston could withstand the scandal of a bigamous marriage.

The sound of a horse's hooves caught their attention.

"'Tis him," Langston said, releasing her and looking out the window into the night. "Good. He is doing what I hoped and coming to the carriage. 'Tis the advantage of having the only light."

Sam swallowed the fear rising in her throat, not for herself, but for Langston. She prayed the man waiting outside the carriage was not her husband come back to haunt them.

Following the plan they had prepared, Sam stepped from the carriage to meet the lone rider. The clouds chose that moment to open and provide a window for the full moon to shine through. Silver limned the rider.

"Samantha," a melodious tenor said in ironic greeting. "I see you are prompt as always."

Sam's stomach lurched as her world sank beneath her feet, sending her plunging into an abyss of despair. Her prayers had been ignored.

It took all her courage not to let Charles Davidson realize how utterly annihilated she felt. Being weak himself, he recognized it in others and never failed to exploit it, and she had to be strong for Langston's sake.

"So, Charles, all these years you have been alive. I suppose I should not be surprised, since you left shortly after you learned I was pregnant. You never did like responsibility."

"Tut, tut, Samantha, don't be bitter. It will mar your beauty." He dismounted and walked towards her, the horse's reins held in one hand.

"Where have you been these past ten years?" she demanded, all the remembered suffering and deprivation she had experienced after his disappearance lending strength to her words.

He shrugged, and the wind picked up the edges of the cape on his coat. She noted that he was warmly and fashionably dressed. His boots were polished and appeared new, his dark hair secured under an expensive beaver hat. The horse, too, was a sign of prosperity, as she well knew. The cost of stabling a horse in London was exorbitant.

"A number of us escaped in a lifeboat. We eventually reached one of the Caribbean islands, where we were rescued. Seeing no reason to advertise my survival, I made my way to New Orleans. It was an adventure, and a very profitable one."

"Why come back now?" Even as she asked, she knew. Someone, probably Huntly, had found him and told him about her marriage. The marriage that was no longer valid.

"Don't be any more naive than you must, Samantha. It was never one of your endearing qualities," he sneered, "though the years have been kind to you, Samantha. No wonder you are the toast of London."

Sam's lip curled in disgust, both at him and at herself for ever thinking he was worthy of her affection. "Is that why you summoned me, to comment upon my looks?"

His features twisted, the moonlight accentuating the beak of his nose and the hollowness of his cheeks. "No, dear wife. I have come to offer you respectability."

Here it was, she thought. The culmination of all her fears. She was a bigamist.

"How do you propose to do that? Fake your death again?"

"Such vituperation," he drawled. "No, I shall not go that far twice, but I could be induced to disappear again before anyone else is aware that Langston is not your husband."

It seemed an eternity since this afternoon, when she and Langston had discussed the possibility that the summons was from someone wishing to blackmail her. Neither of them had admitted that the person might actually be her husband.

"What did you have in mind?" she asked.

"Fifty thousands pounds."

"What?" She gaped at him. "You are mad. That is a fortune."

"True," he said calmly, "but your husband—or should I say the man who thinks he is your husband—is as wealthy as Croesus. He will pay it in order to keep the taint of bigamy from his proud family name. Imagine the scandal."

Oh, Lord. She could imagine it too well. It would be the end of everything Langston had spent his life achieving.

"I... I don't know," she murmured, wondering what Langston was thinking as he listened to this. "I need to think. I may have to tell Langston."

"I have no doubt of it," Davidson said. "Just make sure you impress upon him the fact that I will expose you both with no qualm whatsoever if my demands are not met."

"How do I contact you?" she managed to ask.

"*I* will contact *you.*"

It was his way of keeping the upper hand, and even though she realized this, there was nothing she could do to thwart him. He held all the cards, by virtue of his very existence. In a daze, Sam watched mutely as her former and only husband mounted his horse and rode away.

She stood there, dazed, until Langston's arms closed about her, and then she sank into his embrace. Her entire body shook. "It was him. It was really him," she said, her words muffled by his greatcoat.

"Come back to blackmail you," he said, wry humor flavoring the words, taking Sam by surprise.

"How can you find this amusing?" she demanded. "He will ruin you. The scandal will destroy your bill." Her voice became a whisper. "And we are no longer married."

"That is exactly what he wants you to think."

She stepped away from the warmth and comfort of his arms and stared at him. "That is the truth. I know your Runner has found nothing, but *I was there.*"

"You were young. It could have been a hoax, and you never would have realized it."

"We were married in a church. I gave you the name, everything." She was trembling violently.

He pulled her back into the security of his embrace and smoothed the stray tendrils of hair away from her face. "I know, my love. But an experienced and devious man, as Davidson has proved to be, could easily have duped a young girl into believing the wedding was real." He sighed and stroked the smooth curve of her neck.

His words caused hope to flare in Sam's breast, only to die instantly. "It would be wonderful to think that beast is not my husband, but I remember the man who married us. He was a tall, thin fellow, with full lips and shoulder-length brown hair. He was real, believe me.''

''His name was Josiah Thomas,'' Langston said quietly, ''and he is nowhere to be found. 'Tis as though he has disappeared off the face of the earth.''

''If only Charles would do the same,'' Sam murmured, clinging to Langston as he led her back to the carriage.

She took her seat inside the vehicle and stared morosely out the open window at the night sky. What neither of them had said, although she knew it in her heart, was that she had to leave him now. She could not stay with him when they were not wed. If Charles revealed himself, as she had no reason to think he would not, the servants would gossip and Amalie would hear. She would not put her daughter through that.

And there was Langston. Everyone in the *ton* knew about their marriage, a marriage that was no longer valid. The scandal of Charles's return would ruin him. She could not let that happen. She had to leave him quickly and hope that by doing so the uproar would be short-lived and soon forgotten. It was the only way she could think of to protect this man she loved, to protect everything he had spent his life accomplishing.

Tomorrow she would tell him. For now she would cherish every second they had left.

Desperately she turned and pulled Langston's mouth to hers.

CHAPTER TWENTY-ONE

THE NEXT MORNING Langston opened the door connecting his rooms with Sam's and stopped in his tracks. "What the devil are you doing?" he roared.

Startled, Sam dropped the chemise she was folding to put into her trunk. She had thought him at the Commons.

"Jon!" she gasped.

"And what a surprise I am," he said, nearly snarling as he advanced on her.

"Um...yes. I mean, no. I mean, I thought you would be at the Commons most of the afternoon, trying to get a final vote on your Poor Laws."

"That is to be next week."

"Oh." In her anxiety this morning, she had misunderstood him.

Wrath shot from the brown depths of his hooded eyes, and his lips were a grim line.

"You were going to leave while you thought I was gone," he said flatly.

"I have to, Jon. You must see that." She took a step toward him, stopped by the fury emanating from him. "We are not married."

"You don't know that," he stated coldly.

She sighed and turned away to sink into a chair. She rubbed her temples, feeling the onset of a headache. She was not surprised. It had been several months since the last one, and they were sometimes triggered by anxiety.

"I saw Charles with my own eyes. Had I wanted to, I could have touched him." She shuddered with revulsion. "And to think I married him. How could I have been so stupid?"

He strode to her, kneeling down beside her, putting the small velvet box he was holding on the nearby table before capturing her hands with his. "You were little more than a child, Sam. You could not have known what he was really like. 'Tis in the past. Forget it." He lifted her face with one hand and held her motionless when she would have looked away. "I will not let you go. I did not want this union, but now that we are in it, I refuse to dissolve it."

A tiny sob escaped her as she searched his expression for the truth of his words—and saw that it was so. He would never let her leave. She knew it was his pride and arrogance that formed his resolve.

"What about Amalie?" she asked. "I do not want her involved in a scandal. Or Stephen."

"Sam, Sam," he murmured, shaking his head. "You forget how unhappy Stephen was before you came. And you forget how worried you were about Amalie's future. Money can buy a future for her, and it can lay to rest a great deal of scandal."

"What about your political work, Jon? Can money keep that from being ruined?"

His eyes shifted from her piercing gaze. She longed to stroke the frown from his forehead, to ease some of the burden she had brought to him. But the only way she knew to do that was to leave, and he would not let her.

When he looked at her again, determination hardened his jaw. "Huntly is behind this, and if he did not do something now to try to discredit me, he would do it later. I won't lose what you have given Stephen and me because of him."

Sam stared at Langston, afraid of reading too much into his words, but the hope she had clung to throughout the past weeks was expanding in her heart to the point of actual pain.

"What are you trying to say?"

"That there must be something we can do to thwart the man who *claims* to be your husband, and in the process thwart Huntly."

"Why?" she whispered.

He scowled at her. "I've already told you. I won't let you go. I won't let that scum ruin your life or Amalie's or Stephen's—or mine."

Sam sighed. He did not love her, or if he did, he did not know it. But he needed and wanted her and admitted it. It was enough for now.

"What are you going to do?" she asked, knowing that the best she could do for him was to help him outsmart Charles Davidson.

"My Bow Street Runner told me that someone else was also investigating Charles's death. He finally caught up with the person and paid him for the name of his employer. Huntly."

"It does not make sense," she murmured. "If Huntly is behind Charles, why not simply expose to the papers and the world that you are living out of wedlock with me? Have Charles act the part of the cuckold who never stopped loving his erring wife but is not powerful enough to fight the Marquis of Langston for her favors?"

"Why not, indeed?" Langston rose and paced the darkened room. "That would be the logical thing to do. If done properly, it could ruin my chances of re-election to the Commons, thus killing my Poor Laws bill. And if you did leave, you would be playing right into their hands. Huntly could then have exactly what he wanted—you. With the added benefit that I would be ruined."

Sam swallowed hard as fear formed a knot in her stomach. Everything he said was true.

"A falling-out amongst thieves," she said softly, rising and going to where he stood by the mantel. She put her hand on his arm and looked into his eyes. "Could it be possible that Charles is double-crossing Huntly?"

He looked sharply at her. "Perhaps you have hit on it. Fifty thousands pounds is a fortune to anyone."

"Except you," she said wryly, before adding, "To Charles it would be enough to risk angering Huntly."

"If only we could find the man who conducted that wedding ceremony." He frowned into the flames. "Winkly should be contacting me soon. I sent him a message this morning telling him about Davidson's appearance."

"Oh, Jon." Sam sighed, wishing with all her heart that they did not have to go through this. "Perhaps it really would be better if I moved back to my house in Covent Garden until everything is resolved."

He turned on her like lightning, gripping her shoulders. "I won't let you go. And if we truly are not married, then I will move heaven and earth to make it so. You are mine!"

He pulled her to him and took her mouth in a hungry, demanding kiss that denied everything but their need for each other.

Her heart raced and blood pounded through her veins. The waves of passion emanating from him crashed over her, and she sank into his arms, forgetting her fears, forgetting everything but the caress of his lips and the warmth of his hands.

It was much later that Lottie's knock roused them from a light sleep. Yanking the covers to her chin and ignoring Langston's chuckle, Sam yelped, "I will ring when I need your help, Lottie."

For good measure, Lottie rattled the doorknob. Sam tensed, dreading the entrance of Amalie's old nurse and preparing to duck beneath the covers.

"Don't tease your mistress," Langston said, humor lacing his voice, which was deep and gravelly from their spent ardor.

"Yes, milord," Lottie said through the door in mock subservience.

Sam did not relax until she heard her servant's receding footsteps. Only then did she murmur, "She has the devil of a sense of humor when it strikes her."

Instead of answering, Langston swung his legs off the bed and padded to the table by the chair where Sam had sat earlier. He picked up the velvet box he had placed there two hours before and returned to Sam. Sitting on the mattress so that she rolled against him, her pelvis curled around his buttocks, he opened the lid.

Curious about what he was doing, Sam raised up on one elbow and peered inside. Ice-cold sparkles dazzled her eyes. It was a treasure trove of jewels.

Sam stared, breathless with awe, as he dipped his hand into the rainbow glitter and lifted out a necklace dripping with diamonds. Without a word, he draped it across her breasts, so that the cold metal and jewels rested against her skin in a cascade of fire. Next he took out a ring with a single canary-colored diamond sparkling in a swirl of gold.

He lifted her left hand and slipped the ring on her finger until it rested against her plain gold wedding band. "This is the Rundell engagement ring," he said softly. "I just retrieved it from my mother. Along with the rest of the bride jewels."

Sam looked at him in amazement. "Bride jewels?"

He nodded, lifting her hand and kissing the ring and her fingers. "I would have had them sooner, but Mother had put them away for safekeeping at the castle."

She held her hand in such a way that the magnificent stone caught and reflected the light. "How beautiful," she breathed.

Picking out a pair of diamond ear drops, he said, "Mother particularly wanted you to have the ring, Sam. It seems that she is more than reconciled to our union. She is thrilled with how happy Stephen has become, and that alone would make her support it."

Sam smiled gently. "Stephen and Amalie have both thrived."

"We all have," he murmured, nuzzling her ear. "Now, turn your head so I can put on these baubles."

When he was finished adorning her, he stood back and admired her. Diamonds dripped from her neck and encrusted her wrists, ears, and fingers. They even glittered on her ankles.

"How decadent," Sam said, giggling. "Surely your mother never wore all of these at the same time."

A wicked glint entered Langston's eyes. "If she did, I am sure it was a temptation beyond my father's power to ignore."

Sam laughed and moved away when he reached for her. But not for long. Murmuring and chuckling, they began their lovemaking anew.

Much later, he helped her take off the jewels and return them to the box. He caught her hand just as she started to remove the engagement ring and brought her fingers to his mouth. "No, Sam. That must stay on you for all time."

Her heart skipped a beat, and she had to blink against the tears of happiness that clouded her vision. If she had not known better, she would have thought he had been moved by their words and actions.

In a voice barely above a whisper, she said, "I shall cherish it all my days."

He dropped her hand and cleared his throat. "When I return from Parliament, I expect to find you here."

"I thought you were not going there today," Sam said.

"I was not, but have reconsidered. Ravensford is very likely there, and I intend to ask him to look discreetly into the procedure for procuring a divorce." His jaw hardened as he paused by the door to his rooms. "If we find you truly are married to Davidson, I will start divorce proceedings immediately. Meanwhile, we must wait on Winkly's communications before showing our hand publicly."

Sam stared at him, her expression revealing her unease. She knew better than to argue with him when he was in this mood. All she could do was bide her time and remember her patience. And pray.

All she wanted from life was here. She was married to the man she loved with her whole heart, and she was mother to two beautiful children whom she would die for. There was nothing else she wanted, and she was willing to fight to keep the treasures she had found.

WHEN CHARLES HAD NOT sent word by the next afternoon, Sam began to worry. The man she remembered was selfish and rash. He would have acted upon his threat by now. But there was nothing she could do; she did not know where he was or how to find him.

In a desperate effort to ease the torment, she decided to go to the Commons and listen to Langston's speech. He had read it to her last night, and it was superb. It was his last chance to persuade the Commons to pass his Poor Laws before the next elections.

She arrived and made her way to the back of the gallery, keeping the hood of her cape pulled forward to shade her face. Langston did not need the complication of having it known that his wife was in the audience. Their marriage was so controversial her presence would draw attention from his words.

No sooner did the speaker recognize Langston than another man rose and interrupted.

"If it pleases the gentlemen of the Commons," the man said, "before Lord Langston begins his repetitious speech on his infamous Poor Laws, I would like to bring to everyone's attention the caliber of man he really is."

A hush fell over the assembly. Sam inched her way forward, wondering what was happening. Who was this man, and why was he stopping Langston?

"Mr. Hobson," the speaker said, "I have not recognized you. Please sit down."

Mr. Hobson made an obeisant bow. "What I have to impart is of great importance." He paused dramatically. "His lordship the Marquis of Langston is married to a bigamist, gentlemen."

"Dare say we would like to share in his arrangements," one wit said. This was met with several guffaws.

"No," Mr. Hobson said, frowning fiercely. "This is not a joking matter. Lord Langston's wife, Mrs. Davidson, is still married to another man. Her husband, reputedly dead at sea, is in reality very much alive. In fact..."

There was a stirring at the door and a figure entered. Sam leaned forward, her hands gripping the balustrade. It could not be.

"...he is here with us today." Mr. Hobson gestured with his hand. "Gentlemen of the Commons, may I introduce Mr. Charles Davidson, the

first and only legal husband of the Drury Lane actress Samantha Davidson.''

Pandemonium broke out.

Sam, horrified tears blurring her vision, fled the
gallery. How could this have happened? How could
Charles have dared so blatant a move? And at the
expense of his fifty thousand pounds!

CONSTERNATION AND FURY consumed Langston in
equal portions. Hobson was Huntly's man, and the
three of them, including Davidson, had successfully conspired to defeat his Poor Laws. Staring
around the Commons, Langston was wise enough
to know that even if there were a chance the vote
would be with him, it would be days before this furor died down and the vote could be taken. He did
not have days.

Swallowing the bitterness of failure, he strode
from the room. He could do no good here. He
could not even refute Davidson's claim to be Sam's
legal husband.

The only thing he could do was find Sam before
the gossip and scandal reached her. He knew her
well enough to be sure that this latest evidence
would send her from his home without thought for
anything but the harm she was doing his political
future.

He arrived home minutes later and took the stairs three at a time. Without knocking, he entered her room. It was just as he had thought—she was packing again.

"This is becoming a bad habit," he said, slamming the door shut and striding forward. He yanked her into his arms and crushed her mouth against his.

They were both breathless and hot with passion before he allowed her to speak, and then only to murmur as he lifted her skirts and fitted himself to her. Backing her to the wall where he propped her for leverage, he surged into her, reveling in the feel of her legs wrapped around his waist.

When they stood, lost in each other's arms, their hearts still pounding, he tipped her head so that their eyes met. Her glorious mane of hair cascaded over his arms, tempting him to bury his face in it. He wanted her more than he wanted life itself.

"Don't ever try to leave me again. I will lock you in a room and throw away the key if I must."

Tears welled up and ran down her cheeks. She gazed at him, all her love and all her worry for him reflected in the depths of her eyes.

"Not even for Amalie and Stephen's sakes can I do this to you," she whispered. "I have to leave. You must let me go."

"No," he growled, crushing her lips again.

He moved against her, as insistent as though they had not just made love. Sam sobbed as her body awakened.

"Stop, Jon," she pleaded. "This is passion. 'Tis not enough to ruin your life for."

He held her closer, demanding a response she wanted to refuse. His mouth nipped at hers.

"'Tis beyond passion," he murmured. "'Tis beyond reason."

He swept her into his arms and carried her to the bed. As he joined her, he vowed, "You are mine. And I will keep you no matter what the cost."

THAT NIGHT the carriage jostled and bounced on the uneven road as it made its way to Drury Lane. Sam had one last performance before she retired from the stage. Acting was hardly a fitting profession for the Marchioness of Langston, though Jon respected her reason for giving the theatre so much notice. However, in the final analysis, his public service had to come first.

Her decision to leave the theatre made no odds now.

By the light of the carriage lantern, she read from a scandal sheet: "Respected Member of Parliament, the Marquis of Langston, wed to bigamist actress."

"I will sue the owner of that trash," Langston vowed, taking the cheap paper from her nerveless fingers and crushing it into a ball before tossing it out the window.

Sam sighed. "The damage is done."

"I will be damned if I let any ragtag excuse for a newspaper intimidate me. All we have to do is ignore it."

"But 'tis true," Sam said quietly, wishing with all her heart that it were not.

He turned to her, and in the shifting light of the carriage she could see the flash of anger in his eyes and the taut line of his jaw. "You will divorce him, if indeed he is your husband."

"He is," she wailed softly. "We were married."

"An unrecorded marriage performed by a man who is nowhere to be found." He shook his head. "No, Sam, I think that, given time, we will discover that you were never wed. I think it was a hoax to gain Davidson your favors."

"If only that were true."

He pulled her into the curve of his shoulder and held her tightly, his warmth penetrating the layers of clothing between them. In spite of her misgivings, Sam found comfort in his clasp. She also found courage.

The scandal sheets would be all over London by now, and everyone at the theatre tonight would know about her bigamy. Still, she would go on. She would hold her head high and give the performance of her life.

Several hours later she stood in the wings and waited for her cue to enter. Taking several deep breaths to still the butterflies rioting in her stomach, she squared her shoulders and lifted her chin. Right on cue, she floated to the center of the stage.

"Boo!"

"Get rid o' the doxy!"

Splat! A large, ripe tomato hit the hem of Sam's previously pristine white gown. Another hit her shoulder. An orange bounced off Edmund Kean, who had been standing beside her. He jumped for safety. The other cast members ducked or ran behind the stage.

Mortification brought twin flags of bright color to Sam's cheeks as she turned to face the audience. Before she could open her mouth to berate them, a tall, lithe figure vaulted to the stage and sped to her. Langston. He had come from his private box to protect her from the unruly crowd.

He whipped off his immaculately tailored black coat and wrapped it around her shoulders for protection. Then, putting his arms around her to shield her further from the vegetables and fruit still being thrown, he tried to steer her off the stage.

But Sam was beyond reason. Seeing her husband risk everything to come to her rescue strengthened her resolve to face down the men and women shouting obscenities at her.

"Move away," she ordered Langston, who continued to try to direct her behind the curtain.

With a violent twist of her body, she was free of him. She strode to the front of the stage and glared out at the audience.

"Listen to me!" Her voice rang out imperiously, making many of the rowdy group pause in surprise. "Who are you to condemn me for something you know nothing about?"

Several men made catcalls. A few women rose and left. But the majority remained silent, a mix of curiosity and expectation on their faces.

Langston's coat still hung from Sam's shoulders, and juice from a tomato stained her gown. Her hair had come unbound and fell in unruly waves down her back, and her hands shook from intense anger. But she held herself like a queen, and like a queen's subjects the mob gave her obeisance.

"Every one of you has things you wish undone, things you are ashamed of, and if you think not, then you think dishonestly. How dare you condemn me for loving a man I thought I was free to wed! How dare you—I repeat—how *dare* you malign a man who has done so much for this country and the people of England? For by attacking me, you malign him!''

In the stunned silence that followed her words, Sam went to Langston and took his arm, then sailed from the stage without a backward glance. When they were safely behind the curtains she collapsed against him.

''I ... I am so ... sorry,'' she whispered into the folds of his once immaculately tied cravat. ''I never meant this to happen to you.''

''Damn it, Sam,'' he said, his voice low and intense. ''What happened is nothing to me. That rabble tried to hurt you.''

Burrowing her head into the warmth of his chest, she murmured, ''It does not matter about me. Oh, I am so sorry.''

''Shh,'' he said, stroking her fall of chestnut hair. ''I am fine. You were magnificent. I am only sorry they did that to you.''

Sam gulped back the tears rising in her throat. '''Tis not unexpected. An audience is always fickle. 'Tis just as well. I shall not miss the stage near as much after this.''

Admiration for her bravery overwhelmed Langston. ''My courageous darling.''

In spite of her strong words, Sam clung to him as undeniable despair overcame her. Everything was going wrong. All her hopes and dreams were going awry, and there was nothing she could do to stop it.

Feeling her shoulders tremble with sobbing, Langston cursed viciously. Then he put one arm under her legs and the other at her back and caught her up. Ignoring the curious and startled gazes of the rest of the cast, he strode past them, outside and to the carriage, with Sam held to his heart.

He continued to hold her all the way to his Town mansion. When they were safely in the drawing-room, he had her sit on one of the numerous straw silk-covered settees, then ordered Peter, the foot-man, to fetch Mistress Lottie and the children.

He handed Sam his handkerchief, which she used to blow her nose, making him smile tenderly at her. "You are the only woman I have ever known who could do so undainty a thing without marring her beauty."

Sam smiled tremulously at him, wondering why he was being so tender to her. But before she could speak, the door opened and the children, both in nightclothes, entered with Lottie close behind.

"Papa," both children said, Stephen beaming at his father and Amalie smiling shyly.

"Your lordship," Lottie said, curtsying, her eyes darting to Sam's disheveled figure. "What is going on?"

"Well you might ask," Langston said, putting an arm around each child and looking at them in turn. "I have a question for each of you, and I want you to answer truthfully.

Both gave him a solemn nod.

"Stephen, how would you feel if Sam left us?"

"Left us?" Devastation ravaged his young face. "Surely she won't do that. I...I love her. I don't care what you feel, Father."

Langston could not suppress a wry grin. "I did not think you would, son." He turned to Amalie. "And how would you feel if your mother took you from here?"

Amalie's sleep-softened face crumpled and she clung to Langston's arm. "I won't go. I am happy here. I...I love you like a...a papa," she whispered, her blue eyes shining.

He hugged her to him and looked over her head at Sam, who had stood and was staring openmouthed at them.

"What are you trying to do, Jon?" she asked.

He held her gaze, releasing the children and taking a step toward her. "You were going to leave after tonight. No." He held up a hand to silence her when she would have spoken. "Don't deny it. It was in your eyes and in your tears."

"You are right, and I still intend to. This little scene changes nothing."

He took another step towards her. "I think it does," he said quietly. "But more important, *why* do you intend to leave?"

She clenched her hands into fists to still their shaking. "Because I must. You saw what happened. You will be ruined if I stay. Ruined."

He took another step closer. "Why does that matter, Samantha?"

She met his implacable gaze and wondered why he was doing this to her. Why was he putting her through torture for the second time this evening?

"Why, Sam?" he persisted.

A tiny spurt of anger energized her. He must know her answer, yet he persisted in exposing all her weaknesses to his scrutiny.

"Love," she stated. "And why are you doing this to *me?*"

He caught her in his arms, then held her slightly away so that his brown eyes stared into her gold-green ones. "Love, Samantha," he murmured against her lips. "Love."

CHAPTER TWENTY-TWO

SAM TOOK a deep breath to ease her anxiety and pushed open the library door. Inside, Langston stood with two other men, one in shadows, one with a black wool cap crushed in his hands.

Langston turned and extended his hand to her. "Sam, come here."

Gladness permeated his tone and lessened some of her nervousness. His news could not be bad.

"M'lady," the man with the cap said, bowing.

He had a lined face and pointed chin that combined to give him the appearance of a weasel. Yet, there was no slyness or guile in his eyes when he openly returned her scrutiny. However, she had no doubt that he could be formidable when he chose.

"This is Winkly, the Bow Street Runner," Langston said by way of introduction.

Sam nodded at the man and extended her hand. He raised it to his lips, an action that was somehow endearing. She smiled.

"Yer as beautiful as they say," Winkly said, grinning.

"Thank you," Sam said.

"She has always been beautiful." The other man stepped from the shadows.

"Josiah Thomas!" Sam gasped.

He bowed with a flourish. "At your service, my lady."

"Yes," Langston said, putting an arm around Sam. "Winkly tracked him down by looking for Charles Davidson's old acting troupe, the one he left just before marrying you."

"Acting troupe?" Hope began to burgeon in Sam. "Mr. Thomas is not a real vicar?"

"'Xactly," Winkly said with a smug grin.

"My dear lady," Thomas said, "forgive me for deceiving you, but Charles paid me well."

"And I am paying you better to come forward with your story," Langston said cynically.

"Precisely, my lord," Thomas said with a theatrical shrug.

"Davidson should be 'ere shortly, guv," Winkly interjected. "I tracked 'im down an' told 'im to meet us here, or I'd arrest 'im for falsifyin' church records."

Loud voices came from the hallway. Langston smiled triumphantly and said, "That must be him now."

The library door opened. "A Mr. Charles Davidson," Hampton announced, his nose in the air, his whole being radiating disdain. He stepped aside to ensure that when Davidson went by him the two did not touch.

Davidson entered, his countenance turning pasty as his eyes darted to each person. He stopped dead in his tracks.

"Exactly," Langston said, relishing the cad's discomfiture.

"What is the meaning of this?" Davidson blustered, edging back to the door.

"You won't get out that way," Langston drawled. "It has been locked, and I am the only person Hampton will open it for."

"Charles, old fellow," Thomas said jovially, although he surreptitiously wiped his palms on his yellow breeches. "Been a long time. Heard you drowned in the Atlantic."

Davidson scowled. "Shut up, Josiah."

"Reckon 'tis a fallin' out amongst thieves," Winkly said in an eerie echo of Sam's words.

Casting his wife an admiring glance, Langston gave Davidson a pointed look and said, "Something like what happened between you and Huntly."

Sam made her way to a chair some distance from the activity. There was no part for her to play here now, but she needed to hear Charles Davidson admit the falsehood of their wedding in order to fully believe it.

Davidson shrugged. "Can't blame a fellow for trying. If you had paid me, I would be a rich man."

"You did not give me a chance," Langston said sardonically.

"Well, that wasn't my fault," Davidson said defensively. "Huntly grew impatient." A sly grin moved over his face. "However, given the proper incentive, I would be willing to admit to the falsehood of my marriage to Samantha."

Langston's bark of laughter rent the air. "That's rich, but I don't need your compliance, Davidson. I have Thomas's."

"How do you know he's not lying?" Davidson asked.

"'Cause *I* done me work," Winkly said harshly. "And I don't take kindly to the likes o' you impugning me reputation."

Now it was Langston's turn to feign indifference. "So you see, Davidson, your being here is only a formality. We do not need you."

Langston paused to let his words sink in. It was true that he could disprove Davidson's claims about the marriage, but he also knew that if the man chose to remain in England and continue to bandy about his previous relationship with Samantha, things would never settle down. For both Sam's and his sake, he had to make Davidson leave the country.

"Then why did you summon me?" Davidson demanded belligerently.

"To make you an offer that will benefit us both," Langston said.

Suspicion narrowed Davidson's eyes. "Such as?"

"Such as, I will buy you passage back to New Orleans and provide five thousand pounds to set you up."

Davidson's eyes widened. "What's the catch?"

Langston's mouth twisted. "You board the ship this afternoon."

"What? I cannot do that!"

Langston turned to his desk and picked up a sheet of paper. "In that case, you may go. As for you, Thomas—" he held out the paper "—this is a draft on my bank. 'Tis yours as soon as Winkly confirms that you have signed a statement about your role in my wife's false marriage to Charles Davidson."

A grin split Thomas's face. "No sooner said than done, my lord." He cast a glance at Davidson. "I am no fool."

"Precisely," Langston drawled.

A muscle worked in Davidson's jaw. "Will you keep Huntly from coming after me? After all, if I do as you want, I will be double-crossing him."

"And this would be the first time, I suppose?" Langston said wryly.

His sarcasm was lost on Davidson. "With fifty thousand pounds I could have disappeared off the face of the earth. Five thousand is not the same."

In a deadly voice, Langston said, "I will see that Huntly never bothers you again."

Davidson swallowed hard, then nodded. "You have a deal."

"Good," Langston said briskly. "Winkly will see that you fulfil your end of our bargain. You may go now." He rang for Hampton, who unlocked the door.

"Come along," Winkly said briskly. "And don't be tryin' nothin'. I 'ave a pistol and I know 'ow to use it."

Brandishing the weapon, he ushered the two men from the room. As soon as the door closed behind them, Sam shot up and ran to Langston.

He caught her to him. "You are free, my love."

"Charles and I were never married," Sam breathed, leaning against Langston for support. "Amalie is illegitimate."

She stared up at him, happiness over her freedom warring with the dismaying knowledge about Amalie. "What shall I tell her?" she asked in a whisper.

Langston shook his head in bewilderment. "Tell her that I am her father. She does not need to know you and Davidson were never married. I planned to make her legally mine, in any case. This merely provides all the more reason to do so quickly."

Looking at the love and compassion in her husband's dark eyes, Sam sent a prayer of thanks heavenward. "I love you, Jonathan St. Simon, Marquis of Langston."

He hesitated only an instant. "And I love you, Samantha, Marchioness of Langston."

WITHIN DAYS the scandal sheets carried a new story:

> Samantha Davidson never married to man who fathered her daughter. Marquis of Langston legally wed to beautiful actress.

Sam sighed as she read the paper. It was not what she would have liked to see, but it was better than what the rags had said two weeks earlier. Now, if only she could keep Amalie from seeing them.

"Throw it in the fire," Langston's deep voice said from the doorway behind her.

Whirling around, she ran to him. "Langston, I thought you were at the Commons."

He held her tight. "You always think that."

She grinned up at him. "'Tis because that is where you usually are." Sobering, she asked, "How is it going?"

He grimaced and released her. "It could be better, but it has been worse. With Davidson's recantation, the initial furor has begun to die down. At least now there is a chance the bill will pass."

Taking his hand, she led him to a chair by the fire and pushed him into it before kneeling beside him. She held his hand to her cheek.

"I am so glad my past has not completely ruined you."

He smiled down at her. "Well, we are not out of the brambles yet."

She sighed. "I know." Softly she asked, "What will you do about Huntly?"

Langston frowned, staring at nothing. "There is only one thing open to me. I shall challenge him to a duel of honor."

Disgust stiffened Sam's spine. "Is that the only answer you men have?"

A lopsided grin curved Langston's sensual lips. "It would seem so. Sam, I cannot haul Huntly into court, because legally he did not do anything wrong. And if I let him get away with what he did, then he will try something else later." He shook his head at her defiant glare. "I know you do not like it, but 'tis the only way."

Sam snorted. Getting to her feet, she stalked away from him, anger making her movements jerky. Then, turning around, she pinned him with her gaze and demanded, "How do you plan to challenge him?

He met her glare without flinching. "The usual way."

"Don't be facetious," she ordered, furious with him for making light of so serious an undertaking. "He may kill you."

"Ah," he said, understanding dawning. "Here is the crux. You are worried. Do not be. I am an excellent marksman and swordsman."

Samantha fought the urge to break into tears. She backed away from him, knowing that the instant he took her into his arms she would be lost.

"You arrogant fool," she muttered, wiping at her eyes.

"I am. I admit it," he said, advancing on her with a roguish grin. "But not without justification."

She groaned and sidestepped his arm. "Men."

He sobered, the intensity of his gaze telling her that he was not going to change his mind. With a sigh of resignation, she let him catch her.

"If you have to do this, then I have to be there," she said from the circle of his arms.

He reared back in shock. "No!"

She met his glare defiantly. "Then I will find a way to be there without your permission."

He studied her for long minutes. "You would, too."

"Yes, I would."

He groaned in resignation. "I would rather know where you are and that you are safe. All right. You may come, but you must stay in the carriage during the duel."

"Thank you," she said meekly, rising on tiptoe to kiss him.

ONE WEEK LATER to the day, Langston started across the dew-drenched grass of Hampstead Heath, the most popular spot in London for clandestine duels. The sun was a hazy yellow ball in the early-morning sky, its warmth not yet felt.

Huntly stood thirty feet away, his second assisting him to take off his coat. Beneath, he wore a black shirt, a more difficult target to hit.

Langston's mouth twisted in a humorless line. Huntly was a coward and a rodent to the end.

"He must be scared," Ravensford said in tones meant to carry across the field. The abrupt jerk of Huntly's head indicated that the earl's endeavor was successful.

Langston shook his head, chuckling. "You would try the nerves of a saint, Ravensford."

The earl shrugged. "Isn't that the reason I am your second? To discommode your opponent?"

"None other."

Huntly's second conferred with Ravensford while both opponents drew and tested their swords. Feeling the finely balanced weapon, Langston was glad Huntly had chosen them.

Thirty minutes later he was still glad, even though sweat dripped from his brow and burned his eyes. Huntly was a good swordsman.

Langston sidestepped and parried a deadly assault, but he was not fast enough, and the tip of Huntly's sword caught in the billowing fabric of his sleeve. The keenly honed blade sliced through linen and flesh alike without encountering resistance. Langston leapt back as blood flowed from his arm.

It burned where the steel had pierced, but he knew it was only a flesh wound. He renewed his attack.

From the closed carriage, Sam watched the two men dance over the green, their stockinged feet covered with mud and water. She knew they had removed their boots in an attempt to counter the slick grass. Still, to her horror, Langston slipped. She stifled a scream. He regained his balance just in time to avoid being run through by Huntly's sword. Sam sighed in relief.

She almost wished she had not coerced Langston into letting her come. Seeing the blood-lust in both men's eyes and realizing how close her husband had come to death, she could hardly bear to watch any more. Her only consolation was that Langston had spared no expense for the attending physician. Sir Reginald stood ready.

Suddenly the two swords clashed. Light flashed from the burnished steel. One blade sailed into the air. Sam clapped her hand over her mouth, stilling a triumphant shout.

Langston glared at Huntly, the tip of his blade resting lightly against Huntly's Adam's apple. All he had to do was push. Just a little push and the wretch would be gone. The temptation was great.

"Go ahead, Langston," Huntly said, fear making perspiration break out on his forehead and upper lip. Very softly, for their ears only, he added, "Kill your son's real father."

Pain crushed Langston's chest. Excruciating pain.

"That is right," Huntly said softly. "I was Annabelle's lover."

The tip of Langston's blade pierced Huntly's flesh. A trickle of blood slipped down the man's neck and dripped onto his shirt.

With his free hand, Langston wiped the sweat from his brow while keeping his sword at Huntly's throat. He stared into Huntly's eyes. Only an inch more, and he and Sam would pack up the children and go to the Continent while the scandal died down and his father worked to clear his name.

God, how he wanted to end Huntly's miserable life.

"I have known since Stephen's birth that you were his father," Langston said at last, his voice low. "And I have learned to love the boy in spite of that knowledge."

Huntly's eyes widened in desperation, and Langston knew with certainty that the man had only told him because he hoped it would save his life. But Huntly had achieved his goal. Langston could not kill a man who was so pitiful.

He stepped back and dropped the sword to his side. "Your life was in my hands," he said clearly. "Remember that in the future, because if you breathe one word of what you just told me or try again to hurt my wife, I will hound you to the ends of the earth—and I will kill you."

With that, he turned and walked away.

"Langston!" Sam's scream of terror reverberated through the fog-shrouded morning.

He lunged to the right, and felt the slight brush of cold steel against the side of his head. Huntly had tried to run him through the back.

Whirling around, he raised his sword in self-defense. Huntly ran onto it.

"Bloody..."

Langston pulled the blade out quickly and knelt to press his hands against the gaping wound in Huntly's chest. Blood pumped around and through his fingers.

"At...at least," Huntly said, his voice thready and weak, "now...I will join...her."

His eyes closed.

Langston stared down at him. Sir Reginald had to push him away in order to reach the wound.

"Will he live?" Langston asked in a voice of infinite exhaustion. So much had happened.

Still working feverishly, Sir Reginald shook his head. "No. The sword pierced his heart." He glanced over his shoulder at Langston. "I shall list the cause of death as self-defense on your part. With luck, and pressure brought to bear on the Regent, you should not have to flee the country."

Numbly Langston nodded his head, then started for the carriage and Sam and sanity.

Sam leapt from the vehicle and catapulted herself at Langston. He caught her, stumbling backward from her momentum.

"You are all right," she breathed, cupping his face between her hands and kissing him. In the next instant, she broke from him and ripped a strip from her petticoats to bind the cut on his arm.

"I love you, Sam," he whispered, drawing her back into the crook of his arm. "I love you so much it hurts."

She rested her head on his shoulder and burrowed close to him. "I know. 'Tis painful, yet pleasurable."

He nodded, remembering Huntly's words. He had always known Stephen was Huntly's son and had often wondered when Huntly would see fit to divulge that information to the world. But he never had. Perhaps somewhere, deep inside, Huntly had truly loved Annabelle and did not want to hurt the child of that love.

He gazed down at the top of Sam's head, smelling the damask-rose scent that was so essentially her. She loved Stephen, also. And she loved him.

EPILOGUE

SAM ENTERED the library, the fresh aroma of pine boughs coming from the decorated mantel. Red holly berries and mistletoe mingled in a wreath hanging from the chandelier. A yule log burned brightly in the grate, lending warmth and Christmas cheer to the room.

Sam stopped in her tracks. "What are you doing?" she asked as Langston carefully set the portrait on the floor beside the fireplace.

He turned to her and grinned like a boy. "I'm putting away my past."

She looked at the painting of Annabelle and suddenly felt sorry for the dead woman. She had given up so much happiness, never knowing it could have been hers. And now, on this most precious of holidays, the other woman's pain and betrayal were about to be put aside.

"What brought this about?" Sam asked, walking to him.

He wrapped his arms around her and held her tightly. "You."

She smiled. "Me? Because I almost ruined you?"

He grinned back. "Because you taught me to love again and to trust."

She blinked the sudden moisture from her eyes. "I love you so much."

Gently he kissed her, a long, slow caress that curled her toes and warmed her heart.

"I will never let you go, Sam. Even if it means keeping you under the mistletoe until you turn ninety."

"Or a hundred," she murmured. "Oh, and one more thing..."

When she did not immediately continue, he set her away from him and gave her a gentle shake. "Minx. You are trying to goad me."

She chuckled and nodded. "Only a bit. I have very good news." She paused and worry drew her brows together. "At least, I hope 'tis good news." She took a deep breath. "A Christmas present. I am in the family way, Jon."

He gaped at her, then with a whoop of joy pulled her back into his arms. "Wonderful. I could not wish for a better Christmas gift. We shall name him Deverell."

Sam laughed delightedly. "Unless," she said, "he is a she."

He kissed her on the forehead, nose and lips. "Yes, dearest. Unless he is a girl. And by the way—" he grinned from ear to ear "—my Poor Laws passed both houses today."

"We have much to be grateful for this Christmas," she said, happiness swelling her heart and making the future look rosy indeed.

FREE VALENTINE'S BROOCH! $9.95 U.S. retail value

This Valentine's Day Harlequin brings you all the essentials—romance, chocolate and jewelry—in:

VALENTINE *Delights*

Matchmaking chocolate-shop owner Papa Valentine dispenses sinful desserts, mouth-watering chocolates...and advice to the lovelorn, in this collection of three delightfully romantic stories by Meryl Sawyer, Kate Hoffmann and Gina Wilkins.

As our special Valentine's Day gift to you, each copy of *Valentine Delights* will have a beautiful, filigreed, heart-shaped brooch attached to the cover.

Make this your most delicious Valentine's Day ever with *Valentine Delights!*

Available in February wherever Harlequin books are sold.

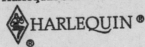

HARLEQUIN ®

Look us up on-line at: http://www.romance.net

VAL9

INSTANT WIN 4229 SWEEPSTAKES
OFFICIAL RULES

1. NO PURCHASE NECESSARY. YOU ARE DEFINITELY A WINNER. For eligibility, play your instant win ticket and claim your prize as per instructions contained thereon. If your "Instant Win" ticket is missing or you wish another, send a self-addressed, stamped envelope (WA residents need not affix return postage) to: Instant Win 4229 Ticket, P.O. Box 9045, Buffalo, NY 14269-9045 in the U.S., and in Canada, P.O. Box 609, Fort Erie, Ontario, L2A 5X3. Only one (1) "Instant Win" ticket will be sent per outer mailing envelope. Requests received after 12/30/96 will not be honored.

2. Prize claims received after 1/15/97 will be deemed ineligible and will not be fulfilled. The exact prize value of each Instant Win ticket will be determined by comparing returned tickets with a prize value distribution list that has been preselected at random by computer. Prizes are valued in U.S. currency. For each one million, or part thereof, tickets distributed, the following prizes will be made available: 1 at $2,500 cash; 1 at $1,000 cash; 3 at $250 cash each; 5 at $50 cash each; 10 at $25 cash each; 1,000 at $1 cash each; and the balance at 50¢ cash each. Unclaimed prizes will not be awarded.

3. Winner claims are subject to verification by D. L. Blair, Inc., an independent judging organization whose decisions on all matters relating to this sweepstakes are final. Any returned tickets that are mutilated, tampered with, illegible or contain printing or other errors will be deemed automatically void. No responsibility is assumed for lost, late, nondelivered or misdirected mail. Taxes are the sole responsibility of winners. Limit: One (1) prize to a family, household or organization.

4. Offer open only to residents of the U.S. and Canada, 18 years of age or older, except employees of Harlequin Enterprises Limited, D. L. Blair, Inc., their agents and members of their immediate families. All federal, state, provincial, municipal and local laws apply. Offer void in Puerto Rico, the province of Quebec and wherever prohibited by law. All winners will receive their prize by mail. Taxes and/or duties are the sole responsibility of the winners. No substitution for prizes permitted. Major prize winners may be asked to sign and return an Affidavit of Eligibility within 30 days of notification. Noncompliance within this time or return of affidavit as undeliverable may result in disqualification, and prize may never be awarded. By acceptance of a prize, winners consent to the use of their names, photographs or other likeness for purposes of advertising, trade and promotion on behalf of Harlequin Enterprises Limited, without further compensation, unless prohibited by law. In order to win a prize, residents of Canada will be required to correctly answer a time-limited arithmetical skill-testing question to be administered by mail.

5. For a list of major prize winners (available after 2/14/97), send a self-addressed, stamped envelope to: "Instant Win 4229 Sweepstakes" Major Prize Winners, P.O. Box 4200, Blair, NE 68009-4200, U.S.A.

MILLION DOLLAR SWEEPSTAKES
OFFICIAL RULES
NO PURCHASE NECESSARY TO ENTER

1. To enter, follow the directions published. Method of entry may vary. For eligibility, entries must be received no later than March 31, 1998. No liability is assumed for printing errors, lost, late, non-delivered or misdirected entries.

   To determine winners, the sweepstakes numbers assigned to submitted entries will be compared against a list of randomly, preselected prize winning numbers. In the event all prizes are not claimed via the return of prize winning numbers, random drawings will be held from among all other entries received to award unclaimed prizes.

2. Prize winners will be determined no later than June 30, 1998. Selection of winning numbers and random drawings are under the supervision of D. L. Blair, Inc., an independent judging organization whose decisions are final. Limit: one prize to a family or organization. No substitution will be made for any prize, except as offered. Taxes and duties on all prizes are the sole responsibility of winners. Winners will be notified by mail. Odds of winning are determined by the number of eligible entries distributed and received.

3. Sweepstakes open to residents of the U.S. (except Puerto Rico), Canada and Europe who are 18 years of age or older, except employees and immediate family members of Torstar Corp., D. L. Blair, Inc., their affiliates, subsidiaries, and all other agencies, entities, and persons connected with the use, marketing or conduct of this sweepstakes. All applicable laws and regulations apply. Sweepstakes offer void wherever prohibited by law. Any litigation within the province of Quebec respecting the conduct and awarding of a prize in this sweepstakes must be submitted to the Régie des alcools, des courses et des jeux. In order to win a prize, residents of Canada will be required to correctly answer a time-limited arithmetical skill-testing question to be administered by mail.

4. Winners of major prizes (Grand through Fourth) will be obligated to sign and return an Affidavit of Eligibility and Release of Liability within 30 days of notification. In the event of non-compliance within this time period or if a prize is returned as undeliverable, D. L. Blair, Inc. may at its sole discretion, award that prize to an alternate winner. By acceptance of their prize, winners consent to use of their names, photographs or other likeness for purposes of advertising, trade and promotion on behalf of Torstar Corp., its affiliates and subsidiaries, without further compensation unless prohibited by law. Torstar Corp. and D. L. Blair, Inc., their affiliates and subsidiaries are not responsible for errors in printing of sweepstakes and prize winning numbers. In the event a duplication of a prize winning number occurs, a random drawing will be held from among all entries received with that prize winning number to award that prize.

5. This sweepstakes is presented by Torstar Corp., its subsidiaries and affiliates in conjunction with book, merchandise and/or product offerings. The number of prizes to be awarded and their value are as follows: Grand Prize — $1,000,000 (payable at $33,333.33 a year for 30 years); First Prize — $50,000; Second Prize — $10,000; Third Prize — $5,000; 3 Fourth Prizes — $1,000 each; 10 Fifth Prizes — $250 each; 1,000 Sixth Prizes — $10 each. Values of all prizes are in U.S. currency. Prizes in each level will be presented in different creative executions, including various currencies, vehicles, merchandise and travel. Any presentation of a prize level in a currency other than U.S. currency represents an approximate equivalent to the U.S. currency prize for that level, at that time. Prize winners will have the opportunity of selecting any prize offered for that level; however, the actual non U.S. currency equivalent prize if offered and selected, shall be awarded at the exchange rate existing at 3:00 P.M. New York time on March 31, 1998. A travel prize option, if offered and selected by winner, must be completed within 12 months of selection and is subject to: traveling companion(s) completing and returning of a Release of Liability prior to travel; and hotel and flight accommodations availability. For a current list of all prize options offered within prize levels, send a self-addressed, stamped envelope (WA residents need not affix postage) to: MILLION DOLLAR SWEEPSTAKES Prize Options, P.O. Box 4456, Blair, NE 68009-4456, USA.

6. For a list of prize winners (available after July 31, 1998) send a separate, stamped, self-addressed envelope to: MILLION DOLLAR SWEEPSTAKES Winners, P.O. Box 4459, Blair, NE 68009-4459, USA.

EXTRA BONUS PRIZE DRAWING
NO PURCHASE OR OBLIGATION NECESSARY TO ENTER

7. The Extra Bonus Prize will be awarded in a random drawing to be conducted no later than 5/30/98 from among all entries received. To qualify, entries must be received by 3/31/98 and comply with published directions. Prize ($50,000) is valued in U.S. currency. Prize will be presented in different creative expressions, including various currencies, vehicles, merchandise and travel. Any presentation in a currency other than U.S. currency represents an approximate equivalent to the U.S. currency value at that time. Prize winner will have the opportunity of selecting any prize offered in any presentation of the Extra Bonus Prize Drawing; however, the actual non U.S. currency equivalent prize, if offered and selected by winner, shall be awarded at the exchange rate existing at 3:00 P.M. New York time on March 31, 1998. For a current list of prize options offered, send a self-addressed, stamped envelope (WA residents need not affix postage) to: Extra Bonus Prize Options, P.O. Box 4462, Blair, NE 68009-4462, USA. All eligibility requirements and restrictions of the MILLION DOLLAR SWEEPSTAKES apply. Odds of winning are dependent upon number of eligible entries received. No substitution for prize except as offered. For the name of winner (available after 7/31/98), send a self-addressed, stamped envelope to: Extra Bonus Prize Winner, P.O. Box 4463, Blair, NE 68009-4463, USA.

SWP-H12CF1

Heartbreak RANCH

Four generations of independent women...
Four heartwarming, romantic stories of the West...
Four incredible authors...

Fern Michaels
Jill Marie Landis
Dorsey Kelley
Chelley Kitzmiller

addle up with Heartbreak Ranch, an outstanding
Western collection that will take you on a whirlwind
rip through four generations and the exciting,
omantic adventures of four strong women who
ave inherited the ranch from Bella Duprey,
amed Barbary Coast madam.

Available in March,
wherever Harlequin books are sold.

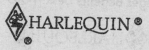

HARLEQUIN ®
®

You're About to Become a

Privileged Woman

p the rewards of fabulous free gifts and
enefits with proofs-of-purchase from
Harlequin and Silhouette books

ages & Privileges™

ur way of thanking you for
uying our books at your
avorite retail stores.

**PROOF OF
PURCHASE**
HPT-PP20

Offer expires March 31, 1997

Pages
& Privileges ™

**Harlequin and Silhouette—
the most privileged readers in the world!**

For more information about Harlequin and
Silhouette's PAGES & PRIVILEGES program call the
Pages & Privileges Benefits Desk: 1-503-794-2499

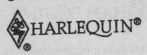

HARLEQUIN®

HPT-PP2C